BOUND FOR HOME

A SWEET CONTEMPORARY GAY ROMANCE

BLAKE ALLWOOD

BLAKE ALLWOOD PUBLISHING

CONTENT WARNINGS

Death of a loved one
Drugging someone against their will
Encounter with prostitution
Librarians

Join Blake's email list to get advance notice of new books and receive his occasional newsletter:

www.blakeallwood.com

MM Romance
By Blake Allwood

Transitions Series
Aiden Inspired
Suzie Empowered (MF Romance)
Bobby Transformed

Chance Series
Love By Chance
Another Chance With Love
Taking A Chance For Love

Romantic Series
Romantic Renovations (1)
Romantic Rescue (2)
Romantic Recon (3)

Melody Series
Melody of the Heart
Melody of the Snow

Road to Rocktoberfest Anthology
Changing His Tune - 2022

Coming Home Series (2023)
A Long Way Home
Family Home
Discovering Home
Finding Home
Bound For Home
…and many more

Novellas
Tenacious
Moon's Place

Romantic Fantasy
By Adam J. Ridley

Big Bend Series
Love's Legacy (1)
Love's Heirloom (2)
Love's Bequest (3)

The Witch Brothers Series
Emerald Earth (1)
Diamond Air (2)
Ruby Fire (3)
Sapphire Water (4)

Science Fiction
By Adam J. Ridley

Superhero Series
Emergence

ACKNOWLEDGMENTS

Special thanks to the following amazing people who helped me get this book finished and into your hands.

Jo Bird: Editor

Renee Mizar: Editor

Ann Attwood: Proofreader

And of course, a big thank you to my husband who puts up with my endless stories and handles the formatting and final publishing of all my books.

PROLOGUE

I COULD FEEL THE thousands of pairs of eyes watching me walk across the stage. My heart beat so fast, I thought it might burst and end me right there in front of the entire crowd. Every step closer to the microphone brought me closer to my dream.

That was when fear began to grip me. I couldn't do this. Not only would I fail, but I'd be the dude who snatched defeat from the jaws of victory. There I stood, hoping no one noticed my trembling hand as I grabbed hold of the mic, about to catastrophically flop in front of the entire nation.

I heard myself tell the audience my name, then asked a few questions. My answers were monosyllabic. Shit, hadn't I practiced with my sister for hours, her asking every ridiculous question she could think of to get me used to answering the judge's questions? I'd even done a practice run at the bar a few times, allowing the drunken idiots to ask questions, but mostly they had been about my dick size. I doubted the judges would ask that here… then again, who knew what might happen on reality TV?

God, if you're listening, just help me get through the song without singing off-key. I looked to the rafters as I sent up my little prayer, only to be nearly blinded by the stage lights. Oh, crap, what if I forgot the words? I was sure I'd forget the words. *God help me, I can't feel my tongue. Oh wait, there it is. It's the lump that feels like a cotton ball in my dry mouth.*

I couldn't do this. I should just leave now. When I turned to walk off the stage, though, I heard the note strike that signified my music was about to start. No song meant as much to me as this one. I couldn't screw this up. I couldn't do that to my granny.

My granny had taken me in when I was just three. While my mother traipsed around the city doing God only knew what, Granny was my rock. She became the one I could always count on for a steady hand and unconditional love. No matter how bad things got, she'd sing me Amelia Denton's song. "Love is just a hug, to keep you safe and strong" was her favorite lyric and one that I felt deeply. The song served as Granny's remedy for when I'd cry for my mom or when I'd have a night-mare. She would pull me into her secure embrace and soothe me with those beautiful words.

The music transported me off the stage and out of the studio, away from all those watching, critical eyes. There were no more cameras, it was just Granny and me, sitting in that rocker, singing that song. I felt myself start to sing and, like when I was a baby, I could feel Granny's strong and safe arms wrap around me protectively.

By the second verse, time had flashed forward, and I saw her lying in her hospital bed. A memory that always lingered just below the surface. The cancer had progressed, and she struggled to breathe, yet still she sang for me.

"And with these arms I hold you, forever in a hug," she whispered in my ear as I watched her slip away from this life.

The tears were flowing down my cheeks as the song ended. The images in my head had vanished, replaced by the four judges sitting in front of me and the audience who'd been stunned into silence. Then a roar of applause echoed through the auditorium, the enthusiastic approval of thousands of strangers wrapping around me like an embrace. And for just a split second, she was there again, my granny with her arms around me, helping make my dreams come true.

I'd done it. On that stage, when it mattered most, I had sung from my heart to the person I loved more than any other I'd ever known. The audience was on their feet, cheering for me. For her.

ONE

CHRIS

THE LITTLE YOU-KNOW-WHAT TOSSED another pile of books onto the desk in front of me. Actually, a mix of periodicals and books. Never mind her job involved separating them before bringing them over to the circulation desk, but damned if she didn't do it to spite me.

Of course, with Audrey being the daughter of the head librarian, there wasn't much I could do other than do her job too. I'd complained twice, and nothing had come of it.

I'd graduated two weeks ago with my library science degree, and I was already itching to find my own library, somewhere I would be in charge, maybe in a small town. I loved the idea of a quiet place where I could help kids and adults alike find and nurture a love of books. Naturally, it'd also be a place I wouldn't have to put up with the likes of a coworker who didn't do any actual work.

Here, in the suburbs of Nashville, all I did was clean up other people's messes.

I gave the tart a nasty look and began sorting the different piles.

"Christopher," my boss yelled from her office behind me. "Can you come here?"

I sighed. When I looked over at the head librarian's wicked spawn, I saw her smirk. This would likely be my demise. I honestly liked her mother. The woman was smart and patient, though maybe too patient considering her daughter was worthless in this job.

"Yes, Mrs. Elliot, I'll be right in."

But not until I cleaned up Audrey's mess. Already, several of the magazines had creased front covers because of how she'd carelessly tossed them on my desk. After I'd sorted out the worst of it, I went behind the circulation desk and entered Mrs. Elliot's office.

I took a seat across from her, my eyes trained on her perfectly maintained desk, waiting for the worst.

"Christopher, are you happy here?" she asked, causing my anxiety to spike.

"Um, I'm not unhappy," I said, and could've kicked myself. I needed to keep this job until I could secure my next one. Unemployed people had a much more difficult time finding a job, and since I was living paycheck to paycheck, I couldn't afford to be unemployed.

Mrs. Elliot took a deep breath, then let it out, and said, "We have a new library branch opening in Crawford

City. It's small, and since the town hasn't had a library since the early nineteen eighties, you'd be starting it from scratch."

"Wait, starting what from scratch?" I asked, meeting her eyes and trying to wrap my head around the bomb–or gift–she had nonchalantly dropped in my lap.

"You just finished your library science degree, Christopher. I like you. Mr. Cummons, the library system's director, likes you. You're a hard worker and you love what we do here. So, naturally, you're our first choice for the position."

"You *like* me?" I asked, thinking of the war Mrs. Elliot's daughter and I engaged in on an almost daily basis.

She smiled. "I like you a lot, actually. I've always been impressed with your work ethic. I had hoped that quality would've rubbed off on... well, anyway, that doesn't matter now. Do you know much about Crawford City?"

I shook my head. "No, ma'am. To be honest, I don't even know where that is." Not that I considered myself a city boy, but I'd rarely ventured beyond the outskirts of Nashville.

The older woman chuckled. "Well, that's not too surprising considering it's a rather small town. It's not all that far from here, and it's pretty country. There's a new mayor in town and he's collaborating with their school district's superintendent to establish a small library. They've asked us to oversee it as part of the Willingbrook Library System."

"That's cool. I always wanted to work in a smaller facility. I think I'm better suited for that environment."

Mrs. Elliot looked at me curiously for a moment, before she asked, "Have you ever worked in a small-town library before?"

I shook my head. "No, I've only ever worked here. I did volunteer at the library in my high school, but that wasn't exactly small either."

"I'm going to tell you now, it won't be anything like what you've done here. You'll be the only employee there because, frankly, we can't afford another person. Mayor Nash has assured me he has several volunteers who will work with you to keep the place operational, but volunteers are not employees. I'm not going to pretend this won't be a difficult job if you decide to take it on."

"I've already decided," I said without hesitation. "Yes, please. I want to do it."

She chuckled. "In that case, the job is yours. Over the next few months, we'll be moving into the new building. Well, not exactly new. An old primary school that sits in the town square is being converted into the library. It's small, but it'll serve its purpose. As lead librarian, part of your job will be helping patrons learn how to request books from our larger system and access the system's e-books."

"That's no problem. I've had to teach several people here how to access that system too."

Mrs. Elliot nodded. "Well, I'm going to remain your direct supervisor, since our library is the closest to that one. You can always call on me if you have any issues."

I was so overcome with joy that I could've danced out of the room. I didn't, though. Instead, acting the part of a professional, I nodded and smiled politely, thanking her for the opportunity. The dancing would come later at home.

I went back out to the circulation desk with a spring in my step and when Audrey looked at me, I laughed, causing her to scrunch up her face.

Getting away from the boss's lazy daughter might just be the best part of my new job.

"Mom? Dad?" I hollered, but the house remained quiet. I'd moved back into my childhood home just a couple weeks ago when I had to leave the dorm. I couldn't afford any of the housing in this part of town since Nashville had begun to encroach on us.

It'd taken a long time. Being on the other side of the reservoir had shielded us for years, but now that a lot of country music stars and other Nashville elite were buying homes in this area, things were quickly changing. The world's largest online retailer also situating a distribution center out here only made it worse.

I shook my head as I thought about it. If Mom and Dad hadn't already owned their home, I had no doubt that none of us would've been able to afford to stay in this area.

"Mom? Dad?" I hollered again as I walked through the house, but clearly, they were gone. I tossed my stuff into my old room, then went to the kitchen. Mom usually left a note on the fridge if they planned to be out long.

Sure enough, I found a note stuck to the fridge with a magnet, right where she'd usually leave one.

> *Son, your dad needed help mowing the Beecham Cemetery. I'm helping him, so just fix yourself something. Dad and I will get something on the way home.*

I smiled. Dad had worked at a factory most of my life, but when it closed down, he had a heck of a time finding work. Mom had been a bus driver since I'd been old enough to go to school, but it didn't pay well, so money was always tight growing up. Still, they always encouraged me to go to college and pursue my dreams, whatever those might be.

I chuckled as I sat down to eat my bologna sandwich. Both my parents worked best with their hands. Somehow, I'd come out the opposite. I was a book geek through and through.

Dad and I measured the same height, but that was where our physical similarities ended. While he looked like a lumberjack, I resembled a beanpole. Sure, I forced myself to exercise every morning before I went to work, but working out in a gym would never even remotely result in a strong physique like my dad had from hard physical labor.

I sighed. Even though I wholly admired him, I'd never be my dad. Thankfully, my parents always just let me be me—a geek who found happiness between the pages of books.

I quickly picked up around the house, knowing if Mom was helping Dad out, they would come home exhausted. Mom had always been a stickler for maintaining cleanliness, and I followed suit. Not wanting her to feel a need to clean when she got home, I vacuumed the living room and hallway, did a quick Swiffer of the kitchen tile, and even mopped. When I was convinced I had the place clean enough, I went back to my room and opened my laptop to do some research.

I still couldn't believe my dream job had fallen into my lap. I hadn't even had to apply for it. Talk about being the luckiest man alive. Now, I needed to learn about this small town called Crawford City that I'd soon be calling home.

Two

Roth

THE STAGE LIGHTS WERE making me feel nauseous. *Why do they have to be so bright?* I wondered for the umpteenth time as sweat trickled down my back.

Ramona Letson and I stood side by side onstage as a hush fell over the crowd, waiting for the results to be announced. The judges had weighed in, but it was out of their hands now. The audience had voted, and that collective opinion of strangers would determine both of our futures.

Ramona reached over and took my hand, and I cringed, knowing how sweaty it must be. "And the winner of this season of *Talented Citizens* is... Ramona Letson!"

The crowd cheered and my heart felt like it grew and shriveled simultaneously, as if I was both happy and depressed at the same time. On the one hand, I felt joy for Ramona and relief I wouldn't have to sing in front of a live crowd ever again. On the other, I'd lost and done so in a spectacular and very public fashion.

I hugged Ramona, who was screaming and jumping up and down. I almost laughed, but forced myself to maintain my composure as I left the stage.

I was met backstage by my family, who, with sad faces, hugged me and told me how sorry they were.

"God, I'm not. Y'all, I've learned one thing the hard way. I'm just not made for this life."

Lettie burst out laughing. "Only you, little brother, would take a loss as a win."

I almost flipped her off, but I wasn't at all sure we weren't being filmed, so I settled for just giving my sister a nasty look.

We had a few things to tie up with the network, and then my family took me back to our hotel. I was so exhausted, I fell asleep in the backseat on the drive. Tomorrow, we'd board our flight and head back home to Nashville.

I hugged everyone when we reached the lobby, thanked them for coming to support me, then barricaded myself in my room. I knew they all thought I was upset about losing, but really, the only upset I felt was learning how much I didn't want to spend my life performing every week as I had during the competition.

I was an introvert, and as such, I needed my downtime. The scores between Ramona and myself were neck and neck throughout the competition and I knew if I had been as outgoing as her and most of the other performers, I'd have done much better on the show. But as the final week had approached, I felt my enthusiasm drain away.

Performing... yes, that was something that I loved, even being an introvert, but never to the degree I had these past few weeks.

The next morning, we all went out to eat before our flight left. To my surprise, I was met at the airport by hundreds of fans. How they knew which flight I'd be on, I had no idea, but it confirmed to me that I would probably be better off finding find a different career path. My parents watched me, concerned, but I figured I'd sit everyone down and explain myself once we returned home and I didn't have fans listening to my every word. Hell, I'd probably be worried about me, too, if I didn't already know what was running through my head.

After the plane finally landed and we'd all piled into my dad's SUV, I turned my phone on, determined to manage all the calls and texts I knew I'd have before getting home. I listened to a few messages from friends telling me how sorry they were, and deleted messages from people I didn't know. On day one of the competition, I'd learned the hard way. Not all fan messages were good! When I'd received pictures of various people's body parts, not to mention texts from a couple of people who said they wanted to do really scary things to me, I'd decided deleting messages and blocking numbers was in my best interest.

I'd erased so many messages that I almost deleted the voicemail from Princeton Records. Although I still felt sure I would be better off walking away, I decided to listen to it anyway, just in case.

"Mr. Gallo, we'd like to meet with you to discuss a potential record deal. Can you come by our office in Nashville this week?"

I listened to the voicemail several more times, before I asked, "Do ya'll know anything about Princeton Records?"

"Yeah," my brother Sam said. "I think some pretty big-name country artists have signed with them, including a few who lean more toward pop music. Why?"

"I just got a message asking if I'd be interested in making a record with them."

The family all started talking at once and, as usual, I was too overwhelmed to say much. Finally, Mom said, "Okay, calm down, everyone. Sweetheart, how do you feel about that?"

I chuckled. My adoptive mom had been through enough therapy sessions with us as kids, she often sounded like a therapist herself. "I'm not sure, Mom. I mean, I'm really tired and I didn't think I'd want to pursue anything more, especially anything as intense as the competition has been."

"Are you gonna call them back?" Lettie asked. "If nothing else, just to see if it's a legit offer or not."

They all started asking questions again and I finally put my hand up. "Y'all, you know I'm not one for this sort of stuff. I'm totally wiped out too, so I need to sleep for a few days, then I'll find out what's going on. I'll fill you all in on it as soon as I know something."

That seemed to mollify them for the moment. Being the only introvert in a family of major extroverts, with the exception of Jesse maybe, they'd all learned the hard way. If they pushed me too hard, I'd completely shut down, and no one would get anything out of me.

I turned my phone off before any more messages could pop up, and just enjoyed listening to my family talk about what might happen if I got a recording contract. Of course, Lettie was all about getting to ride in fancy cars, meet famous people, and live in big houses.

Sometimes, I thought maybe my sister should be the famous one in the family, since she enjoyed bling, didn't put up with shit from anyone, and had such a big personality anyway. Seeking the limelight wasn't Lettie's style, though. I likened her to more of a behind-the-scenes string-puller, which was definitely a useful skill in the music business. I'd probably be smart to keep that in mind if I decided to take the plunge into this business.

THREE

CHRIS

WHEN I TOLD THEM the news, Mom and Dad acted both happy and concerned about my new job. "Honey," Mom asked, "isn't that too far to drive?"

"Yeah, probably. I'm guessing I'll have to find a place to stay in Crawford City."

"Are they giving you a raise, at least?" Dad asked.

When I told them what I'd be making as a lead librarian, both my parents looked shocked. "That's good money, son," Dad said, and I chuckled before I could stop myself.

"I told you it would be when I decided to get my degree. You just didn't believe me."

Dad came over and pulled me into a one-armed hug, the kind he was famous for, and moments later, Mom joined us. "We're so proud of you, son," she said.

"Y'all are squishing me," I said, and laughed when they both squeezed harder. I really did have the best parents in the world.

"Want us to go with you to check out places?" Dad asked, and I immediately nodded.

"Yeah, you know I'm clueless. I'll probably rent one of those old, haunted houses that's about to fall in." Both my parents smiled at the truth of that. "I'll call the mayor's office tomorrow and find out when we can go check out the new library too. I'd like to have some idea of what I'm up against."

It ended up being the next day that we were able to go. Dad had a cemetery to mow in the morning, so I made an appointment to meet the mayor in the afternoon. I'd ended up speaking to him directly when I called, which shocked me. I figured most mayors wouldn't answer their office phones. Although based on our short conversation, I highly suspected I'd called his personal mobile phone.

The area was beautiful with its wide-open spaces and rolling hills. We drove along several creeks and streams, and even passed by an impressive-looking vineyard that I made a mental note to go visit sometime. It all reminded me of going on Sunday drives with Mom and Dad throughout my childhood, always in search of our next picnic location. Our family picnics were my parents' cheap and easy way of getting me outside to enjoy nature, and we never ventured too far from the public parks in and around Nashville. I loved how we'd drive along just the three of us, find the ideal picnic site, and Mom would pull out sandwiches, fried chicken, and whatever leftovers had been in the fridge.

But leftovers always tasted better at a picnic.

After a relatively short drive from home, we pulled up in front of the town hall. The old brick building in what looked to be a typical railroad town square wasn't huge by any means, but then, neither was Crawford City.

The structure had clearly seen better days, but you could tell some recent work had been done to ensure it'd last a while longer. I appreciated the effort toward historic preservation and, looking around the small, town square at the older buildings that appeared to be in decent shape, it seemed the folks here valued their local history.

At first glance anyway, Crawford City appeared to be a well-maintained and active small town. Most storefronts had businesses in them, and several people gathered at a café not far from what I assumed was the new library, given what Mrs. Elliot had told me about it.

Seeing a new construction project up the street came as a surprise, one that gave me hope for the little town. The impressive hotel looked modern yet mimicked the rest of the old town's quaint feel.

"Yeah, I can be happy here," I said quietly to myself.

I left my parents at the car as I rushed up the town hall steps, and nearly ran into an older man repairing the railing. I smiled as I zipped past him to the upper floor where the mayor's office was located.

When I went to pull open the door, though, I found it locked.

I quickly looked at my watch. I was on time. Maybe the mayor was running late, so I sat down at the top of the stairs to wait.

A few seconds later, the old man I'd almost collided with came up and greeted me. "Are you Christopher Asbell?" he asked.

"Yes, sir," I said, perplexed.

He reached out his hand, and said, "I'm the mayor, but you can just call me Doc."

"Doc, the mayor?" I said out loud before I could stop myself and the man chuckled.

"I was the town's doctor before I became the mayor."

"Oh," I said. "That explains it then. Why were *you* repairing the railing?"

He chuckled again. "Well, it's part of the job when you don't have a budget for a construction crew."

"I see..." I was beginning to have a sinking feeling in the pit of my stomach about what the library was going to look like.

He unlocked his office and I sat on an ugly green office chair while I waited for him to get comfortable. "So, is it still okay if my folks and I go over to the library? I wanted to get the lay of the land before we started adding books."

Doc smiled at me. "Of course. We haven't officially been given the keys yet, but seeing as it's my son-in-law who is contracted to do the renovations, I figure we can get in without any trouble."

Son-in-law? It felt as though I'd stepped into some time warp and been transported back to nineteen-fifties small-town America where everyone knew everyone. And where townsfolk might not be so open-minded, then or now. I felt my shoulders tense as I began to worry a bit about my safety. I mean, I'd been out of the closet since high school, but I didn't really go out much or pursue men, but in small town, Tennessee you could get outed pretty quick, and being in a rural community could mean it wasn't safe.

I was really beginning to reconsider my decision. I hoped the mayor didn't notice how cold and clammy my hands were when he handed me a key he'd taken off his keyring.

"If you don't mind, I'd like you to bring that key back to me." He quickly wrote down an address. "That's my home. My husband or I will be there, and you can drop the key off when you're done.

"Your husband?" I asked, then immediately felt em-barrassed by my shocked tone.

The man looked at me and gave me a half-smile. "Yes, my husband, Amos."

"You're gay then?"

I think he must've thought I was some homophobe because he looked at me funny. "Yes, we're a gay couple."

"Cool," I quickly replied, relief washing over me like a fresh rain pouring over parched ground. "I was just worrying about an angry mob running me out of town, but I guess if the mayor is gay, that's not as likely to happen."

The older man leaned back in his chair and laughed. "No, we're a pretty open little town. You'll see. My son and his husband are out. We have neighbors who are gay and, well, lately there seems to be more and more of us showing up."

"Really?" I asked, surprised. "I guess you've figured out I'm gay, too, but I don't date very much. Mostly, I've got an affair going with my job."

"You really will once you get set up. I'm sorry we didn't have the budget for more than one person to help run the place. But the levy we got passed to establish the library was contentious enough. If we'd asked for even a half a cent more, we'd have been run out of there on a rail."

"Oh, I wanted to ask about that. My boss told me this is a collaboration with the school district. Will I be going into the schools as well?"

He shook his head. "No, our schools have full-time librarians. Your job will only involve your building, plus any outreach you see fit doing. Trust me, that will keep you busy."

"Why do you think that?" I asked. I'd all but assumed I'd have to build interest in the library.

"Well, mostly 'cause everyone is curious about where their taxes are going. You're also located across the street from the most popular place in town, the Crawford City Café."

"I'm glad to hear there's built-in interest already. That's one hurdle cleared," I said. "I'm eager to see inside the library. My boss told me it's an old school."

"It is. It was the second school building in town, built in eighteen eighty. My predecessor wanted to tear it down and turn the area into a park, but luckily, more level-headed people intervened."

The mayor stood up then and grabbed his tools, clearly dismissing me. "It's a nice spot. Been very important to the neighborhood and our local history too. It started out as a school for our Black kids, then after desegregation, it became our town's only elementary school. In fact, both my husband and I attended school there. Unfortunately, when the school district abandoned it, the building stood vacant for a long time. If it hadn't been for Todd, my son-in-law, basically doing the renovation for free, I'm sure we'd have lost it. Anyway, it'll be really nice to have it being used for something we can all be proud of again."

He walked out the door and I quickly jumped up and followed him. "You'll have to excuse me," he added. "I've got to finish this repair before it gets too messed up to fix. Unfortunately, there's not one cent left in the town's budget this year, which is why I'm getting to refresh my carpentry skills."

I smiled. "Well, I can't say I'm envious of you. Just so you know, if anything breaks in the library, we're screwed, 'cause I'm pretty useless with fixing stuff."

"Oh, now that we've got the building done, repairs will fall on the school district. That's part of our agreement. Lucky for you, they still have a budget."

I chuckled as I waved at the man and went down the stairs to rejoin my parents. I was still having a hard time reconciling in my head a mayor doing his own office repairs, but I guessed when you were running a small town with a small budget, you would have to put all your skills to use.

I saw my parents wandering around the town square, clearly waiting for me. "Mom, Dad," I yelled across the street, and they turned to me. "I'm gonna walk on down. Come when you're ready."

Both of them waved me on. Mom had spotted a quilt shop opposite where we were parked, and I knew she'd make a beeline there. Poor Dad had been pulled into more than one of those stores over the years. Mom had never sewn a day in my life until she and Aunt Lilly got into it over who was best at it while in high school home economics. Mom had taken up quilting then, and even though her sister had long ago lost interest, Mom had only grown more obsessed.

I walked down the sidewalk that spanned the length between the town hall and the new library. There appeared to be a lot of open land around the building, which gave me some hope that if we were successful, we'd have room to expand. I sort of understood why the former mayor would've wanted to turn this into a park too. Maybe we could do some outdoor book groups during spring and summer. I was thinking about summer reading camps when I walked up to the building.

Cute. That was my first impression of the place. It was almost perfectly square with a wide stoop, doors compliant with the Americans with Disabilities Act, and a nice ramp. To my relief, this was nothing like the run-down building I'd expected.

The roof rose dramatically like I'd seen on some older Southern homes. At the very top of the roof was a little belltower, which looked completely out of place to me. From my vantage point, I could see that the old bell was still inside.

I silently apologized to the townsfolk because sooner than later, I was going to ring that bell.

I walked up the stoop, imagining large flower planters I could put up to make the entry feel more welcoming. The mayor had said the school district had a budget, and I wondered if I could tap into it to buy the flowers and planters.

I unlocked the door and walked into a beautiful, airy, and bright space. I'd thought I'd see classrooms but with the exception of a couple offices behind the circulation desk and what looked like a couple of meeting rooms just off the entry, it was open floor plan.

"Oh, this is perfect," I said to the room. "It's just perfect."

My excitement grew the more I looked around. The rooms I'd thought were meeting rooms were exactly that, which made me happy. Having worked in a library for some time, I knew everyone from local businesses to students liked to reserve rooms for various things. Keeping the community coming in and out of the library would keep the place alive and useful.

I went to the circulation desk then and checked out the usability of the space. Clearly, it had been designed without a librarian since there were definite functionality hiccups that would have to be worked around, but that was totally doable. I'd seen worse setups.

I swooned when I entered the large office located behind the circulation desk and saw a large, ornate window that looked out onto the back of the property. Beyond the old school grounds stood a lush forest and I knew I'd be spending a lot of time just staring out that window.

I wished I could just put my bed in here and move in. I'm sure the mayor would *love* that. It reminded me, though, that I needed to check out local apartment listings soon.

Going back out into the main room, I looked around the space for several moments, imagining how I'd lay out the bookshelves. About five years ago, we'd redesigned the library I'd just left and made the shelves shorter. Immediately, the library's traffic increased. People clearly felt less confined with the shorter shelves, and it made the library more inviting overall.

There were bookshelves already built onto the walls between the huge windows. The clever designer also had enough sense to install lower shelves below the windows. I already knew we'd be putting tables in front of the windows and these small shelves were perfect for people to store their belongings while they sat reading or working.

Close to the entrance was an area that clearly used to be the front office for the school. The walls had been removed, but the area remained set apart from the main room. I could envision it being a children's book area with kid-friendly open shelves and a comfortable couch situated under the front window that faced the café across the street.

I was about to head out when I saw a slightly ajar door behind the circulation desk. I wasn't sure how I'd missed that, other than having been distracted by my drool-worthy future office.

I quickly opened the door and headed up an old stairway. I wasn't prepared to find attic space. The room had beautiful hardwood floors that hadn't been refinished, but surely could be. I was imagining all sorts of activities we could hold up here when I heard someone call out from the first floor.

"Yeah, I'm up here. Hold on, I'll be right down."

I quickly dashed down the stairs and came face-to-face with... well, the only way to describe him was sex on legs. A rush of desire swept through me, and I felt my cheeks grow hot and mouth go dry. As I stared at the man whose dirty-blond hair fell into his eyes behind wire-rimmed glasses, giving him just the right amount of a geeky, Justin Bieber look, I had to admit that I might've swooned a little bit.

"Hey," he said. "I'm lost and trying to find an address. I was hoping the librarian could help me." He glanced around the empty room and seemed to hesitate. "Um, isn't this the library? I thought I saw a sign for it."

I laughed. "I'm not sure about a sign, but yeah, it *will* be the library. We haven't opened yet."

"Oh, well, I um... sorry," he stammered, which was cute as hell. Apparently, I wasn't the only one feeling a little flustered, though likely not for the same reason.

He was looking at me oddly, like maybe I had something on my face. I subconsciously wiped across my face, hoping to God I didn't have a booger hanging out of my nose, or something equally mortifying.

"Do you know where this address is?" he asked, holding out a handwritten note.

I was just about to tell him I was new to town and didn't know my way around when I recognized the address.

"That's the mayor's house," I said stupidly.

"Really?" he asked.

"Yeah, I'm headed that way myself."

"Cool, maybe I can follow you."

"Sure, but can't you just put it in your phone?"

He chuckled. "Well, if I hadn't left my charger at home, sure. It turns out, a dead phone is pretty useless."

"Oh, that makes sense," I said, and laughed awkwardly. "If you give me a second, I'll find out if my parents are ready to leave. I rode here with them."

He nodded and I quickly called my dad. "Hey, Dad, are y'all about ready to head out?"

"Um, that's a big fat no!" Dad said in a whiney voice.

"Mom ran into someone she knows, didn't she?" I asked.

"Yeah, her old hairstylist."

"Dear God, we'll be here a week."

Dad chuckled. "So, take your time. We're still in the quilt shop and will be for a while yet."

"Okay. I'm helping someone who needs directions to the mayor's house. I need to drop off the key to the library there anyway, then I'll come find you."

"Sorry for bailing on you, son. We were supposed to come check it out with you."

"Not to worry, Dad, you can come visit after we get it all put together. It's a nice space."

"Good. Well, I'm gonna find a bench to camp out on until your mom gets done talking. I'm sure we'll not be leaving this store until they shut the place down. Have your new friend drop you off back at the car, then text us."

I agreed and chuckled as I hung up.

"Well, seems like I'm footloose and fancy-free. My mom ran into her old hairdresser, we won't be leaving town anytime soon."

The man smiled a cute, crooked smile and I thought he looked a little familiar. I couldn't quite place how I knew him, though.

He pulled his car around while I locked up the library. I typed the mayor's address into my phone, then laughed when the map showed it was only a quarter-mile away.

"You know, we can walk if you prefer."

He looked like he was considering it. "I've already got my car. Why don't we drive?"

I nodded and wondered if maybe I was being stupid getting into a stranger's car. Maybe he looked familiar because he was a wanted serial killer who'd been featured on one of those reality TV crime shows. I probably should've relayed more details to my dad.

I laughed at myself as I got in the car, but I kept the library key in my hand in case I had to quickly revert to self-defense.

FOUR

ROTH

WHAT A CUTE GUY, I thought as I stood in front of the librarian, babbling like an idiot. Just my type too. One who looked adorably geeky and not too muscular, just sort of your average Joe. Not that there was anything average about this guy.

Funny enough, I generally had no interest in pursuing most men. I'd never felt all that driven to date or have sex. There'd only been a couple men who really did melt my butter, so to speak. This librarian, though, was certainly one of the few.

He recognized the address and with his phone, we quickly found the mayor's residence. The large, beautiful early nineteenth-century log cabin was incredible, and the home next to it was just as magnificent. It looked like the owners must've been in cahoots, because there was a nice little garden path connecting the two.

With my family's encouragement, I'd taken the contract with Princeton Records because it proved too good to ignore. Part of the deal included working around my not wanting to be on tour all the damned time. That stance had mostly been driven by not wanting to face my crippling stage fright, but it remained a hard line for me.

They also contacted Jake McCartney, who they hoped would agree to be my new PR manager. Jake managed to talk me into meeting him in Crawford City, saying he had to travel this week and would only be in town for a couple days before flying out again. Supposedly, he needed to check on some project here in the boondocks before he flew to Europe to meet with another client.

I pulled up to the large cabin and parked. "Wow, this is beautiful," I said, and the cute man nodded.

"More than beautiful," he agreed.

When he looked over at me and blushed, my insides basically turned to mush. I really wanted to lean over and kiss him, but that would be ridiculous. People didn't just randomly kiss strangers, no matter how adorable.

We got out and walked up to the front door, but just as I was about to ring the doorbell, we heard people talking. Their voices were getting louder and when the floorboards creaked, it became clear they were walking on the front porch.

When a couple of handsome men rounded the corner, all four of us froze. The adorable man, the one I hadn't thought to get the name of, came to his senses first. "Are you the mayor's husband?" he asked the older of the two.

The man smiled and reached out his hand. "Yes, I'm Amos, and this is my son, Todd. Who might you be?" he asked.

"I'm Christopher Asbell, the new librarian. Your husband asked me to drop the library key off when I was done looking at the building."

Amos nodded and looked at me expectantly. I reached over and shook his hand, saying, "I'm Roth Gallo. I was told to meet Jake McCartney here."

Todd rolled his eyes. "Jake didn't tell us you were coming."

"Well, it's no bother. Come on in, you two, and make yourself comfortable," Amos said. "Tell me, how did you meet?"

"Oh, we're not a couple," I blurted, and could've kicked my own ass for how it sounded. "What I mean is, we just met a few minutes ago. My phone died and I went into the library for directions and ran into Mr. Asbell, who showed me the way here."

He nodded in confirmation, but his eyes were like saucers. "You okay?" I asked.

"Um, yeah. I'm sorry I didn't recognize you until now. You must think I'm an idiot."

I shook my head. "Oh yeah, that. It's okay, I don't expect anyone to recognize me. It's not like I'm famous or anything."

Amos shook his head. "You are, *and* you should've won. I have no idea how you lost to that woman. Hell, she could barely carry a tune."

"Dad," Todd said, but his father shrugged, causing us all to smile.

"Just telling the truth," he said.

I inwardly chuckled, although I disagreed with Amos's assessment of Ramona's talent. I had no idea folks living in the boondocks would've watched the show, let alone been so invested in the outcome.

"So, our boy Jake is reeling you in, is he?" Todd asked.

I smiled. "Well, more like I'm reeling him in. I'm told my record label pulled a lot of strings to get him to even consider me. Apparently, he's one of the best in the business."

Just then a car pulled up and two men got out. "Hey, guys, sorry I'm late. I had to pick Derek up."

The two were practically carbon copies of one another, except the younger one was just a little stockier. Clearly, they were closely related.

"I'm Jake McCartney and this is my brother, Derek," the older one said to me, extending his hand. "I assume you're Roth? It's a pleasure to meet you in person. Thanks for driving out here."

"Thanks for having me," I said, and shook his hand. "And this is Christopher Asbell, the town's new librarian."

"Please, call me Chris," he said, and I didn't miss how he ducked his head a little, almost shyly. Could the man be any more adorable?

"Now that we've got pleasantries out of the way, you all come on in and have some lemonade. I just made it this afternoon, so it's fresh," Amos said, beckoning everyone into his living room.

"Thank you, but I don't want to impose. I just needed to return this," Chris said, and handed the library key to Amos.

"It's no imposition. We've been chomping at the bit for my son here to finish that building so we can get the library open and be a legitimate town. Come on in for some lemonade," he said.

Cute Chris blushed even deeper, but didn't argue.

We all sat around the incredibly comfortable living room while Jake peppered me with questions. Chris sat quietly while sipping his lemonade, clearly uncomfortable. I sort of felt bad for him. He hadn't meant to get caught up in all the hubbub that seemed to follow me around these days.

I related more to him than I probably should've at this point in my career. I was usually the quiet one in groups and around people I didn't know well, preferring not to be the center of attention. The introvert in me envied Chris in a way, being surrounded by books and the quietness of a library all day, although in reality, his job was bound to be very public-facing too.

When Jake took a breath, giving me a break from his questions, I asked Chris when he thought they'd have the library up and running.

"Um..." he stammered. "I don't honestly know. I just got the job last week and today is my first time in Crawford City. I'll need to find housing, though, since it'd be a long commute back and forth to my parents' house."

"You're looking for a place to live?" Amos asked when he came in carrying a tray full of glasses.

"Yes, sir," Chris said. "My car is not the most reliable and I hate driving anyway, so I'd prefer to find someplace here in town."

"Well, we might have just the place, provided you don't mind living with a couple old men."

"And the entire town," Todd added.

"Well, only during the day," Amos said. "Oh, we have three grandbabies that live next door too. You'll need to know they come over daily."

"They're loud too," Todd said, laughing.

Chris just stared at them both, looking confused. "You're renting out a room here?" he asked.

"Yep, that's the idea," Amos said. "We have three grandbabies in Oregon too, and they are growing up too fast. We're going to be spending a lot more time out there, so we need someone to stay here and look after this place."

Todd looked at his dad funny. "I told you I can look after the place."

"Psst," Amos burst out. "You barely have time to look after your own home."

Todd shrugged. "Yeah, you're probably right. Running a business and chasing three kids around is a lot of work."

"Which is why we're looking for someone to move into the top bedroom and housesit for us while we're away."

Chris looked around the room and sighed. "That's a generous offer, but I'm afraid I probably can't afford this sort of place. I only graduated from college a couple weeks ago and I've got school loans, and—"

"Well, like I said—" Amos interrupted, "—we're looking for someone to look after the place for us, so that'll be taken into consideration when we're discussing costs. Besides, if you're going to help us get that library up and running in this one-horse town, then that's worth some investment too."

Chris was clearly embarrassed, and I had to resist the inexplicable urge to offer him comfort. "Thank you, I'll consider it."

"Well, you should at least see the room before making your decision. Come on up, I'll show you."

I watched Chris hesitantly follow the man up the stairs and out of sight.

When I turned back to Jake, he was smiling. "You got a thing for the young librarian?" he asked.

Now it was my turn to blush. "Um, I just met him."

"Yeah, and I recognize that look. It was the same thing for me and my honey. The minute I saw him, I knew he was someone special."

Jake was a lot to handle, and I wasn't anywhere near comfortable discussing my nonexistent love life with him, let alone with other people listening, so I quickly changed the subject. "So, Billy at the record label said I needed to talk you into working with me if I'm going to have any chance at success."

Jake's face bloomed into a smile. "Okay, I got it, stay out of your personal business, but if I sign with you, you need to know I'll be all up in your business and take up residence there."

"He's not joking," Todd said from across the room, and Jake picked a couch pillow up and tossed it at the man.

I was staring at them as if they'd just grown horns when Jake chuckled. "Todd is my best friend. He's also a giant pain in the butt, but whatcha gonna do?"

"I'm not, I just call it straight."

Jake rolled back, laughing. "The only straight thing in this room might be the singer here."

I shook my head. "Nope, afraid not. Been out since I was like fifteen."

"Wow, so you're going into country music, and you're gay?"

"Nope, I'm going into country-pop music, and I'm gay."

"Okay, well, that'll be something of a challenge, but I'm up for it." Jake put his hand out and took mine in a shake. "You're officially my client. Now poor Charlie is gonna have to decide who to reassign to my other reps 'cause I've decided to take you on myself."

I blushed again. "Thanks, that's really nice of you."

Todd laughed again. "Hardly, he knows you're a gold mine."

"Hey," Jake said. "He's also a sister, and sisters gotta stick together!"

That was the first time the kid with him chuckled. "Sisters. Yeah, right."

Jake looked at his brother and burst into laughter. "Well, what would you call him?"

"I'd call him Roth, since it's his freaking name."

"Please, little brother, come on out of the stinking closet. Trust me, the water's fine."

The kid just shook his head, looked at me, and said, "See what I have to deal with."

"You are so freaking lucky to have a brother like me," Jake said, smirking.

I felt too overwhelmed to know what to say. Jake had been cast as a serious, tough to get PR manager. He sure didn't seem that way to me now. He seemed more like a friendly guy you'd meet down at the local bar and enjoy chatting with.

"So, do you live here?" I asked him as my mind wandered.

"Not yet, but soon, very soon," he said, pointing to Todd.

"Not soon enough," Todd said under his breath.

"Is it done enough that I can go see it?" he asked.

"Yeah, I told you we finished painting yesterday. Isn't that why you're here, or did you just pull this poor kid out to the middle of the sticks to be mean?"

"You wound me," Jake said. "This is the best place in the entire state. Small town, gay-friendly, cute guys... what's there not to like?"

"You're lucky Lance didn't hear you say that," Derek, the brother said.

Jake blushed then and looked a bit cowed. "Yeah, he's the cute guy I was referring to."

"Uh-huh," Derek said, but he was smiling. I didn't know who this Lance was, but I was looking forward to meeting him. I doubted there were many people who could cause Jake to back down. His tenacity was undeniable, but I appreciated knowing he had an Achilles heel too. It made him a real person, the sort I wanted and needed on my team.

CHRIS

"SORRY, I'M JUST OVERWHELMED," I admitted to Amos while he showed me the room for rent. He'd seen my discomfort and led me upstairs as much to give me a break as to show me the room. He'd admitted as much when we reached the third floor, then asked if I was okay.

"Well, I can understand feeling that way. That Roth character is a good-looking lad and Jake is always a lot to handle."

I sat down unceremoniously on a chair. "Seriously, I just came to check out the new library and the next thing I know, the singer from TV I've been crushing on shows up? I mean, it's so preposterous. I didn't even recognize the guy at first."

Amos sat on the bed and shrugged. "Well, life is funny sometimes. But, son, here's a clue. That boy puts his pants on same as you, one leg at a time. Don't let yourself get so starstruck you can't let him woo you a little. I can tell he likes you too."

"How's that possible? I'm just geeky, average me. Why would a guy like him even look at me twice?"

Amos leaned back and laughed, his rich baritone voice filling the room. "Son, it takes all kinds. I'm guessing you're the right brand for the singer boy. Now, I'm gonna leave you up here and you can take a look at your leisure. If you like it, it's yours. My husband and I really do need someone to look after the place while we're gone. It doesn't do to leave a house empty for long periods of time, especially one as old and fussy as this one."

I chuckled. "Mr. Amos, just so we're clear, I'm not gifted with a hammer. I'm a book nerd. The most I could do is call someone to fix things."

"Please, just call me Amos. And lucky for you, my son is in construction, and he lives less than five hundred feet away. We really are just looking for someone to keep an eye on things. Besides, there are a lot of good reading spots in this house." He winked at me as he got up to leave.

Once he was gone, I wandered around the big open space. It included a small three-quarter bathroom that was more than adequate for me, and a small refrigerator and microwave. The place really did meet most of my needs.

I quickly crunched the numbers in my head and figured with my promotion to lead librarian, I could afford about a thousand a month, provided I didn't get too carried away buying stuff online. I did have a problem with that. I blushed thinking about the last time I'd gone on a spending spree. I had some really nice clothes for work now, but I'd also had to take an extra job to pay off my credit card.

Yeah, this would be perfect. Besides, rooming with the mayor sounded like a good idea. It might help bring a few more locals into the library who would otherwise feel alienated by an outsider in their town. I knew the mayor thought I'd be busy, but I couldn't see how. Mrs. Elliot told me there hadn't been a library here in decades. It'd take some time for the townsfolk to get used to having one again.

I walked down the stairs and was met by the entire group talking at once. Again, I felt overwhelmed before I remembered Amos's words. They were all just people, like me, including Roth. Why was I so taken with him? I took a deep breath and resolved to just let things happen. If we became friends, great. If not, that was fine too. I was an adult, after all, not a starry-eyed teenager.

When I entered the room, the talking stopped, and everyone looked at me. The resolve I'd built moments ago crumbled. "Well, I should be going," I said, looking to Amos. "Maybe we can meet and talk later about renting the room. The mayor has all my contact information."

I was just about to leave, when Jake said, "Why don't we all go to the café for dinner."

I turned back to the group and, forcing a smile, said, "That's kind of you, but I'm with my family. They're in town chatting with friends. I should probably go meet them."

"Can I drive you back?" Roth asked while standing up.

I smiled and shook my head. "No, I'm good with walking. It isn't very far."

I noticed his face fall, but I needed an escape. If my heart beat any faster, I'd be in danger of it beating out of my chest.

"Thank you all, and nice to meet you," I managed to say as I darted out the front door.

I used the quarter-mile walk between Amos's house and town to clear my head. By the time I reached the quilt shop, I was laughing at the circumstances. I was sure my parents would get quite a thrill out of my awkward meeting with my celebrity crush. Not to mention randomly falling into what felt like the best possible living situation.

My phone rang just as I walked into the quilt shop. I laughed when I saw it was Dad calling me. He smiled too when he saw me enter. "Perfect timing. Fran has just invited us to dinner at the café. What do you think?" he asked.

"Um, sure," I said, feeling like a heel since I'd basically blown off joining the group there. Geez, it was like I'd stepped in it and couldn't get my foot back out.

Mom and Fran, who I'd met before, were still chatting nonstop. Dad hung back and shook his head, before whispering, "They've not stopped talking since they saw each other."

I chuckled. "Dad, I remember Mom going to Fran's shop back when I was little. They didn't stop talking back then either."

"I heard that," Mom said, and turned to us. "I want you to know Fran and I have been friends since we were girls, and we haven't seen each other in a month of Sundays. So, you two just settle down back there."

I saw Fran grin, then Mom linked arms with her and led the way toward the café. Dad laughed quietly next to me, and when the women were far enough ahead, he said, "Well, we've been properly chastised."

"Apparently," I responded. "Hey, I met some people and think I might have a place to live. They'll probably be at the café too, so unless I wanna be rude, we'll probably need to sit with them. Is that okay?"

"Sure, son. Who are they?"

When I told him one was the guy who'd almost won the singing competition we all loved watching together, he called me a liar. Of course, I wasn't lying, but I could understand his skepticism. I wouldn't have believed me either.

Fran led us into the café, and we were about to find a table when Roth and the group came in behind us.

"Hi, everyone. It turns out I got roped into the café after all. Do y'all wanna sit together?" I asked.

"Sure," Jake said. "Ms. Frances, it's always a pleasure, and who is this lovely lady?" he asked, causing my mom to beam.

Fran made introductions between us all, then froze when she came to Roth. "I don't think I've officially met you," she said. "But I do recognize you. Such a shame you didn't win. We were all rootin' for you."

My dad's eyes were already as big as saucers when Mom recognized him too, and they both nodded their agreement with Fran. I looked at Roth, who gave me a little smile, and blushed. I felt like I should do something to cut the awkwardness, though. The last thing I needed was my parents being starstruck and risk letting slip my hard crush on the man.

"Mom, Dad, Amos is married to the mayor, and they've offered me their third floor to rent while I'm getting established here."

Amos shook my parents' hands, then showed us to a part of the café where large groups could sit together. We had just been told to help ourselves to the buffet when the mayor and another man who looked a great deal like him joined us.

Mayor Nash, who I remembered had said to call him Doc, sat next to Amos and the new guy next to Todd. "Hi, I'm Ash, Doc's son and Todd's other half," he said, leaning over Todd to shake my hand.

"Nice to meet you. I'm Chris, the new librarian."

"He's also going to be our new roommate," Amos said to the group.

I blushed. I hadn't exactly agreed to the arrangement yet.

"When did you two decide to get a roommate?" Ash asked his dad, looking confused.

Before Doc could respond, Roth sat down next to me, and all the oxygen left my lungs. Apparently, he'd vacated his seat next to Amos so Doc could sit there. When his arm absently brushed mine, my entire body grew hot, and I completely lost track of the conversation for a while.

"Wow, the food smells amazing. It's like being home for the holidays," he said.

I managed a smile and a nod, but my tongue had forgotten how to work. Oh god, could you have a heart attack just from close proximity to a gorgeous man? Judging by the way my heart was racing, I thought it possible. What if I accidentally kissed him or something?

Far-fetched scenarios of how that might happen—me needing mouth-to-mouth after choking on mashed potatoes, or me falling onto him face-first as I got up from the table—played out in my head. When I couldn't hold back a snort-laugh at my own wild imagination, Roth glanced my way and smiled. He seemed amused, and I thanked God he couldn't read my mind.

As my mind came back online, I picked up bits of conversation happening around the table. Mom and Fran had started back up about quilting. Dad was talking with Amos about what he did for a living, and Doc was explaining to Ash and Todd why they needed someone to manage the house while they were visiting their daughter and grandkids out of state.

"So, when do you start your new library job?" Roth asked.

It took a moment for it to register he'd asked me something.

"Oh, um, I'm not sure. Maybe a month?"

"More like a couple weeks," Doc said. "Todd is supposed to officially turn over the keys to the superintendent this week, then we'll need you here to help set up the shelves and start putting out the books."

"Yeah, my boss wasn't exactly sure of the start date, but she expected it to be soon."

"Do you need volunteers to help set up?" Roth asked.

I almost choked on my food. I heard a soft laugh come out of Doc and he responded for me. "Absolutely. I've got a few volunteers, most of whom are around this table, but we could always use more. Isn't that right, Mr. Librarian?"

"Yes, sir. It'll take me a long time to arrange the materials by myself. The more help I have, the quicker we can open."

"Then count me in."

"Where will you stay?" I asked.

"It's not that far from Nashville. I can come in for a few hours, then drive back home."

"You can also stay at the new hotel," Jake said. "It's not officially open, but we can let you have one of the rooms."

Todd looked at Jake and sighed. "No, we probably can't. The insurance company would have our hides. But how about you stay with us? I mean, you'd have three little hellions to contend with, but we could always use an extra pair of hands."

Amos laughed. "You'll drive the poor kid away before he even gets here. No, he can stay with us as well. We've got plenty of room and no loud, demanding grandchildren living with us."

"Speaking of staying with us, are you really willing to take on housesitting?" Doc asked me.

"Um, I haven't really had time to decide. It is a very generous offer, though."

"Well, let us know. The last time we left town, we had a neighbor's teenager stay, and..."

"And we cleaned for a week before we got the place back to where it was before we left," Amos finished.

Todd and Ash both stifled a laugh, and I could imagine just how bad it'd been.

I was almost too nervous to eat with Roth next to me. Even if I wasn't star-crossed over the guy, he was so handsome that just being within touching distance of him caused all the nerves in my body to short-circuit.

I managed to get a few bites in, however, and more than once, as the group chatted on about various things, Roth and I would exchange a look. He seemed just as shy as I felt, though I still couldn't fathom him actually being interested in me like I was him.

I'd been around my mom in enough social situations to know when her social hour was finally coming to an end. As we finished eating, Dad stood up to go pay, but Doc stopped him. "No, this is our treat today. Your son here is going to save us a great deal of headache, not to mention taking a position we've needed filled for many years. Let us treat you this time."

Dad blushed, which was rare for him. "My boy is something special, sir. So, I guess I'll let you honor him."

I looked at my dad funny. He'd always been like the ideal father. When others complained about unfeeling or inattentive dads, I'd never related. Sure, I'd hated him when I was a teenager because he'd been tough and didn't let me get away with hardly anything. But as I grew up, I learned how lucky I'd been to have him.

That being said, he rarely bragged about me, at least not when I could hear.

He smiled at me, and I looked down, embarrassed. That seemed to be the trend for me today.

As we made to leave, Roth stood up and followed us out. "I look forward to helping out at the library," he said.

I smiled. "I'm happy to have the help. So, I guess I'll see you in a couple weeks?"

He nodded and went back inside. I would've bet lots of money I'd never see him again, but at least I'd have a fun celebrity story to tell my kids one day, one that could be corroborated by my parents and a host of other people in my new community.

Six

Roth

AFTER CHRIS AND HIS family left the café, Jake and Derek took me to see Jake's new condo. Jake had agreed to represent me, and didn't make any bones about it being because I was willing to travel to Crawford City. Truth be told, returning to the small town wouldn't be any hardship if it meant I'd also be spending more time with the cute librarian.

The condo was truly beautiful, and built on the side of town that backed up to old railroad tracks. You could tell they'd used old bricks on the exterior because the building looked like it'd been there for over a hundred years.

The work was mostly done, and Jake was clearly chomping at the bit to get access to it. He and Derek showed me up to the top level, which Jake had already laid claim to as his own. Jake said he and his husband, who attended Vanderbilt, currently lived in Nashville, but planned to relocate to Crawford City in the near future.

The second space they showed me had supposedly been purchased by a famous model. I didn't recognize her name, but then again, I wasn't really into fashion, or female models for that matter.

The third space, the one directly above what would be commercial shops, remained available. Jake didn't even try to hide the fact he was trying to get me to purchase it. Of course, I could've easily reminded him that even though I had a record deal, I still had very little money to my name, but I enjoyed getting a tour of the place nonetheless.

Life got hectic once I returned to Nashville. The record label pulled me in for multiple rehearsals, on top of frequent meetings to discuss which songs would go on the album. They didn't want to pay the licensing fees involved for me to re-record Amelia Denton's single I'd sung for the competition, but that was okay. I'd be happy putting my own original music out anyway.

Even though I wasn't picky about the songs, the label was. They'd have me test a song out, I'd practice it a couple times to make it my own, then if they didn't like it, they tossed it out.

I went through about a hundred songs before we settled on ten.

Here's some trivia I'd learned. Recording was a shit ton of work. I figured it'd be easy. I'd go in, sing a few songs, bam, done. But that was far from how things worked.

What shocked me most about the whole thing was how much I loved it. I liked thumbing through songs I'd never heard before. I loved the challenge of trying to make them feel like my own. I enjoyed working with all the recording professionals, and even liked the bossy managers, although more than once I wanted to tell them to take a flying leap.

Luckily, my grandmother and adoptive parents had taught me better, so I managed to keep my inner diva locked away for the most part.

Before I knew it, several months had passed. I'd frequently thought about the sexy librarian in the tiny town east of Nashville. I'd have happily stolen some hours to go visit, and help set up the library like I'd said I would, but it'd been pretty much day in and day out work since there was such a rush to get the album out.

When the label agreed to let me have some free time for myself since recording had wrapped, I called Jake and told him I wanted to visit Crawford City.

"You mean, visit the town's new librarian?" he asked.

"Well, he's definitely a plus. Have you heard how he's doing?" I asked.

"Chris seems happy. Busy, but happy."

"Cool. I owe him some man hours. I think it's about time I pay up."

Jake chuckled. "Well, I'm sure he'll be happy to get the help. Want me to call Doc and get you on the list? He manages the volunteers for the library since the poor kid is buried with work."

"Yeah, I'd appreciate that. Just please ask him to let me know when to report for book duty."

We chatted a bit more about the label, and Jake, always the one to have his finger on the pulse, told me some things about the album release I hadn't been told by the label. I knew I needed a new manager, someone who was in charge of my career, but things had happened so fast, I hadn't had time to hire anyone.

I decided I'd put my sister on the job of finding someone, since she was currently in some weird funk. I knew it was partially because I wasn't around to harass her as much as usual. We really were best friends.

That night, I stopped by the pizza place she and I both loved before heading to her apartment. When Lettie opened the door, she put her hands on her hips, and said, "You disappear for months, then show up unannounced. If I didn't know you grew up with the best parents on the planet, I'd question your raising."

"You're just mad 'cause you couldn't come to the studio with me." I kissed her cheek and held out the pizza boxes like a peace offering. "Besides, I brought pizzas to bribe you to forgive my absence."

"Please, like you can bribe me with pizza."

I laughed. "Oh well, Jesse is coming over to Mom and Dad's. I guess I could just give these to him."

"Over my dead body!" Lettie exclaimed, and pulled me through the doorway. "Okay, so you know you can bribe me, but it *shouldn't* be that easy. Even when you're busy, you should at least text me back when I text you."

"Um, no. You get mad when I text you after midnight, and more often than not, that's when I get done. I needed to sleep at least some between takes, so you just gotta deal, sis. Besides, I'm here now. So, eat your pizza and get a grip."

Lettie flipped me off and crashed down on her couch, indicating I should bring the pizzas over and sit down on the chair that was usually reserved for me.

"Wanna watch movies and veg with me?" I asked. "It's been an intense few weeks. I need to crash."

"Sure, whatcha wanna watch?"

"Something sweet and romantic that doesn't require me to think too much."

"You're such a softy," Lettie said, but then she called me that all the time and I couldn't really argue. I preferred the proverbial chick flicks much more than the action-packed stuff Lettie and our brothers liked, and I supposed I was a bit of a romantic at heart too.

We kicked back to *Practical Magic*, eating pizza and catching up.

When the movie ended, I helped take the boxes into the kitchen, and was about to leave when I remembered the manager thing. "Hey, sis, I need a favor. I need to hire a manager, someone I can trust to keep tabs on my career. I know you know every freaking person in Nashville, so could you do some research for me? Get me some names?" I asked.

"How much you payin'?" she asked.

"I don't know. I hadn't thought of that. I'm guessing whatever managers get paid. Seriously, Lettie, I don't know crap about the business side of all this."

She laughed. "I already knew that. Okay, I'll do some digging."

"You should reach out to my PR firm too. Jake McCartney is the owner, and he's handling my stuff himself. He might be able to help narrow down the list. Oh, and I'll pay you too, once I figure out how much I've got left in my account."

Lettie shook her head. "You are hopeless, little brother, but no problem, I'm on it. I'll ask Mom too. Ever since you showed an interest in singing, she's had an eye on how the music business operates."

"Cool. Thanks, sis. Oh, and I'm planning to do some volunteering at the town library in a little place east of here. You could come with me if you want and have the time."

"I don't want. I have absolutely no interest in going to some *Deliverance*-like town in rural Tennessee. They'd string me up the first time I opened my mouth."

"It's not like that. It's a cool and accepting place. Surprising and beautiful. Oh, and it's not far from Rock Island. You remember when the family would go up there for day trips?"

Rock Island was one of my family's favorite Sunday spots. The Tennessee Valley Authority owned it, and it included an old cotton mill that looked very much like the exterior of the new condo building Jake had shown me in Crawford City.

Lettie nodded. "Text me when you're going, and I'll think about it."

I smiled. That was my sister's way of saying yes when she didn't want to commit to something, but we both knew she would do it.

"Oh, just so you know, Jesse's been offered a job over there somewhere, maybe at Lebanon's hospital? You should talk to him too. I'm sure he's gonna be looking for a place to live around there."

"That's big news. Why didn't anyone tell me?" I asked, feeling put out. Usually, our family was the oversharing kind.

"'Cause you've been MIA for months now. I'm sure Mom or Dad would've told you if you ever called."

"Or Jesse could've," I said pouting.

"Don't get your panties in a wad. He's been as busy as you. Give him a call and tell him I told you, then he can give you all the boring details."

I laughed. "You are such a mess. I'm sure since this is something he's been working toward for like a million years, he doesn't think it's boring."

"Which is why *you* should call him. You'll be interested and happy about it. I swear, hearing him drone on and on about how nice the hospital is, how much he likes the area... blah."

I shook my head and let it drop. Lettie was who she was. Love her or leave her. That's all that could be done. My family and I, we loved and accepted her with all her flaws and rough edges.

When I got into my car, I sat there and immediately dialed Jesse. "Hey, brother, you got a minute?" I asked as soon as he answered.

"Um, what time is it?"

"Like nine o'clock. Were you already asleep?"

"I was. Why are you calling me this late?"

"I just found out from our bigmouthed sister that you got a new job and didn't bother to tell me about it. Have I been demoted out of the family or something?"

Jesse humphed. "You went quiet on us, little brother. But, yeah, I'm gonna be working up in Lebanon at a hospital that Vandy has taken over. I'll be one of the night shift docs in the ER."

"Cool, that's kinda perfect 'cause I've hung out in Crawford City, not far from there, and I like the little town. You looking at living in Lebanon, or do you want something further out?"

"Haven't thought about it, to be honest," he admitted. "Are you going back to Crawford City?"

"Probably in the next week or so, and I've personally seen a beautiful new condo building downtown. It would be perfect for a doctor who works too much and doesn't have time to mow."

"It'll need to be quiet and private, though. I'll be sleeping during the day."

"I think it will be. There's some famous model on the second floor and my PR guy is on the top floor. It's my understanding the two of them aren't there very often, since their jobs involve a lot of travel, so it's almost like you'd have the place to yourself."

"Hmm, sounds interesting. Text me the information. For now, I need to get a few more hours sleep. Got to go in tonight at one, then back on sevens the following night. Can't wait till this residency is over."

"Yeah, yeah, we've all heard you say that before."

He laughed. "Love you, little brother, and don't forget to text me. I'd like to take a look at the condo."

I hung up and was happy to have connected with two of my three siblings. Sam was more difficult to reach and with a baby under a year old, I didn't dare call him until tomorrow, when I knew I wouldn't be as likely to wake my nephew up.

I got home and went into the living room, where Mom and Dad were watching TV. "Y'all are up late, what's up with that?"

They both turned to me, and Dad smiled. "We don't go to bed before ten, son. You're making us out to be older than we are."

"Hey, if the shoe fits."

Mom got up and gave me a kiss on the cheek. "You had dinner yet?"

"Oh yeah, I stopped over at Lettie's, and we ate pizza and watched old movies."

"That's good, dear, I know she's been missing you."

"I missed her too. And why didn't anyone tell me about Jesse getting his dream job?"

"Oh, well, we haven't seen you," Dad said. "But he seems happy about it."

"Yeah, I called and woke him up. I saw a place not far from Lebanon that might be perfect for him. He, Lettie and I are going to go and check it out soon. You two should come too.”

“Maybe,” Mom said, then yawned. “Oh, baby, you talked about sleep and cursed me. I think I’m gonna turn in.”

She kissed my cheek again and headed to bed. Dad turned the TV off and asked me how things were going.

“I’m good, Dad. Glad most of the recording stuff is done. They’re doing post-production now, so, at least for the moment, I’m off the hook.”

“Good, you need a break. Well, I’m gonna go to bed too. Let us know what your schedule is, and we’ll get the family together for dinner one night. I know they’ll all want to hear about how the recording went.”

“Thanks, Dad. I will.”

Not for the first time, I thanked God that I’d landed with the Ramirez family. My bizarre, multiethnic, overbearing, and incredibly supportive family. My three siblings and I had all come to our adoptive parents at different ages as kids, and Jesse and Sam were the only two biologically related among us. We five couldn’t look more different—our parents who were Latinx, my sister was Black, my brothers biracial, and me White—but I thought our differences made us stronger as a unit, and we’d become as tight as a family could be.

I went to my room then and answered a few emails, checked on social media to make sure I hadn’t missed any important messages there, and then crashed myself.

The moment I closed my eyes, my thoughts were filled with a certain sexy librarian, and my heart began to beat fast at the idea of getting to spend some time with him again. Maybe this time, I could get to know him a little better.

CHRIS

"MRS. ELLIOT, IT'S TOO much. I know the budget is stretched thin, but I saw over three hundred and fifty patrons yesterday. And that was in less than six hours."

"Chris, I know, but it's like I told you yesterday and the day before, we are strapped to the max. The fact that Crawford City has a levy to support your branch is nothing less than a miracle. The entire system is struggling to stay afloat."

I sighed into the phone. "I need at least one more full-time librarian, plus a part-time person to manage the volunteers. Even if I had that, we'd be stretched to meet the community's needs."

I'd had this same conversation with Doc the night before too. It'd been playing on repeat between us since day one, because the library was barely staying above water with all the patrons we served on a daily basis. Correction: *I* was barely staying above water.

Doc had been spot-on when he said we'd be busy. The levy barely paid for me and the building, so I knew asking for anything was futile, but I felt desperate. At least no money had to go toward buying books, since those had been brought in by the library and school systems.

"I need some help, at least a little, so I have time to arrange some of the children's activities," I pleaded to Mrs. Elliot. "Maybe if I wasn't spending three and four hours a day reshelving books, I could get further with my other duties."

"I could send Audrey," she suggested.

I cringed. "No offense, but I said I needed help, not someone to make my life miserable."

Thankfully, Mrs. Elliot chuckled. "You know she misses you. Now that you're gone, she's having to do all the work herself."

That made me smile, despite my frustration. If there was no relief to be had, it didn't matter how big a fit I threw, it just wasn't going to happen.

"Okay, I've got at least another hour's work here before I can go home. But please, promise me you'll keep working on increasing our budget. If I don't start opening up earlier, I'm afraid they're going to come at me with pitchforks and torches."

"Just make sure they don't burn any books with those torches," she said, then chuckled again. "Seriously, though, at least the community is embracing its library."

"Yeah, that's not a problem here," I said, knowing that in a lot of other places, libraries were struggling to stay open. Not financially as much as from lack of community interest.

After a few encouraging words from Mrs. Elliot, as was her daily custom to lift my spirits, we hung up and I began to clean up from the day. Books lay strewn across every table. All I had the time and energy for was to put the books on carts, roughly organize them to minimize my work for the following day, and quickly run the vacuum to at least keep the dust down to a minimum.

A cleaning service paid for by the school district came in three days a week, so janitorial duties weren't exactly in my job description. But with all the foot traffic each day, it wasn't enough to keep the floors clean and it definitely wasn't enough to keep the restrooms clean.

Doc and Amos both volunteered at least once a week, and there were a few others who came in regularly as well. For the most part, though, our volunteers were more work than help. Most came to socialize and read the books while on duty, but a handful were helpful. I just needed more of the latter.

I had yet to find anyone who could consistently shelve the books correctly, which nine times out of ten meant I had to spend time helping patrons find misplaced material.

I plopped down on the oversized beanbag chair, which had become part of my nightly routine while reshelving children's books and sighed. It wasn't like I was complaining. I loved this job, to be honest. It was just I didn't feel like I was able to *do* my job. Me running around putting out fires all day every day didn't promote reading. If anything, it discouraged it.

I'd just finished putting more books away and was about to wheel the last cartful to the circulation desk when the library phone rang. I wouldn't normally answer it, but no one ever called except Doc or Amos.

"Hello?" I answered.

"Hey, Chris, I just got a text from Jake asking when you wanted Roth to come volunteer."

Just hearing his name made my body flush with anticipation. The prospect of seeing the handsome reality TV star again made my heart beat fast and sweat break out across my skin.

Then I wondered when the hell would I fit him into my crazy schedule. "Did Jake tell you what he wants to do?"

Doc chuckled. "No, just that he's available to come out."

I groaned. "Well, we could have him do a public reading or something. Do you have about five or six people who could plan and manage an event like that?" I asked.

"Well, yeah, but, son, I don't think he's coming to entertain a bunch of folks. I think he wants to see you."

"Me? What makes you say that? Did Jake mention something?"

Doc laughed. "You're as clueless as they come, son. He's got a crush on you. Why don't you schedule him to come some evening to help you organize after you close? That way, you can spend some quality time to-gether."

I sighed. "Even if you're right, I don't have much time to spend with anyone at the moment, no matter how much I'd like to."

"Okay then, how about Saturday afternoon? He can help you clean up and get things shelved so you've got the whole day off on Sunday."

I hadn't had a day off since I got here. Sundays were supposed to be my down day since we were closed, but I usually spent it catching up on the stuff I'd fallen behind on during the week.

"Okay, that'll work. Have him come out on Saturday but tell him not to show up until after six. If he comes in before that, I'll never get everyone out of the library."

"That's probably true. The boy's only gotten more popular since the show ended, especially since the girl who won ended up losing her recording contract. Did you hear that she threw a whiskey bottle at the owner of the recording studio?"

"You and Amos are like starstruck kids. Yeah, I heard, but only because your husband has told me like six times."

Doc didn't even try to deny it, but I could hear the smile in his voice. "It's not fair you know us so well."

"Well, I do live with you both. Well, that isn't really true. I sleep there, but I live here."

"True enough. Okay, we'll see you in a few minutes. Amos put your dinner in the microwave. Make sure you eat it tonight. He worries that you aren't eating properly and are working too hard."

"I swear you two are worse than my parents. Are you in cahoots with them or something?"

I could tell by his silence they'd actually been talking. "Geez, I should've known. Anyway, I'll be home in about thirty minutes."

I laughed when I hung up. Mom and Dad had really hit it off with Doc and Amos. Fran had also joined forces somehow, and they were all three working to get Mom and Dad to sell up and move to Crawford City.

Truthfully, it was a good idea. Their home had tripled in value in the past few years, and since I wasn't living with them any longer, they could get a much nicer and smaller home here for about half the price of theirs.

Mom still loved her bus-driving job, though, and Dad had his yards and cemeteries to maintain, although that seasonal work would be ending soon. He'd still have to mow and clean up leaves for some of his more affluent clients who were obsessed with their yards, but come November, he was usually off until spring.

I locked up the library and began my nightly walk home. Often someone would invite me over to the café for dinner, but by seven at night, the food was on its downward slide. So, lately, I'd declined most of the invitations.

I did enjoy meeting the different townsfolk in the mornings, though, before I went to work. The café was perfect for that, and since I didn't usually eat but once a day unless Amos saved a dinner plate for me, I could get away with a big, Southern breakfast at least a few days a week.

I loved it when Amos cooked traditional Caribbean food, and happily dug into the black beans and rice, pork chops, and fried plantains he'd left for me in the microwave. I'd just taken my last bite when Doc came into the kitchen and sat across from me.

"So, you know Amos and I are headed out of town this weekend to spend a month with our daughter. Are you sure you're gonna be okay here by yourself?" he asked.

I laughed. "I'm a grown man, Doc. Besides, with all the food Amos has frozen for me, I could live a year without having to go shopping."

Doc chuckled at the truth of it. His husband, according to Amos's son, Todd, had turned over a domestic leaf when he and Doc got married. For every meal in the past month, Amos had made me an extra plate and stuck it in the freezer for when they'd be gone.

It was almost like the man thought I'd starve without someone to watch over me. Not that I didn't appreciate his thoughtfulness.

"Jake texted me back and said this weekend works for Roth coming to visit. I guess Roth's brother and sister are coming with him, so we've invited them all to stay here. Just put them in the guest bedrooms on the second floor."

"Wow, really? Why is his whole family coming?" I asked, suddenly feeling nervous for some reason. It wasn't like I was meeting my boyfriend's family or something.

"Well, apparently, his brother just took a job at the hospital in Lebanon."

"Another doctor?" I asked bemused. We had four doctors and quite a few nurse practitioners living in Crawford City already.

"Yeah, he's going to be one of the ER docs there."

"Well, that's cool, but it still doesn't explain why he's bringing them here."

"Oh, well, Jake wants Roth's brother to see the empty condo downtown. He's going to need to live fairly close to the hospital, and Lebanon isn't far from here."

"Okay, that makes more sense," I said.

"I'm sorry to leave it with you to handle, but we are itching to get out to Salem and see our grandbabies. I swear they grow bigger every day. Lisa's still a little jealous her brother's kids are getting more of our attention, so it's time to head out and do our duties as grandparents."

I laughed. Todd and Ash's little ones were a full-on handful. The grandpas tended to take baby duty on Sundays, which translated to another reason I tried not to be home. The kids were fun to be around, but I'd rather spend my slow day chasing down misplaced books than chasing toddlers.

I'd spent enough time with the triplets to begin forming a bond, though, and Doc swore up and down one of them called me Uncle Chris the last time they visited. Of course, I was almost sure that was to get me hooked enough to take on babysitting duties.

The rest of the week proved so busy, I basically forgot Roth and his family were coming until Saturday. Before Doc and Amos left for the airport, they fixed breakfast for me, gave me a detailed sheet of how to keep the place up, and reminded me our houseguests would arrive at the library that afternoon to volunteer.

After being assured the beds had clean sheets and reminded again that Amos had left plenty of food in the freezer for everyone, I dashed out the door to open the library for our usual Saturday morning rush.

EIGHT

ROTH

LETTIE AND JESSE BOTH eyed me warily as I became more and more agitated the closer we came to Crawford City.

Lettie spent most of the trip talking about how we were going into *Deliverance* country and acted silly almost every time we passed a dilapidated area, like there was some redneck just lying in wait for us. I'd swear that woman was a total drama queen, but her dramatics did help get me out of my own head a little.

"What has gotten into you?" Jesse asked after Lettie had squealed when she saw some old dude picking up his mail from a mailbox.

"Nothing," I said irritably. I had invited my siblings to come with me on a whim, mostly to ensure I didn't scare Chris away. He'd seemed taken aback after recognizing me from the show that I wanted to show him I really was just a regular guy. Why exactly I thought bringing my siblings along would help convey that message was lost on me now, though.

Even at their most low-key, my family could be a lot to handle, even for me. Dramatics aside, Lettie was easy to get to know, but not always easy to like. Jesse was easy-going, smart and calm, but our sister had a talent for riling him up to beat the band. And truth be told, I would've never invited our brother, Sam, even if he didn't have a baby and wife at home. I loved him dearly, as I did all my siblings, but his wacky humor could take some getting used to.

"Someone's touchy," Lettie said, and grinned wickedly at me from the front seat. Jesse always complained he got car sick if he didn't drive, and Lettie always claimed the passenger side anytime we went somewhere, so as usual, I rode in the back.

Somehow, I'd hoped that the two of them being up front would keep the spotlight off me. I should've known better.

"You gonna fess up about why you're really dragging us out to the middle of nowhere, or do we have to wait and find out for ourselves? 'Cause you know, if it's a boy, it's best we know everything before meeting him."

"Geez, you're both so freaking nosy. Why did I think it was a good idea to bring you?"

I knew Lettie was right, though. I needed to prep them now that they'd figured it out, otherwise, they really would embarrass me. Not that they still wouldn't do that intentionally, but I could only control so much.

"Okay, so I met a guy when I went to Crawford City last time, but he's shy and didn't know how to take it that I'd been on TV, and I think that intimidated him a little. I was hoping by bringing you two that he would see me as normal."

Jesse laughed out loud. "You brought Lettie along to help you show some guy that you've got a normal life? You have met our sister, right?"

I laughed when Lettie hit Jesse on the arm. "Hey, I'm normal compared to you two. People naturally like me."

"Like getting away from you," Jesse said under his breath, and I chuckled. In typical little-brother fashion, I reveled in instigating their squabbles. Of course, they almost always figured out my plan and I'd end up getting a tongue-lashing.

"This guy's different," I said, steering the conversation back on track. "I think he's worth... special effort."

Lettie and Jesse shared a knowing glance and shook their heads. Then Lettie chuckled. "You are so lucky you told us 'cause had I met this guy cold, I would've embarrassed the crap out of you."

I sighed. "I honestly didn't think you'd figure me out."

"Dude, you thought we wouldn't notice you crushing hard on a guy?" Jesse said. "You've always been an open book."

I shook my head. "Yeah, I should work on that."

They both laughed since I'd been saying that very same thing since high school.

"Okay, tell us about dream boy, so we're prepared," Lettie said.

"Well, he's a librarian. Tall and slim, cute in a nerdy smart guy sort of way."

"Yeah, that sounds like your type."

I gave Lettie the eye. "He's also shy, which isn't the kind of guy I usually go out with. At least, I think he was around me. It's hard to tell what's natural shyness or just feeling overwhelmed being around someone they've watched on TV. Hell, I felt some of that my first week on the show."

"Well, that's easy to overcome. Once he sees you're a weirdo, he'll be like, 'Oh cool, he's not a big star, he's just a freak.'"

"Thanks, Lettie, you're so helpful."

She stuck her tongue out at me and turned back around. That signaled the end of harassment time, and it was back to Lettie giving Jesse grief about whatever they had been fussing about before. Lettie and Jesse were only about a year apart, so they had the most in common among us siblings. They were polar opposites personality-wise, but they seemed to mesh like twins and were actually quite close.

I laid my head back on the headrest and closed my eyes. I thought of the four of us, and Mom and Dad, and how strange things had been when I'd joined the family. I'd been too young then to realize how I was blessed with having an openminded granny who thought people should be exposed to all sorts of cultures. Grandma Gallo had friends and dated men of different ethnicities when I lived with her, which in retrospect had made fitting into my new multicultural home easier when I came to live with the Ramirezes.

What hadn't been easy was getting used to all the noise. Lettie was loud. Like, *really* loud. All the time. She had two volumes, asleep and yelling. She'd mellowed a little as we'd grown older, but the woman was still intense.

My brothers had become more mature with age, although Sam remained a complete goofball. The boys came to live with our parents and Lettie when they were still quite young, so this was the only family they knew.

I proved the oddball of the bunch. Being an introvert, I tended to want to hide in my room for hours at a time. Of course, Lettie wouldn't hear of that. I'd been her baby brother from the start. As far as the girl had been concerned, I'd arrived on their doorstep because she'd convinced our parents that she needed another sibling, and no one could convince her otherwise.

As a result, she and I had become close. Closer than the rest of the family, at least at first. Slowly, she'd pulled me out of my shell. Through Lettie, I learned to allow my new parents to be my Mom and Dad. Then, after watching her interact with our brothers and learning what it meant to have siblings, I began to allow them in too.

Now, they were all my family. They were my go-to people when something happened in my life, good, bad, or otherwise. If I needed someone to talk to or cheer me up, I called Sam, who would say something ridiculous, and I'd end up laughing. If I needed someone with their head on straight who could help me see the big picture and talk me through a difficult situation, I called Jesse.

Lettie? She was my playmate and always had my back. She was who I went to when I needed some downtime or someone to hang out with. She had always been there for me, and I knew she always would be, and it went both ways.

Mom and Dad remained our foundations, the glue that held us Ramirezes together. I was the only one among my siblings who hadn't changed surnames upon being adopted, but that'd just been semantics as far as my parents were concerned. They respected my decision to keep my birth name, which I'd done to honor my granny. She remained a huge presence in my life, even all these years after her passing, and I still felt a deep connection to her every time I sang.

My parents fully supported my pursuing a career in music, though it wasn't seamless. I had completed my junior year of college when, to everyone's surprise, I dropped out to pursue singing. That sent the Ramirezes into hyperdrive. I kept telling Lettie if it wasn't for me, Mom and Dad would be on her like stink on poo. She would always laugh and thank me profusely for taking some of the parents' focus off of her, acting like she was bowing before me. Instead of nagging me, though, Mom and Dad channeled their concern into support—a *lot* of support. At least one of them would show up at almost every performance I had, which was great. It only became embarrassing when they'd give me a standing ovation after each song. But even that paled in comparison to the time they showed up at a gay bar on drag night.

I still had no idea how they found out I was performing there. When I saw my six-foot-three-inch straight as an arrow father and petite mother enter the bar dressed to the hilt like drag queens, I literally stopped singing mid-song. The DJ bitch from hell noticed where my attention landed and pulled my parents up on stage. If I hadn't had an issue with stage fright at that moment, I would have after that.

The pictures from that night were blown up and hung over the fireplace. A memory I'd rather have forgotten placed front and center for the world to see.

Of course, I knew that wasn't really about them being in drag as much as it was a declaration of how they loved me unconditionally, no matter my orientation. I hadn't told them I was gay until I graduated from high school, but I remembered how we had all gathered in the living room for our typical Ramirez family after-dinner talk when I stood up and made the announcement.

My mom kissed me on the cheek, then in a matter-of-fact way said, "Oh, honey, we've known that for years."

When I looked around the room, I saw my dad and siblings all nodding. "Well, shit, you guys could pretend to be surprised."

I remember my dad saying, "Watch your language, son," and feeling a mixture of relief and underwhelm that my big coming out had been anything but, I sat back down and the conversation shifted to Jesse describing something medical he'd seen while in medical school.

That night, though, my parents came to my room and, as they always did when something important needed discussing, sat on either side of me with their legs up on the bed. They assured me that nothing could stop them from loving me. They both accepted my sexuality and were happy I'd decided to come out. "It never pays to keep things like that inside," they told me, and then each kissed me on the forehead, another typical Mom and Dad thing to do, and left the room.

In the years since, my sexuality had never been an issue in my family. It was merely an aspect of me that everyone accepted, and no one gave much thought to, other than when Lettie would point out a cute guy and then go ask for his number on my behalf. I honestly couldn't tell sometimes if she was genuinely trying to help me find a boyfriend or just took pleasure in seeing me turn beet red from embarrassment. Probably both.

As we neared Crawford City, I pointed out the library and told Jesse where to park. We all got out and walked up to the door, but when I tried to open it, it was locked.

I knocked, but no one came.

"Did he forget we were coming?" Jesse asked.

I looked at my watch. "No, Jake told me to be here at five after six. Chris needed time to close up, so people didn't crowd in to see me," I said, blushing.

"Well, it looks like he flew the coop," Lettie said. "Maybe we should walk around to the back door."

"No need," a voice said from behind us. I turned around and saw the man I remembered was Todd coming up the steps. "We had an emergency at the library and Chris is at the clinic with Ash helping get things squared away. He knew you'd be arriving soon and sent me to meet you here."

"What happened?" Jesse asked.

"Nothing major, just a kid running around the library who ran into one of the shelves."

"How badly hurt?" Jesse asked, clearly in doctor mode.

"Just a couple stitches. My husband, Ash, is a doctor and is treating the patient now."

"Should we leave and come back later?" I asked.

Todd chuckled. "I think if you're willing to wait, that would be best," he said, then turned to my brother. "You're Jesse, right?"

"Yes," Jesse said, cocking an eyebrow. "Do I know you?"

"No, but your brother told Jake you're interested in the condo, so naturally he wanted you to get a tour. I would show you now, except it's getting dark, and I know Jake would prefer you see it in daylight. You're staying at my dad's house tonight. Do you want to follow me over there and you can get settled in while we wait for Chris to come home?"

I glanced toward the library's entrance and thought that was probably the best idea. So, we followed Todd to the home I'd visited when I'd been here last. He showed us the guest rooms before going downstairs.

When we came back down ourselves, I could smell something cooking. "My dad left these for you all to warm up, so I decided we'd at least get you fed while you're waiting," Todd said as he pulled food out of the microwave and served us at the table.

"Your dad made dinner for us?" I asked, confused.

Todd just laughed. "Yep, he's become Danny Domestic. Anyway, y'all enjoy. I'll let Chris know you're here and that he can just meet you at home."

He left shortly after that saying he had kid duty.

"How did you meet these people?" Jesse asked as soon as Todd was out the door.

"Well, through my PR manager. It's all very..."

"Weird," Lettie finished for me. "Who just lets you stay in their fancy log cabin for free? Are these your whacked-out fans that're gonna try to kill us in our sleep?"

Her dramatics made me laugh. "I don't think I have those kinds of fans."

"Well, can't be too sure. I say we leave now before they're given the chance."

Just then the front door opened, and Lettie gave me her uh-huh look.

"I've seen enough horror movies to know how this shit ends," she whispered. "Black girl gets it first every damned time."

"Shh," I said to Lettie, trying to hush her. Once she got something in her mind, though, there was no hope of convincing her otherwise. My sister had an overactive imagination, which coupled with her flair for the dramatic led to over-the-top reactions sometimes. It was a wonder she hadn't become an actress.

As soon as the poor guy walked into the house, Lettie jumped up. "Look, he's covered in blood. Listen, White boy, I will kick your butt. Don't you try nothing, you hear me?"

Chris looked shocked and alarmed by my crazy-ass sister, then glanced down at his shirt and sighed. "I didn't realize, sorry. The kid I helped had a head wound. It's a long story, but he's fine. I'm going to go up and get changed."

"You come down here with a chainsaw and I'm gonna beat your ass with that lamp," Lettie said, gesturing to a side table. Jesse and I both just shook our heads and remained silent. We'd learned over the years to just let Lettie be Lettie in the moment, then we'd smooth it all over later.

"Scout's honor," he said, raising his hand and giving the three-finger salute. "I don't even know how to use a chainsaw."

"That's exactly what a chainsaw murderer would say!" Lettie exclaimed as she stood with her hands flailing in the air.

Chris glanced at me, and I rolled my eyes, then he chuckled. "You're probably right, but there's three of you and I'm a wimpy librarian, so I'm pretty sure you could take me."

Lettie eyed him and, clearly confident she could, in fact, take him, she nodded and sat back down at the table. That was Chris's cue to leave, and he dashed up the stairs, but not before glancing my way again with a small smile.

Jesse and I turned our attention back to our dinner, but Lettie refused to eat. "The sexy man who led us here could be trying to poison me, too," she said.

"Lettie, please. Todd is gay and has a doctor husband and three toddlers. I doubt he wants to kill you."

"Every damned slasher movie, the White boy says the same thing. Nope, I'm not falling for it."

"Whatever. I'm eating. This smells delicious," Jesse said, causing me to laugh out loud.

Jesse and I finished our food while Lettie sat on the other side of the table from us. Mostly, I thought so she could watch the stairs. I'd never seen her this freaked out before. Maybe all that *Deliverance* talk on the car ride here had actually gotten to her.

"Lettie, these aren't scary people. They're actually some of the kindest folks I've ever met, Chris included. There's really no reason to be flipping out."

"No reason? We're in the middle of nowhere, sitting in a beautiful home a stranger led us to, and there's kids with head wounds and blood everywhere... it's just too weird."

"Maybe for you," Jesse said. "You should come hang out with me in the ER sometime."

"Oh no, brother, blood and snotty stuff ain't my thing. All that needs to stay inside the human body, as far as I'm concerned."

Jesse chuckled and finished his meal. He leaned back just as Chris walked down the stairs.

"I'm really sorry y'all. I had plans for you to help out at the library, but, well, things happen."

"You okay?" I asked, seeing the tiredness around his eyes.

He smiled, although it was clearly forced. "No, to be honest. I'm wiped out and still feel a little on edge from the whole thing."

"Would you like us to leave?" Jesse asked.

Chris shook his head. "No, I'd prefer you to stay. I'm afraid I'm not going to be much entertainment, though."

"There's no need, we can entertain ourselves. You go get some rest," Jesse said.

"Why don't I show you your rooms first."

"No need. Todd already did that."

"Cool. I see you've already had dinner. Do you need anything else?" he asked.

When we all shook our heads, he pointed toward the living room and where the TV and remote were, then he disappeared up to his bedroom.

"Well, that sucked," I said quietly.

"Yeah, sorry, little brother," Jesse said. "But he really did look like the world was resting on his shoulders."

"He did. Oh well, they've got some cards over here. Do you wanna play a game? For old times' sake."

We cleaned up the dishes and took each other on with our family's version of Rummy until we, too, decided to go to bed.

NINE

CHRIS

T HE DAY HAD BEEN too much. We'd had our usual Saturday crowds, and even though the volunteers were able to manage most of the traffic, I felt worn out by closing time. Knowing I'd see Roth that evening, though, gave me the extra energy I'd needed to push through the afternoon.

Around five, a woman I'd never seen before came in with three kids. I didn't pay much attention, but after sprucing up the periodicals, a never-ending job in this town, I came back out to the main room and noticed the woman had disappeared. Her kids, however, were sitting in the children's area reading.

Well, that's okay, I thought. The kids appeared content, maybe Mom had gone to the restroom or stepped outside to make a phone call.

About thirty minutes later, the little girl, no more than five, came over to the circulation desk and asked to use the restroom.

"Where's your mama, honey?" Elinore Rose, one of my regular volunteers, asked her.

The little girl shrugged, so Elinore and Betty, her sister-in-law who had come in to visit with her, took the little girl to the restroom.

Before they returned, the youngest boy began running around the library, pretending he was a cowboy riding a horse. I considered leaving my post to track down the mother and looked up at the clock. Five thirty, just thirty more minutes and I'd be able to close the doors and be done with this day.

The volunteers came back out with the girl, and I saw Elinore walk toward the little boy. He saw her coming, but she didn't get to him before he ran headfirst into the corner of the shelves while looking the opposite way.

We all stood there, momentarily stunned in the sudden silence, until the boy started wailing. Then everything happened at once. Blood from the gash on his head spurted all over the place. A quick-thinking volunteer called the clinic, telling them we had an emergency. Others went searching for his mom, who'd completely disappeared from the library. I ended up trying to comfort the boy, thus getting covered in blood, while Elinore and Betty looked after the other two kids.

The mom was found in the backseat of a car parked halfway down the street, necking with a guy from the next town over. I was told later that either one or both of them must be married to other people because they looked guilty as sin and the moment the woman got out of the car, the guy quickly dashed away.

As soon as the mom arrived at the clinic, she began yelling about her son being allowed to hurt himself on public property and how she planned to sue the city. Of course, Ash had already called children's services and when a representative showed up asking questions about why she'd left the child unattended, all her hollering quickly changed to excuses about just stepping away for a moment.

The kids had been allowed to go home with their mother, but I knew children's services would be paying them a visit soon enough. I felt frustrated and angry for the woman putting her young children and us in such a position, but my volunteers did me proud by rising to the occasion. Hopefully, nothing like that would ever happen again at the library, though.

By the time I got home, still wearing my blood-soaked shirt, I was exhausted, and knew I wouldn't be good company. Todd had texted me, letting me know Roth and his siblings had arrived and were settled at the house. I was determined to muster up enough energy to entertain them when Roth's brother let me off the hook.

I was sure had they shown up any other night, I'd have found the energy to hang out, or at least better contend with Roth's clearly wigged-out sister. After a quick shower, though, all I could do was check on them, then drag myself back upstairs to crash.

I slept hard and woke up early the next day ready to make amends for my turning into a pumpkin the night before. I decided to cook one of the few meals I could actually do well. Breakfast for four, coming right up.

TEN

ROTH

I WOKE UP TO the smell of frying bacon and slipped out of the guest room and down the stairs to find Chris standing at the kitchen stove cooking.

"Hey, you feeling better?" I asked, making him jump.

"Well, I was," he teased. "Ask me again when my heart comes back down off the ceiling."

He smiled over at me. "I'm fixing breakfast as an apology for ditching you all so early yesterday."

I chuckled. "We came here to help you at the library, not because we expected you to entertain us all evening."

Chris shrugged and began plating the bacon. "If you've got time today, I'm sure you can still help, if you want to. I didn't get the chance yesterday to clean up the library, so it's a total mess, I'm sure."

"I'd like that. In the meantime, can I help with break-fast?" I asked, hoping he'd let me just so I could spend some time with him. He seemed so laid-back this morning, and he didn't have the same look of terror he'd had when he first figured out who I was, which put me at ease too.

"Sure, if you want to put the coffee on, that'll help."

When he showed me where everything was, I went to work making the coffee. It was strange to be working on such domestic stuff together with a man I didn't really know. So, to minimize the awkwardness, I began asking questions.

"What made you want to be a librarian?" I asked.

Chris had a smile on his face when I turned toward him. "It's not just one thing I can put my finger on but rather a lot of small things. I mean, I like books and reading, of course, that's a basic prerequisite. I also enjoy helping people find a book that lights them up, and the highlight of any day is when a reader comes back in and can't stop talking about how amazing a story was that I'd recommended. How about you? What made you want to be a famous reality TV star?"

I almost choked. "Nothing, actually. I hope I never, ever step foot on another reality TV show stage as long as I live. But I was born to be a musician, that's the dream."

I recognized the confused look he gave me because everyone wore that same expression upon learning I didn't relish being onstage like most singers. "Not a per-former?"

I sighed, knowing instinctively that I should probably shut up. My career was too new to be putting out my life's story unfiltered, but there was something about Chris that prompted me to confide in him.

"No, I'm not a huge fan of performing, but I get serious stage fright."

"Oh, yeah, I saw you talking to Amelia Denton about that." He blushed then and I hoped he wasn't about to revert back to being starstruck around me. "I can't believe I'm making small talk about you hanging out with Amelia Denton."

I smiled. "Seriously, it's pretty overwhelming for me too. Amelia had a big influence on my life and that of my grandmother. In fact, it was thinking of my granny that helped me overcome my stage fright during the show."

Chris gave me a sad smile. "Yeah, they talked about your grandmother on the show. She sounded like an interesting lady. I barely knew mine."

Chris put the eggs next to the bacon on the platter, then leaned back against the countertop. "My grandma died when I was little, but I have some memories, mostly of her watching me. She used to have groundhogs that played outside her house. We had a routine of watching them before she'd make me a snack and put me to bed for my nap." His smile at the memories warmed my heart. "I used to dream about the groundhogs. I thought they were big monsters who'd eat me, and my grandma could keep me safe from them. So, to me, she was some sort of superhero. Anyway, so, I hope you like scrambled eggs. I forgot to ask."

"I like eggs however they're made. Mostly, I'm just enjoying your company."

Chris blushed again. "I'm not very exciting, I'm afraid. Just a small-town librarian."

"Oh, I don't know, you seem to be more than that to me." I was just about to step toward him and hopefully tug him into a kiss when my nosy sister walked into the kitchen.

"You're making breakfast?" she asked.

Chris broke our gaze to look over at her and nodded. "Yeah, I woke up early since I went to bed before the sun officially went down. I have biscuits in the oven, store-bought, but they should be done in a moment. Then we can eat."

Lettie looked at him like she was going to argue about not trusting him, but something changed in her expression when she looked between him and me. "Is the coffee done?" she asked.

"Not quite. I just turned it on," I admitted.

Lettie sighed and sat down on the island stool.

"Apologies for not making proper introductions last night. Chris, this is my sister, Lettie. Sis, meet Chris, Crawford City's librarian," I said. Chris gave her a little wave in greeting, which was absolutely adorable.

"So, Chris, what's your deal? You work in a library, but you came home covered in blood. Level with me. Are you really a serial killer?"

Chris barked out a laugh, clearly caught off guard. "No, not unless murdering a bowl of cereal counts. But for real, I do love to read about them. Have you read the last book by Clifton James?"

Lettie's mouth dropped open. "*Darkness Invades You?*" she asked.

"Yep. I read it right before I came to work here. I recommend it, but it still creeps me out."

"My God, me too. I froze the damned book after reading it and still haven't taken it out of the freezer."

Chris laughed out loud. "I hear his next book is supposed to be a romance. Can you imagine him writing romance novels after that book?"

"Dear God, I shudder to think."

Chris pulled the biscuits out of the oven and transferred them into a cloth-lined basket. The island had four stools and it appeared Chris meant for us to eat there, so as soon as he put the plates out, Lettie and I began to scoop up food.

"Shouldn't we wait for your brother?" he asked.

"Nah, Jesse will sleep another hour, at least. He's not a morning person, especially since he's been working night shifts at the hospital."

"Cool," Chris said, and sat on the stool across from us. "I probably should've served you at the table. We can move if you like."

"No, this is great," I said. "Lettie and I are used to eating this way. Our parents' house has a similar island."

"Speak for yourself. I like things a little formal from time to time," Lettie said, tongue in cheek. The woman didn't know the difference between formal dining and fast food.

"Seriously, we can move to the table. Do you want me to get out the china?" Chris asked, sounding panicked.

Lettie couldn't hold back a laugh. "No, dude, I'm pulling your chain, just sit down. I'll get us all some coffee."

The moment she stood up, Chris's face fell. "I'm sorry, I'm just not used to hosting others. I've only lived with Doc and Amos for a short time, but they'd be appalled by my lack of social graces."

Lettie filled each of our cups before returning the pot to the coffee maker. "We didn't grow up with high-tea-type parents. We're more down-to-earth folks, so this is more comfortable," Lettie said.

"High-tea parents?" I asked. "Where do you even come up with these terms?"

Lettie rolled her eyes at me, but couldn't hide a grin. "Shut up, you understood what I meant."

That seemed to ease any remaining tension in the room enough that we were able to enjoy the morning, chatting about everything from the library to Lettie's newest art project. Luckily, no one brought up my recording contract. The topic would likely be unavoidable at some point, but I didn't want Chris to shut down again over being starstruck. I wanted him to see the real me as we got to know each other.

We'd just finished eating when the doorbell rang. Lettie and I took the dishes to the kitchen sink while Chris went to get the door. Jesse walked into the kitchen as Chris walked out and helped himself to coffee, declining any breakfast.

A few moments later, Chris walked in with Jake close behind. "Oh my god, you fixed breakfast?" Jake asked, and Chris chuckled, telling him to help himself, which Jake did. I stood while everyone else sat at the island, and made another round of introductions.

"So, Jesse," Jake said between mouthfuls. "I understand you're looking for a place to live. I'm happy to run you by the condo to take a look. We've officially opened, and the place is now on the market. My husband and I are moving in after he finishes school, and the other condo owner is already living there. In fact, I think she's there now. We can meet her, if you like."

Jesse shrugged. "I'm not sure what I'm looking for. I'm just finishing my residency, then I'll be working in Lebanon. I should probably get something there, but I'll admit, the drive here is pretty spectacular."

"It really is," Jake agreed.

"Well, if you want, we can go after we finish breakfast."

"Then we can all go help Chris at the library," I quickly added, to remind my sister and brother we did come to volunteer.

Lettie groaned, but didn't say anything, which was good since I was ready to tell her off if she tried her normal wiggle out of work tactic.

I convinced Chris to join us on the condo tour, so he rode with us, while Jake led the way to the downtown building that backed up to old railroad tracks. The ground level housed local shops and a surprisingly elegant small hotel, which Jake said his mother-in-law ran. The condos were separate, but occupied the same top floors as the hotel.

The vacant condo was beautiful. It'd been built to resemble a loft more than a condo, with modern lines, beautiful wooden beams, and brick construction. Jake explained that an old mercantile originally stood on the site, and after it burned down, they wanted to build something that honored the original architecture. They'd done a remarkable job, as far as I was concerned.

Jesse seemed impressed, too, although I could tell he was trying to downplay it. Lettie had long ago lost interest, and was just about to walk back down the stairs of the building when she ran into the upstairs neighbor. "Oh my god!" she exclaimed so loudly, we rushed to see what was going on. "Jennifer Cole?"

Of course, Jesse just rolled his eyes at our sister and went back to touring the condo. Jake smiled, though, and invited the woman inside.

"Jen, I'd like you to meet Roth Gallo, my newest client. This is his sister, Lettie Ramirez, and their brother Jesse is around here somewhere. Jesse is considering purchasing the condo. Everyone, meet Jennifer Cole, one of my closest friends."

Jesse was in the kitchen when the introductions were being made, so he hadn't seen Jennifer yet. I recognized her from the millions of magazines Lettie seemed obsessed with, and she looked even more radiant in real life than in her photos. She was known for wearing wild-colored contacts more often than not, ones that gave her a feline look, but today she either had in regular contacts or none at all.

Her eyes were large and light brown, which contrasted so beautifully with her darker skin. The woman truly was stunning. No wonder she'd become such a famous model.

When Jesse joined the rest of us in the main room, he stopped in his tracks. I'd known my serious, levelheaded brother most of my life, and I'd never seen him speechless or spellbound. Not until today.

Only then did I notice the same expression on Jennifer's face as well. The two stood awkwardly staring at each other, until Lettie cackled, breaking the spell. "Well, should we give you two a room?"

Jesse turned his *I will kill you in your sleep* expression on our sister and I couldn't help but join in her laughter.

"Jennifer, it's a pleasure to meet you," I said to help alleviate some of the awkwardness.

She turned my direction and gave me the most charming smile. "It's entirely my pleasure, and please, call me Jen. Jake," she said, turning to him and waving toward my brother, "I approve. The bronze god can buy the condo. Give him the family discount."

Lettie laughed even harder, and I could tell even though we'd just met Jen, the two were likely to become friends.

Jen invited us all to join her for an early lunch at her stepmother's café. It took a moment to realize she meant the buffet place down the street. When Chris declined, saying he needed to get to work at the library since he had so much to do, I didn't hesitate to say that I'd go help him.

Everyone, including Jen, looked at me funny, as if volunteering to help at the library was the last thing anyone should want to do. That wasn't my real motivation in going, though. Regardless, no one said anything to me, and before long, we were walking as a group toward the restaurant and the library.

ELEVEN

CHRIS

I HAD FUN WATCHING the family dynamics between Roth and his siblings. Being an only child, I'd never had those kinds of relationships. Despite their teasing, I could tell all three of them cared deeply about each other.

I figured when Jen got involved, they'd all be distracted enough that I'd be able to slip away and get work done at the library. I was trying not to stress too much over it, but because of last night's chaos, I really was hours behind in getting the place fit for opening on Monday.

I felt relieved when Jen invited the group to eat. Not having to show a bunch of new volunteers what to do meant I'd get the work done faster just doing it myself.

It surprised me when Roth offered to help rather than stay with the group. Being so generous with his time impressed me, even though I internally whined a little as we all left the condo building. As much as I wanted to spend more time with him, I had a lot of work to do, and the gorgeous man was a walking distraction.

When the group separated, I led Roth to the back entrance of the library and unlocked it. I'd learned the hard way, it was best to go in unseen on Sundays, because if anyone knew I was there, they'd pound on the front door and ask to come in rather than wait until the next day.

Unfortunately, our large group had made quite the scene coming down the sidewalk, so I was already dreading being interrupted and having to send people away. There was absolutely no way I could fudge the rules and let someone in if I had any hope of getting the tons of reshelving done by tomorrow.

When we walked in, I quickly locked the door behind us, and prayed no one had seen us enter. When I turned toward Roth to say as much, my heart skipped a beat. I realized in the moment that this was the first time we'd been truly alone together since having met. I shook my head to get rid of the insane notions of kissing him.

"Um..." I stammered, trying to get my wits about me. "So, do you have experience working in a library?" It was the same question I asked every new volunteer, because everyone who volunteered for me were novices. The library had been closed for years so, naturally, no one had any experience.

"Well, yeah, actually," Roth replied as he rubbed the back of his neck the way people did when they were a bit embarrassed.

"Really?" I asked, unable to mask my surprise.

"Yeah, I was in the honor club in high school, and had to volunteer so many hours a week to keep my membership up, so I worked in the library."

"That's so cool. Does that mean you know how to shelve books and periodicals?" I asked, all of a sudden excited that I might actually have real help for a change.

"That's mostly what I did."

"Oh god, thank goodness. In that case, I'll go collect all the books and periodicals spread throughout the library, and you can be in charge of putting up the periodicals while I sort the books."

By the time I gathered all the misplaced books onto carts, Roth had completely reorganized the periodicals area and moved on to putting away the magazines.

We worked silently, and I thought for what had to be the hundredth time I should get a radio to play when working alone here. "Do you want me to put some music on? I can use my phone."

Roth grinned over at me. "That'd be nice."

The guy's smile nearly undid me. I quickly turned my attention toward my phone to avoid embarrassing myself. "So, what do you like?" I quickly looked up at him, feeling dumb. "Sorry, I didn't think. You probably like country, don't you?"

He laughed. "Some. I also like jazz and some blues. I tend to listen to modern pop the most, though."

I must've looked shocked, because he laughed again when he saw my expression. "You think just because I sang country-pop during the competition that I only like country?"

"I guess I did assume that. Do you like Adele? I have her on my playlist."

"I love Adele!" he said. "Yes, that's perfect for shelving books."

I laughed then. "Dude, I've thought that for years."

I quickly hit play on my playlist after plugging in my phone over at the circulation desk, then returned to finish up organizing the books to be reshelved. I was just about to roll a book cart into the stacks when Roth finished the magazines.

"Do you want me to do the reshelving?" he asked. "I'm happy to go for it."

I stared at him a moment too long. A war raged inside me. On one side, I wanted to believe he did indeed know how to shelve the books properly, and on the other, I had no desire to have to go back and fix a problem created by trusting him blindly. That side won.

"Cool, I'll help you. That way we can get done faster."

He gave me a side glance that left no doubt he understood my real motivation in working together. Still, I'd still rather him be annoyed than have to chase my tail for the entire week searching for mis-shelved books.

We started in the cooking section. There was a cooking competition going on at the local Methodist church, so there were a large number of cookbooks that'd been pulled. I did a quick look over the section to make sure there weren't any books out of place and then began shelving them. Without my prompting, Roth turned around to the shelf opposite mine and began shelving the books about arts and recreation.

"Clearly, you know the Dewey Decimal System," I said, before I realized just how geeky that sounded.

Roth laughed. "You think my librarian didn't force me to memorize it before I was allowed to shelve books?"

I smiled back at him. "As any librarian worth their salt should. It's such a pain to chase down mis-shelved books. That's why I usually do the reshelving myself, even if it means staying late and coming in on my day off."

"I know all about that too. Once a week, Mrs. Patterson forced all the volunteers to walk through the shelves looking for anything that was put up wrong. It ended up saving us a ton of work, and we divided our time up by section. We'd do 0 to 100 one week, then 100 to 200 the next, and so on."

"That's a great idea," I said. "We did that at my former job, but only when we had extra time, which was basically never. I should put the volunteers on that. Maybe that would be a good way to train them on the system too."

I was just about to tell him I'd like to have him finish reshelving the rest of the cart when I heard someone knocking at the front door.

"Damn," I said before I could stop myself.

Roth looked concerned. "You okay?" he asked.

"Oh, fine. It's just every Sunday, the only day we're closed, there's someone who wants to come in. I swear it makes it impossible to get anything done. Not to mention, this is supposed to be my day off so I'm not really even here."

"Why don't you tell them to leave or just ignore it?" he asked.

I sighed. "Well, it's not that easy. I mean, I'm trying to make the library an important part of the community, and technically we're supposed to be open *every* day of the week, but we really can't afford another person. I feel obligated to at least be available."

Roth nodded his understanding. "Well, if it helps, I've got this. I promise not to reshelve things wrong and if I'm not sure on something, I'll skip it. If the amount of that person's knocking is any indication, it's an emergency."

"Always is," I said on another sigh. "Okay, you've got shelving duties. Thanks, Roth, you really are helping me."

He nodded and I could tell he was getting back into the zone, as I called it. Shelving books was monotonous and boring, but if you were lucky, you could get into a zone and finish in no time.

When I neared the front door, I took a quick peek out the side window adjacent to the entrance and was surprised to see the mother of the three kids from yesterday standing there. What the heck was she doing here, never mind on a Sunday? I didn't open the door.

I quickly went to the circulation desk, grabbed my phone, and dialed the sheriff's office. When Maelyne, their weekend dispatcher, answered, I told her the lady from the night before was knocking on the door.

Just then, even from the circulation desk, I could hear the woman jerking on the door and screaming that she knew I was in here.

"Oh dear," Maelyne said, apparently hearing the woman through the phone. "Just hang back and don't open that door. Darren, our deputy on duty, is just down the street from the library. I'll send him now."

I hung up just as Roth, who was looking rather wide-eyed himself, came up to the desk.

"What's going on?" he whispered.

"Unhinged mom from last night is back," I whispered back. "Deputy is on his way to find out what she wants."

"Any way she'll get in?" he asked when she began pulling on the front door again.

"Nah, it's pretty stable. She'd have to take a sledge-hammer to it to get in without a key."

"She could break the glass and get in through a window?" Roth asked.

"Yeah, but hopefully the deputy will get here before she tries that."

Luckily, the door rattling soon stopped. I heard the woman talking to someone and hoped it was the deputy. I sure didn't like the thought of it being someone from Roth's group.

I quickly put my hand up to ask Roth to stay put, and I slipped into my hiding spot at the side window and peeked out. The deputy was talking to the agitated woman, who gestured wildly as she spoke. I heard her say something about a bear before she started crying.

With that, the deputy led her away from the front entrance, then a few moments later, I got a phone call from Maelyne.

"Honey, the mom is saying her youngest left a teddy bear somewhere in the library and the poor baby is hysterical and won't stop crying until she gets it back."

"Oh, I haven't seen it, but I'll look. If you give me a minute, I'll call back to let you know what I find."

Maelyne was a seventy-something-year-old woman full of spit and vinegar. I'd met her a few times since her sister volunteered here at the library, one of my few volunteers who was great about helping people find their books.

After hanging up, I did a quick search of the children's area and not finding the bear, I was about to call her back when I remembered the little girl running around the library before she'd said she needed to pee. I began going up and down the rows until I finally found the little bear sitting in a corner of the library not far from where the girl's brother had been injured.

I called Maelyne back and told her I had the bear. "But I don't want that woman in here, especially right now when we're closed," I told her.

"Oh, no. Darren wouldn't do that. I'll have him come around the back and you can hand it to him from there."

"Thanks, Maelyne. I owe you one."

"Just doing my job, honey," she said happily.

The deputy was at the back door just moments later, and he took the bear apologetically. "I've told the woman she needs to stay away from the library for the time being until things settle down, but I'm guessing she basically does what she wants. If you see her again, don't hesitate to call us if need be."

I nodded and sighed. "Yeah, okay, thanks for helping."

He winked at me and disappeared back down the stairs to where I assumed the woman was waiting.

When I came back in, my stomach was upset, as it had been the night before. Once again, I was dealing with an insane situation and still had a ton of work to finish.

To my surprise, however, Roth came toward me pushing an empty book cart.

"You're finished already?" I asked.

He shrugged and smiled. "I'm pretty fast. It became a challenge for me when I was in high school. If I got done early, Mrs. Patterson would let me spend the rest of my volunteer time reading." He chuckled then. "She called it 'getting to know the material time.'"

"She sounds pretty awesome."

A sad expression crossed Roth's face. "She was beyond awesome. Unfortunately, she had cancer and we lost her the year I graduated."

"Oh, that's tough." I looked around the library then, unsure how to deal with the emotions of the moment. "Well, I owe her for what she taught you, that's for sure. That would've taken me an hour to finish."

Roth grinned a little mischievously. "Remind me to show you my secret someday. There's a method to my madness."

Like there'll ever be another day this handsome music star comes back to my Podunk little library to volunteer again, I thought to myself.

"Well, if you're finished with that, I've got to do some work at the circulation desk. The only thing left to do out here is running a vacuum cleaner and cleaning the restrooms."

"I'm happy to help with either one. Just point me toward the cleaning supplies."

I looked at Roth like he'd just lost his head. "You mean you *want* to clean the restrooms?" I asked, dumbfounded.

"Sure, why not? I mean, you do have gloves, right?"

I nodded and led him to where I kept the cleaning supplies and unlocked the door. I kept it locked rather than risk some of the kids opening it and getting too close to the chemicals stored inside.

Roth quickly slipped on the gloves and grabbed the toilet bowl brush, chemical cleaning solution, and the bucket before he walked toward the restroom.

I shook my head as he disappeared inside without even acting like it was a big deal. I secretly decided I'd go in to make sure he'd actually done the cleaning before leaving, but even his willingness confused me. Most of my volunteers had flat-out refused to ever clean the restrooms. In fact, only Doc and Amos were consistently willing. So, having a famous singer willing to take it on perplexed me.

Oh well, *don't kick a gift horse in the mouth*, my granny always used to say. So, I went into my office and began organizing and putting paperwork together for the following workweek.

TWELVE

ROTH

I WOULDN'T PRETEND THAT my desire to volunteer was anything less than wanting to spend time with the cute librarian. I wasn't someone to jump into a relationship without really getting to know someone first. Now that I'd been in the competition, I was even more leery of people's intentions and why a potential partner would want to be with me.

I had thoroughly enjoyed my morning watching Chris react to things. First, being able to spend quality time with him as he cooked breakfast. Then, seeing how he bantered with my crazy-ass sister.

His reaction to all of us meeting Jen was curious, though. I'd glanced at him when Jesse all but fell over when he first saw her. Chris was quiet and appeared stand-offish, but he'd also clearly enjoyed the show as much as I had.

Spending time with him in the library had been my favorite part of this entire trip thus far. Since the competition, it'd felt as if people had different expectations of me, like I'd somehow become incapable of being a normal person.

I admit to feeling disappointed when Chris assumed I wouldn't know anything about how library books were organized. Had he thought I'd never set foot in a library before? Being able to shock him first by knowing how to shelve, and second by being fast at it had been fun, though.

As for the restrooms, well, I'd never minded cleaning. My parents were sticklers that everyone in the family take turns with bathroom duty, so I knew my way around a toilet bowl brush. Knowing Chris would likely be impressed by my willingness to tackle the restrooms was a total plus. By this point, I was determined to show the guy I was more than his assumptions about me.

The restrooms ended up being less work than cleaning at home. Of course, my older brothers were both slobs when we were growing up. I assumed they were better now, considering Jesse had become a respected doctor, and Sam's wife hadn't left him yet. And trust me, if Sam was as nasty as he had been growing up, no one would've stayed with him long enough to start a family.

I chuckled as I thought of my brothers. Both so different, but I loved them equally. They were as much a part of me now as any siblings could be. As I wiped down the sinks, I smiled thinking about how much fun it was to see Jesse lose it over Jennifer Cole.

She was drop-dead gorgeous, and seemed like a lot of fun as well. She certainly had my brother's number, and she and Lettie were all but joined at the hip as they walked down the street toward the café. My sister could be a bit much at times, but she was an amazing human being, and she needed a friend just as intense and maybe just a little wild as she was. I only knew what the public said about Jen, but I got a gut feeling that Jen might just be that kind of person.

I finished up and after putting the cleaning supplies away, I found the vacuum and began that job. It only took me a moment to figure out why cleaning was important to Chris. The place was a mess.

I found half-eaten food in the children's area even though *No Food or Drink* signs were posted all over the library. The floors were dirty too, which wasn't a shock since the place resembled a worksite more than a library from the front.

I guessed if there wasn't enough money to hire help for Chris, there also wasn't enough for proper landscaping, and the grass that'd been seeded was clearly coming in sparsely. The sidewalks out front had clearly flooded after a big rain and the dirt that spread across them as mud was being tracked into the building.

By the time I finished vacuuming, I was determined to attempt to remedy the situation. If nothing else, I'd ask Jake what he could do to help. He clearly had an investment in the town. Surely he knew someone with vastly more money than me who could afford to cover costs to put some sod down and otherwise spruce the outside up a bit.

Hell, now that I thought about it, maybe I *could* afford that. I had received an advance when I signed with the record label. I already knew I sucked at keeping my eye on the business side of things, which was why I needed a manager, but I'd never been very good at managing my finances. In fact, I hated it. So, to avoid accidentally blowing it all, I'd dumped most of my advance into my savings account, only pulling enough into my checking to ensure I had enough at my disposal to get by without worrying. I hadn't looked at the account since then.

I made a mental note to check it, though, when I got home. Maybe Jake could refer me to an accountant to manage my finances for me. The only reason I hadn't done that yet was because I'd heard too many stories of celebrities who'd lost everything when an unscrupulous accountant had gained access and ripped them off. But I trusted Jake's judgment and if he recommended someone, they'd be reliable.

I sighed as I finished up a section of the carpet. I'd been bemoaning a rich person's problem and I had no right to feel anything other than gratitude over my financial situation. I would learn to manage my money like an adult, end of subject.

I was just about to vacuum one of the last bits of carpet near the entrance when another knock sounded on the library door. Chris was in the office behind the circulation desk and hadn't heard it. Peeking out the side window, I saw my brother and sister standing on the stoop. I tapped on the window and held up a finger to let them know I'd be out in a moment, then fetched a broom and bucket of water and met them out front.

"You two need to clean the dried mud off this sidewalk. People are tracking it into the library."

Lettie looked at the broom I handed her with disgust, but Jesse took the bucket of water, and, without question, headed toward the mud slick and began pouring the water on it. "I think there's a water tap around the side," I told him. "If you can just slosh water on it like you're doing, that might help more than anything."

Jesse nodded and I left them to work. When I turned around, I saw Chris standing at the entrance, smiling. "You gave your siblings grunt work?" he asked as I went up the steps.

I blushed and returned his smile. "Well, and kept them from tracking more dirt in. I'm just about to finish the carpets. I just have the area here and in front of the circulation desk. Is there anything else you'd like me to do?" I asked.

He shook his head. "No, once you're done with that, we're finished for the day. This would've taken me all day to do without your help."

"Really? Then you're free for the rest of the day?" I asked.

"I guess," he said contemplatively. I could tell he was trying to figure out if he'd forgotten something.

I left him to stew on it while I finished vacuuming. I heard my siblings at the entrance just as I turned the vacuum off, so I met them at the door to prevent them from coming in and tracking mud all over the clean floor.

"Hey, I'm just about done. I'll be out in a few minutes."

"Good," Jesse said. "Jen and Jake invited us for drinks with them and Jake's husband at a local winery. I'd like to take them up on the offer."

"Cool. Do you mind if I invite Chris?" I asked.

Both my siblings smiled mischievously, but they each shook their heads. "No, the more, the merrier," Lettie said.

I went back inside after telling Jesse and Lettie I'd meet them back at the house soon. I figured Chris and I could walk back, since it really wasn't that far.

I put the vacuum cleaner away and when I closed the door, Chris came up behind me and locked it. "That was more help than I could've dreamed of having," he said. "Thanks, Roth. I owe you one."

"Well, can I collect on that now?" I asked, and winked at him. "We're going to some winery down the road. Come join us?"

Chris's face took on a crimson blush. "Sure, I guess that's okay."

We walked out of the library, and Chris was locking up when a car raced past us. A glass bottle came sailing through the air and barely missed my head before shattering on the steps.

I had just enough time to see a wild-haired woman toss the bottle and caught sight of her license plate number before she sped away.

"Damn, you okay?" Chris asked as he examined me, then took stock of the broken glass.

"I'm fine. I'm guessing that was your friend from earlier."

"Something's wrong with that woman," Chris said with a frustrated sigh. "I'm going to have to go report this and sweep up the mess."

"Why don't you give me the key to the cleaning closet, and you go make your call. I got a good look at her and even memorized her plate so I can tell the authorities when they get here."

Chris handed me the keys after unlocking the door once again and took out his phone to call the sheriff's office.

By the time I'd swept up the glass, the deputy had arrived, and I relayed what I'd seen and the plate number.

Before he left, the deputy said to Chris, "You need to watch your back, son. That woman, Lorna Bailey, is blaming you for all sorts of stuff. It's public knowledge she was caught fooling around on her husband. Apparently, he's left her and is staying with the kids at his parents' place, and she's blaming you for it. She's clearly not wanting to take responsibility for her own actions, which in my experience makes her more dangerous."

"Can you do anything about her throwing a bottle at our heads?" I asked.

"If the plates prove to be hers, then I'll bring her in for questioning. Still, keep your eyes open and be safe," he said before walking away.

Chris and I walked quietly back to his place. I could tell the disturbed woman had him on edge, and I wished I could do or say something to ease his worry. Truth be told, though, I felt just as uneasy. Luckily, my sister was enough to distract anyone, and by the time we were all headed to the winery, she'd already gotten Chris to laugh. Mostly by her teasing Jesse about Jen Cole, supermodel to the world and my brother's new obsession.

"I'm not obsessing," Jesse complained when he heard me say something to that effect to Lettie. "I've just never met anyone like her. She's beautiful and funny too."

Lettie caught my eye and winked. "Yeah, funny too."

Jesse nudged our sister like he did when he was trying to get her to shut up, which only got her going even more. If past experiences were any indication, our trip to the winery would prove an eventful one, especially if Jen came. I hoped my brother and sister's teasing would be enough to distract Chris from thinking about the bottle-throwing incident. Hopefully their antics would get it off my mind too.

THIRTEEN

CHRIS

I DIDN'T REALLY HAVE time to be running around the countryside. I could've used a few more hours just sketching out some of the library programs I'd yet to have time to consider, much less plan. But after the mother from last night tried to clock me with a glass bottle, I decided I deserved the break.

Besides, what fool would give up a chance to have drinks with Roth Gallo? Jesse drove and Lettie sat in the front seat, putting Roth and me together in the back. For the most part, Jesse and Lettie argued or teased one another the entire way to the winery.

Roth was sitting close and more than once, our hands bumped into one another's, or his shoulder would press against mine. Each accidental touch sent electric currents pulsing through my body. How could I feel so attracted to someone I hardly knew?

That wasn't how it usually worked for me. Up until now, I'd blown off my intense attraction to Roth as a celebrity crush, but that excuse had worn off after spending the day together. Not that I knew how a celebrity was supposed to act, but I was pretty sure the laid-back, don't mind cleaning a public restroom sort of guy like Roth wasn't it.

On the drive, Roth had taken my hand in his, and when I didn't pull it away, he glanced over at me shyly and smiled. I knew I was blushing, and having gotten to know his sister, I was very happy she was in the front seat and too preoccupied with harassing her other brother to have noticed. Feeling his fingers laced with mine felt like heaven and I didn't want to let go.

As soon as we climbed out of the car at the winery, I was immediately taken with the inviting streamside setting. The building itself had been an old mill, and seeing its giant paddle wheel still turning sent my creative mind into hyperdrive.

"This should be the setting for a novel," I said out loud, not even thinking.

"For real," Roth said as he came up behind me.

Jesse and Lettie joined us in watching the wheel turn for a bit before we all walked up the front steps and into the building.

The mill's interior had been turned into a gift shop full of fun kitchen gadgets and wine-themed décor. Even on my ridiculously tight budget, I couldn't resist buying a sweet little pillow that said, *Books and Wine are My Addictions of Choice.*

Jake and Jen came in with a man I hadn't met before who Jake introduced as his husband, Lance. Just as I was making my purchase, Lance had talked the woman behind the counter into letting us see the second-floor art gallery.

While I wasn't an art connoisseur in any way, even my untrained eye could appreciate the magnificence of the paintings on display. I listened as Jake told Jesse about Matt, the artist, and how Matt and Logan, a vintner, had fallen in love and transformed this place into an award-winning winery.

"It's really spectacular," I said as I walked over to where a window, bordered by two huge, beautiful paintings, looked out over the mountain stream that turned the water wheel and provided the mill with power.

The paintings had clearly been made for this spot in particular, because even though they were both abstract, as you backed away from the window, you could clearly see they were artistic renderings of the landscape from that vantage point. The idea of Monet and his Water Lilies came to mind.

The winery was only a few miles outside Crawford City, and I couldn't help but hope that I'd eventually get to meet the couple who owned this beautiful place. If the decorative pillow I bought was any indication, maybe they were book lovers and would come visit the library.

Lia, the woman who apparently ran the gift shop, suggested we walk around the winery property and told us about a beautiful chapel located a quarter of a mile from the old mill. "If you'd like to see the vines themselves, that's about another half-mile in the other direction," she said.

Jake began bragging about how beautiful the chapel was, and how he and his husband had been married there, so the group decided to go in that direction. As we stepped outside, though, Roth asked if I minded going to look at the vines with him instead. "I think I'd rather save the chapel for another day," he said so only I could hear.

"Sure, I'm open to anything," I said, not thinking what that must've sounded like.

Roth's smile turned a bit naughty, and he said, "I'll keep that in mind." That, naturally, caused me to blush a deeper red than the wine.

"Hey, y'all, we're going to go the other way," Roth called out to the group. "We'll meet back up with you in a bit, okay?"

He didn't wait for their response, just took my hand and led me toward the vineyard. I half expected to hear his sister calling after us to wait up, and although I liked her and thought it'd be fun to get to know her and the rest of the group better, I was happy when no one followed us.

We walked quietly down a dirt road, enjoying more of a contented silence than an awkward one. Once we reached the edge of the meadow, opposite the old mill, the road became framed by large trees that provided a beautiful canopy over us. "It almost feels like we've gone back in time with the old road and gristmill," I said.

"It's pretty romantic, huh?" Roth asked.

"Yeah," I agreed, and let out a wistful sigh.

Roth reached over and took my hand then and we continued down the country road until we came to a beautiful old barn. "Lia said that's where they process the wine."

"Yeah, and there's the vineyard," I said, pointing toward the neatly arranged rows that rose up a steep hill with a southern exposure facing the old barn.

"Wow, beautiful," Roth said as he stared up at the rows of grapes that climbed the hill.

Seeing the wonderment on his face, I was more taken by his beauty than the scenery. "Gorgeous," I whispered.

When he turned and caught me staring at him, I became embarrassed. It wasn't like me to be so forward, and I was about to pull away, but Roth didn't hesitate. He cupped my face in his hands and moved in for a kiss.

Maybe it was the place, maybe it was the man or the day I'd spent with him. But right then and there, he wasn't a famous singer any longer, not some unattainable celebrity. He was simply a kind and beautiful man who I'd struggled all day not to kiss.

When our lips touched, fireworks went off in my mind. He smelled like the woods and something more cologne-like. The two scents mixed so well together, I felt intoxicated.

The kiss started off tentative and soft. But the moment his aroma swept over me, I deepened the kiss and before long, we both became ravenous, almost as if we couldn't get enough of each other.

Finally, I pulled back. Although the move cost me, I knew I needed to stop now or risk losing control. As much as I'd like to pull this gorgeous man into the woods for some privacy, what started as the best kiss of my life didn't need to end in us being treated for poison ivy in unmentionable places.

"I've wanted to do that since I met you," Roth said as he leaned his forehead against mine, breathing hard.

"Me too," I said quietly, because I'd yet to get my full voice back after such an intense moment.

Roth straightened and met my eyes. "I really like you, Chris. I was afraid you'd think I'm too much 'cause of how crazy my life is right now."

I couldn't help but snort out a laugh. "You mean you were afraid your celebrity status would scare me away?"

Roth looked at the ground, but I didn't miss seeing the flash of vulnerability in his eyes. "Yeah, sort of. I mean, I'm not the most suave man anyway, and when you pile all the other stuff on top..."

"You get someone who's amazing," I finished for him. "The thing is, Roth, I'm a really simple guy. I've got no talent to become famous for, and even if I did, I don't have any desire. My dream is to run a little library in a Podunk town, and that's why I'm in Crawford City."

I took his hand again and we walked toward the barn, where I saw a bench sitting out in front. Once we were seated, I told him what had been concerning me since I'd met him.

"I don't know if a famous singer and a small-town librarian have any future at all. I'll never want to live in a giant mansion or drive flashy cars. What I do want some-day is a regular house with a kitchen, bedroom, and a little reading room with a comfy chair and maybe a fire-place. Anything more doesn't really matter to me. Some-one who wins huge singing competitions will probably want a lot more in life than that," I said, and glanced at Roth, who was watching me.

After a long pause, Roth sat back on the bench and looked out over the vines. "I'm just a regular guy, Chris. I'm plain and simple too. Besides, I didn't actually win the competition, I'm second best." He laughed then. "Seriously, though, I haven't really thought about where I'll live. You seem to have thought about that a lot more than me. I mean, I want a place for my family to come visit, and I want to live in a nice place, but I don't think every famous person wants or feels a need to live large. I mean, Amelia Denton lived in a simple suburban house for years before she bought a mansion in Brentwood."

I smiled as I listened to him. He'd sung Amelia's song in the competition, but then he'd also had classes with her, so it didn't surprise me that he'd compare himself to her. I had no idea where Amelia lived or what her former house looked like, but I'd made my point and Roth seemed to understand my concern. I didn't want to be a celebrity's husband.

"I know I'm being silly, but I wanted you to know I'm not very fancy before we take things any further."

"I'm not very fancy either. So, maybe we can be not fancy together?"

"I'd like that," I said, giggling at the silliness of his statement. "Let's be unfancy together."

We walked back toward the mill, and this time, as we held hands, it felt different. More intimate and thrilling somehow. Maybe this thing between us wouldn't go very far, but surely, it couldn't hurt to get to know each other better. That, at least, was what I kept telling myself. Deep down, I figured I'd have a pretty serious heartache when this inevitably ended, but as my dad always said, "You only live once, might as well do the best you can with it."

FOURTEEN

ROTH

I WASN'T NORMALLY THE assertive type in relationships, but with Chris, that didn't seem to be the case. I'd wanted to kiss him since I met him, but had forced myself to behave. When I glanced over and saw him watching me with the same look of desire on his face that I felt, though, my resolve crumbled.

I almost expected him to pull away, but when he didn't, what I'd meant to be a chaste kiss quickly turned lava hot. Heat coursed through me at the feel of his lips devouring mine, causing my insides to melt for this man.

If Chris hadn't pulled back, I wasn't entirely sure where things would've ended up. Probably with us rolling around in the woods, if I was honest. Our honest conversation on the bench afterward proved eye-opening, but also confirmed some things for me. I had sensed Chris felt insecure about my being a celebrity, even though I still didn't think of myself that way, but I appreciated his candor about it. When he told me everything he wanted out of life, it was as if he'd recited my personal goals list, too, other than the one missing item of having a music career.

As we walked back toward the old mill, hand in hand, the air seemed lighter. It was like something magical had been switched on inside me, something warm and tingly and full of possibility, and I could hardly contain my excitement.

Unfortunately, our lovely evening was fading as quickly as the sun that had already begun to set. Jesse had to work the next day, so we really needed to get back to Nashville. When we pulled up in front of Chris's house, I got out and followed him up to the front door.

"I'm not ready to say goodbye," I said, pouting a little.

"Me either, but we both have lives. My day will begin pretty early tomorrow, and I suspect yours will be busy too."

I smiled and was about to lean in to kiss him goodbye when it hit me. I had absolutely nothing to do while waiting for the record label to contact me. "Actually, I'm free for a while since I've finished recording my album. If you'd like some help at the library, I'd love to offer my services. Free of charge, of course."

I winked at him, but Chris eyed me skeptically. "You want to come volunteer at the library, like full-time? Surely you have better things to do than witness me trying to corral volunteers and books all day."

The man really had no idea that he'd charmed me. "It's not like I don't have experience, and I had a good time helping out earlier today. In fact, shelving all of those books kept reminding me of my happiest memories in high school."

"I don't know. Where would you stay?" Chris asked, biting his bottom lip. I could sense I was winning him over to the idea, I just needed to figure out logistics in the next few seconds.

"I'd offer to let you stay here," Chris continued, gesturing toward the house, "...but that seems like a bit too much. I mean, working together is too much too, but I'm not going to turn down the opportunity to spend more time with you. And obviously, I'm desperate for help at the library." He chuckled as he finished that statement.

"Well, it's settled then. I'll ride back with Jesse and Lettie tonight and I'll drive over tomorrow, then you can put me to work. Don't worry about lodgings, I can stay in Jake's hotel."

"I mean, if you're serious, how long do you think you can stay in town?"

I could tell he was beginning to think about how to utilize me at the library, and that filled me with joy. I hated not having a direction in life, and I'd been going at my music career so hard for so long that I'd never had to contend with downtime. I'd promised both Jake and the record label I wouldn't be moonlighting until the record was finished and distributed, so I couldn't exactly get a job even if I'd wanted that. This way, I wouldn't be going against my contract or agreements, and I could still keep busy, not to mention remaining in Chris's orbit.

"I'm not sure how long or when I'll have to get back, but I can ask the record label. Lettie is working on helping me find a manager. Once I have one, I'll be able to keep better tabs on my schedule."

"Why don't you just hire Lettie to be your manager?" Chris asked. Of course, he was joking, but the moment the words left his mouth, I realized how perfect my sister would be for the job.

Lettie was smart, talented, and knew every damned person in Nashville. She put up with absolutely no shit from anyone, including me. "Damn, Chris, I hadn't thought of that." His smirk told me he thought I was being sarcastic. "No, really, that's a brilliant idea. You might have just saved my ass."

I looked back at the car where my siblings were waiting on me. Lettie caught my expression and gave me her *don't be talking trash about me* look.

I laughed and she immediately got out of the car.

"What are you saying about me?"

"None of your business," I hollered back.

She stomped up to the steps and, hands on her hips, said, "I was being very good and letting you both say goodbye, but you've had your chance. Come on, little brother, time to go home."

"See, she's already managing me, and I haven't even mentioned it to her," I said to Chris, and he laughed out loud.

"Said what to me?"

"That I should hire you as my manager."

Lettie was never at a loss for words. Witty, sarcastic, infuriating, yes, and always ready with a quick retort. Now, though, she just stared at me, mouth agape and eyes wide.

"You want *me* to be your manager? Are you serious?"

"Chris just suggested it, and yes, I think you're the best possible person for the job."

She looked to Chris, who was still smiling from the exchange, for confirmation that I wasn't just blowing smoke. When he nodded, she said, "I mean, I would be freaking awesome at it, not to mention, I'm like a mama bear when it comes to protecting you. But work for you? I don't know..."

Lettie looked as if her mind was wheeling like a windmill in a hurricane, and I took the gift of her being lost in thought to say a proper goodnight to Chris.

"I'll see you tomorrow," I whispered into his ear. "I'm going to drag my sister back to the car now before her head explodes."

"Good idea," Chris whispered back, stifling a chuckle. "I'm looking forward to tomorrow."

"So am I. Night, sweetheart," I said, and kissed him deeply, hopefully conveying the passion I felt for him.

"Okay, that's enough for a first date," Lettie said as she grabbed my hand and pulled me toward the car.

"Bye," I managed to say before she shoved me in the back seat.

From the car, I could see Chris laughing again, and that was the image I took with me. A beautiful man, framed in the doorway of a magnificent old cabin, with joy radiating from him. I really did have it bad for the guy. To my surprise, Lettie sat quietly most of the trip back. If I were to guess, she'd ponder on the job offer for an hour or so, then she'd make me spend the night at her place, and come morning would drill me for my thoughts and motivations in hiring her. Lettie could be spontaneous, but clearly she recognized this was no time for making impulsive decisions.

With our sister completely lost in her own world, Jesse and I chatted about Jen, and he peppered me with questions about her career. It made me laugh internally, not only because Jesse had never shown any interest in fashion or celebrities, but also because Lettie was much more of an expert on the subject than I ever would be.

Jesse was cute, being so over the moon for Jen. I mean, I could totally understand being smitten by a gorgeous supermodel. But my very levelheaded brother didn't just fall for any pretty face he met. I enjoyed telling him what I knew about her.

"Jesse," I finally said. "I don't want to burst your bubble or bring you down from your supermodel high, but she's known for discarding men like used tissues. If you do ever go out with her, just know it's unlikely to last long."

Jesse's face fell, but he nodded. "It's not like I've got time to be dating anyone anyway. I've got a new job. I'll be working nights," he said, practically making a list of reasons not to pursue her. "Thanks for bringing me back to earth, Roth."

"That's a bunch of bullshit," Lettie burst out. "Just because she hasn't met a guy that keeps her furnace lit doesn't mean you aren't that guy for her. Geez, and the person cautioning you to be careful is a famous singer currently wooing a small-town librarian? Did you not see Roth's tongue down the guy's throat earlier? Yeah, real cautious."

She rolled her eyes at me and, in a show of compassion, laid her hand on Jesse's arm. "Brother, if you like her and she likes you, don't even hesitate to get to know her. I can assure you that Jen Cole wants to find someone worthy of her love, same as any of us, famous or not. There is a whole lot more to her than just a pretty face."

Jesse let the conversation drop after that, but I could tell Lettie's words had struck a chord. I had to admit, she wasn't wrong. Whatever challenges Jesse might face in dating Jen might be the same as what Chris and I would encounter if my career were to take off. I'd been trying to help my brother steer clear of future heartache, but really, who was I to throw cold water on his potential happiness? I sure as hell wouldn't want someone doing that to Chris and me.

As I suspected, Jesse dropped me off at Lettie's place after she talked me into staying the night. We laughed about how enamored Jesse was with Jen Cole and, with a new level of interest, we Googled her to learn more about her career.

"She's actually perfect for him," I said, after we'd read several articles about her. "She's a strong and no-nonsense person, just like him. But she also seems to have a sweetness about her as well. They're almost like two peas in a pod."

"Which," Lettie added with a sigh, "...could be great, or horrible."

I glanced over at my sister and saw an expression of sadness I hadn't noticed before. "What aren't you telling me?" I asked.

She shook her head. "Oh, nothing. I had a short fling, but it fell apart. We were just too alike."

"Did you take him to meet Mom and Dad?" I asked.

She smiled. "No. It didn't last that long. Really, it was just a fling, not sure why I got so worked up about it."

I grabbed my glass of wine, brought the bottle over to refill hers, and sat next to her on the couch. "Okay, so spill. Who is the mystery man?"

Lettie looked shy all of a sudden, which in and of itself was newsworthy. My sister rarely kept things close to the chest, not between the two of us. "It's probably best that I don't tell anyone, even you. He just went through a high-profile divorce and got joint custody of his two kids. I'd rather keep this one to myself than jeopardize things for him."

I thought for a moment before I gasped. "Jaydon Hayes?" I asked.

Lettie squared me with a look. "Damn, you know me too well. Seriously, not a word. We started dating before the divorce was final and if his ex-wife found out, it could hurt him with his custody case."

"How the hell is it going to hurt his custody case? I mean, it's well-documented that the man was cheated on repeatedly. His ex-wife doesn't have a leg to stand on in that regard."

"You only know what's in the tabloids. The reality is more complicated, and she accused him of having an affair too. The truth is he and I didn't start dating until they'd been separated for months, but that hardly matters now. Just trust me." She put her hand up to stop me talking before I could respond.

Jaydon Hayes, the famous sculptor, had moved to Nashville after marrying his wife. He was tall, incredibly handsome, charming, and had a Jamaican accent so sexy that I would happily listen to him read a dictionary. I'd met him a couple times when I'd gone with Lettie to her art friend's parties. I liked him instantly, and I suspected nearly everyone who met Jaydon Hayes fell in love with him. That, apparently, included my sister.

"Lettie, tell me more about what happened. This stays between you and me, I promise."

She drank the entire glass of wine, then put it down on the table and leaned back into the couch, putting her feet in my lap. Of course, I knocked them down. "Don't put your stinky feet on my lap, we've talked about this. I'm here to listen, not be your personal ottoman."

She laughed like she always did when this scene played out. "Okay, so Jaydon and I have been friends, as you know, for years. His wife, Octavia, and I even sort of liked each other, as much as anyone can like her. Luckily, she was never jealous of me, so she didn't freak out around me like she did when other women came anywhere near the man."

"Yeah, she did seem sort of paranoid and possessive. Last time I attended an art party with you, she was drunk and railing at Jaydon about flirting with the host."

Lettie sighed. "We'd just started dating when I pulled up to his home one night and saw a man parked across the street, taking pictures of Jaydon's house and car. I got out and threatened to wallop the man, and he admitted he was a private detective hired by Octavia. Their divorce was being finalized and she was on the verge of losing the custody battle in court. Jaydon said he didn't want to do anything that gave her ammunition against him, so he only wanted to date on the down-low until things had settled. I blew a gasket, telling him I wouldn't be any man's secret, and he blew back, saying I was being selfish. Maybe I had been, but it's too late now anyway. We broke it off."

Lettie poured another glass of wine but just swirled it around, not taking a sip.

"I can't blame you for standing your ground, but I can't really blame him either for being cautious. Their personal business is plastered all over the Internet. If I'm honest, I'd think you wouldn't want to get caught in the middle of all that either. The press will crucify anyone who tries to date him, all the more so before the dust settles on their divorce."

"So, what? You think I should've just rolled over and kept our dating a secret? If that were the case, I'd still be dating him, and you wouldn't even know it."

I shrugged. "I don't know what to tell you. I mean, until you're ready to be in a long-term relationship, I'd say it's better if you didn't put it out for the world to scrutinize. At the same time, you'd run the risk of it dragging on in secret too long. Seriously, I'd never date a closeted gay man. I want to be myself, not live a lie. So, I get where you're coming from too."

Lettie sighed and leaned over to hug me. "I really do like him, and his kids are sweet despite the evil crow that gave birth to them."

"Then why don't you compromise?" I asked. "Get to know him quietly, maybe take him up to Crawford City and the winery? I doubt anyone will know him there, and even if they do, I doubt they'll care enough to call the paparazzi."

"I'll think about it," she said noncommittally, and climbed back over to her side of the couch. "So, your turn. What about the cutie-pie librarian?"

I laughed. "I'm going to go back and volunteer at the library for a while. Hopefully, that will give me some time to get to know him without having to contend with any of my career hoopla."

"You show your face during the day, and word will spread in no time that you're there," she said.

"Yeah, I've thought about that. I'm going to help Chris in the early mornings and late afternoons, when the library isn't as busy, until the locals get used to seeing me around. Later on, I thought I could start going in during the day to read to the kids or do an activity with them or something. Since I'll be in town, I can even pretend like I'm interested in Jesse's condo and help him set it up."

"Jesse's condo? You've already decided it's his?" Lettie asked, chuckling.

"Please, you know after seeing how enamored he is with Jen, there's no way he's going to let that place be sold to anyone else."

We both laughed. "And when they have kids, maybe they can combine the two and make it one large compound."

"You think there's a real chance of that?"

Lettie shrugged. "No idea, but it's fun to think of Jen Cole as my sister-in-law. Oh my god, we could have so much fun shopping in Paris, and maybe when she gets tired of some of her beautiful designer dresses, she could hand them down to me."

I laughed at the far-off look in her eyes. "You've already begun planning all this out, I see."

"Well, of course I have, little brother. Besides, if I'm going to be your manager, I need to look stylish and gorgeous."

"Of course," I said. "So, you've decided to take me up on the job offer?"

"I'd be really good at it. We can try it out, and if it doesn't work, I'll help you find someone who will."

"Do you know what it takes to be a manager in this business?" I asked, concerned all of a sudden I'd jumped into asking her too soon.

"No, but I know plenty of them. I'll call around tomorrow and ask questions. None of them will be surprised that I'm considering the position. It's not that uncommon for siblings to run management for famous people. In some ways, it's an advantage 'cause we can yell at each other and still work things out."

"Are you planning on yelling at me?" I asked, knowing that wasn't her way.

"Only when you need me to, dear brother."

That night I went to bed excited about what it might mean to work with Lettie. She already had my back and was the first person I turned to when I needed something important or just needed to talk. As long as she didn't hate it, this could work out perfectly for both of us.

FIFTEEN

CHRIS

NOTHING SHORT OF AMAZING. That was how it felt coming to work on Monday with absolutely nothing to do but show up. I spent the morning brainstorming programs I could offer the kids this summer, provided I was able to tie down a couple volunteers to lead them.

I could also offer evening readings in the area between the library and city hall. I had visions of inviting food trucks and having different areas dedicated to different genres, but I'd probably have to hold off. Even if Roth came through as a volunteer, I couldn't imagine having the time or budget to plan such an event.

By late afternoon, I hadn't heard from or seen Roth, so I assumed maybe he'd changed his mind. I pushed down the disappointment, although I scolded myself for getting too excited over something I should've known would never be.

I had just locked up the front when I heard knocking at the back door. *Strange*, I thought, and my first inclination was to call the sheriff's office to report the crazed woman had returned. The deputy had left just an hour before after he stopped by to inform me the woman's license plate had come back as registered to her husband.

When I peeked out the little window, however, I was happy to see Roth standing there.

"Hey," I said after opening the door. "I didn't expect to see you here so late."

He looked a little sheepish. "Well, I'm not one to go back on my word, but I also didn't want my presence creating chaos, so I decided to come after hours and help you organize."

I leaned over and kissed him. "I'm glad you're here. I was about to give you up for lost."

"Nope, here and ready for work!" he said, holding his hand up. "Unless you want to do a little more kissing."

I blushed. "More kissing for sure, but after we finish putting the library back to rights."

We worked quickly through the piles of books. It'd been a slow afternoon after everyone had come early to get the gossip about Saturday's injured kid situation. So, I'd already collected most of the books onto the book cart and even organized a few.

While I spruced up the children's area and got the periodicals squared away, Roth shelved the entire book cart and within half an hour, we were completely done. Fortunately, the school sent over a cleaning crew on

Mondays, so I didn't have to worry about the restrooms or carpets tonight.

"Hey, since we finished and it's still early, do you want to run over to the café for dinner?" I asked.

"Sure," Roth said just as his stomach growled loudly.

I laughed. "I'd say your stomach is in favor of the idea too."

Mondays were the slowest day of the week at the café, so we were able to eat uninterrupted and, to the best of my knowledge, no one seemed to recognize Roth. Mrs. Cole filled the buffet one last time between five thirty and six, so most of the food was still hot and fresh.

"I love the fried chicken here," I said as I began filling my plate.

"Me too. The last time we were here, I wanted to eat like ten pieces, but I didn't want you to think I was a pig."

I laughed. "My mom would've fallen in love with you if she'd seen you eat that much. She's always concerned I'm not eating enough. I swear she thinks a man under two hundred pounds is emaciated."

"Speaking of that, how do you stay so fit?" Roth asked. "If I worked across from a place like this, I'd be as big as the building."

That Roth had noticed my body, and proceeded to give me a subtle once-over while waiting for my answer, caused me to feel tingly all over. "I don't eat much, to be honest. I mean, when I do, I can pack it away, but most days I'd forget to eat altogether if it wasn't for Amos and Doc riding me to do so. I also get a lot of exercise running around the library. I haven't measured it, but

I'm guessing I get in close to ten thousand steps a day, probably more when the library is left in shambles."

We ate in companionable silence, both of us enjoying the fresh hot chicken and the homemade potatoes and gravy. Hearing my mom's voice, like Jiminy Cricket in my head, I also forced myself to get a helping of broccoli and green beans. My mother remained a stickler for her family to eat more vegetables. I'd learned long ago to eat them just to avoid a battle, which I always lost.

When we left the café, we held hands and walked back down the street toward the hotel. "So, are you already checked in?" I asked.

He nodded. "Yeah, it's an amazing place. I booked a room for the week, and thought we could play it by ear after that. Wanna see it?"

"See your room?" I asked, my heartbeat picking up speed. My tingly body and worried mind warred with each other over my answer, and my heart ultimately won out. "I need a little time. I mean, I know you probably aren't used to guys holding back, but it's been a long time for me. I'm not ready for more yet."

I blushed and would've found an excuse to get away, considering how embarrassingly stupid I must've sounded, if Roth hadn't been holding my hand. Gay guys were supposed to be all about sex, at least that's what my scattered dating history had shown me, but I'd never felt comfortable just jumping into bed with any man. I was, in every way, a relationship person.

More than once, that had destroyed any chance of scoring a second date. I'd tried fucking without thought once and hated it. I didn't want to repeat that, even if it meant I'd be alone for the rest of my life.

Roth must've sensed my unease, because he dropped my hand and wrapped his arms around me in a hug. He stayed silent for a moment, just holding me in his comforting embrace, and I melted against him. "We don't need to rush into things. I like you, Chris, and I want to woo you a little. If and when getting more physical feels right, for both of us, we can go there." He kissed my temple, and I sighed in relief that he seemed to understand how I felt. "For now, I genuinely just wanted to show you the hotel room. It's beautiful and modern, not anything like you'd expect to find in a rural small town. No strings, just a tour."

I nodded into his shoulder and when we entered the hotel, its beauty and thoughtful design blew me away. They'd retained historical components of the place, including exposed brick walls and huge wooden beams, with understated elegance, like what you'd expect to have seen in a hotel in the early 1900s.

Exquisite Edwardian style furniture sat around the great room, and the reception desk looked like it'd been a bar in a pub before it landed here.

"You're right, this is different than I would've expected in a small town," I said as I looked around in wonder.

Roth led me to his room, and again, the elegant design shocked me. It was a two-room suite with a bedroom and living room, as well as a small kitchenette and dining table.

"Do you want to watch TV?" Roth asked.

"Sure," I said, feeling nervous all of a sudden.

"Popcorn or no?"

"I'm still bursting at the seams from dinner, so none for me."

Roth turned the TV on and sat down on the couch, motioning for me to do the same.

Before I could get too anxious about us being in his hotel room, Roth put his arm around me and pulled me into his side. "This is nice," he said, and when I glanced at him, he had a genuine smile on his face.

That helped me relax a bit. The only problem was I really wanted to kiss him again. I turned toward him and when his gaze met mine, I allowed myself to do just that.

I hadn't ever just made out with a guy before, but I totally got the appeal now that I was doing it.

Everything about Roth seemed to set my nerve endings on fire. Not for the first time, I lamented not being able to just enjoy going all the way with a man I desired. If he wanted me even as half as much as I wanted him, I had no doubt we'd be dynamite together.

That was when it hit me. This man was more than just a quick fuck. I'd never felt this infatuated with a guy this early in the game, and that scared me. I pulled back and abruptly stood up. "I should probably get back home," I said, sort of stammering.

"Are you okay?" Roth asked.

"Yeah, just, well... I um..." My brain had short-circuited, and I didn't want to admit I'd begun developing serious feelings for him so soon.

"I'll see you tomorrow, right?" I asked stupidly as I moved toward his door.

"Yeah, tomorrow morning. Want to meet for breakfast?"

"Sure. Why don't you come by the house?" I asked as I reached for the doorknob. "Is eight too early?"

"Nope, perfect," he said calmly from the couch. He must've recognized my spooked deer in the headlights look, because he made no move to get up.

I waved and said goodbye as I slipped out the door. I beat myself up all the way back to the house. I wouldn't be at all surprised if he ran off and never showed his face around me again. Why couldn't I just get out of my own head and let myself go? Why did I have to let my emotions get in the way of what should be a natural thing?

It wasn't like I didn't want Roth with every fiber of my being. It wasn't like I didn't already fantasize about what we could do together behind closed doors. But what did I do the minute I was alone with the man, mere feet away from a bed? Bolt faster than a frightened rabbit, that's what.

"Fuck!" I said out loud, then quickly looked around to make sure no one had heard me. Luckily, I had cut through the wooded area between the library and the cabin, so I was alone. I took a deep breath and let it out slowly, forcing myself to calm down.

"It doesn't do any good to make yourself sick. You are who you are," I whispered to myself. "If Roth likes you, he'll give you time to get more comfortable. If not, he'll disappear and that'll be that. Either way, you'll know if he's worth it."

As I lay in bed that night, staring at the ceiling, I thought about how Roth had reacted to my multiple freak-outs that evening. Concerned, comforting, reassuring. The complete opposite of the majority of men I'd been out with before who'd grown annoyed and even ranted at me for leading them on. One guy even upped and left the restaurant in the middle of dinner when I'd told him I never had sex on a first date.

The only romantic relationships I'd had, as brief and largely unromantic as they were, had started as friendships before sex entered the picture. Would Roth be willing to consider allowing us to develop that part of our relationship first? Let me get to know him more before things turned physical?

I seriously doubted he'd even consider it, but I owed it to myself to ask. I just needed to work up the courage to be that direct with him. Besides, even if we didn't move beyond friendship, we all needed friends, right? Even famous people.

Having a plan to move forward without destroying everything before it even started, I fell asleep feeling almost hopeful. I just hoped Roth would be up for the challenge.

SIXTEEN

ROTH

I WALKED THE SHORT distance from the hotel to Chris's house the next morning, mostly because it was beautiful out and not yet too hot to cause me to melt. I also needed to burn off a little nervous energy, not knowing what frame of mind I'd find him in after he bolted last night.

When I arrived, Chris had just taken the food off the stove, and gestured to a stool at the kitchen island for me to sit down.

"So," he said as he began to plate the food. "I've been thinking about us, and I'm not going to be upset if this is too much for you."

That he'd used the term "us" wasn't lost on me, and he seemed to be working up courage for whatever he was about to say next. He put the skillet back on the stove, and grabbed the coffee before coming back to the island.

He poured us both a cup and then returned the coffee pot before continuing.

"I'm not very good at the dating thing. In fact, I sort of suck at it. I'm not into Grindr and jumping in the sack with someone the moment they meet, which is probably weird for a gay guy to admit, but it just freaks me out."

Chris made eye contact with me then, worry lines creasing his adorable face. He seemed to be trying to gauge my reaction, but wanting to give him the space to say all he needed, I just nodded for him to continue.

He took a deep breath, and said, "So, I'd like to work on being friends, if that's okay. I mean, eventually, I'd like it to become more if we both want that, but for now, I'm..."

When I could see he was struggling with how to elaborate further, I placed my hand over his. "Chris, just so there is no doubt in your mind, know that I want you. You're handsome and smart, and you make my insides feel all squishy," I said, hoping to make him laugh.

When he did, I smiled and continued, "But I'm perfectly fine with giving you time. I'll admit that I've never had a guy who's interested want to try being friends first." I shrugged as I thought about it. "Maybe that's why my relationships always fall apart or never go anywhere. So, I'm onboard with being friends before becoming boyfriends, especially if that's what you want and need. You're a really good kisser, though, and I don't want to give that up, okay? I mean, friends sometimes kiss each other, don't they?"

Chris chuckled. "I'm not so sure about that, but I like kissing you too," he said, giving me a quick peck on the lips. "Thank you for understanding. Hopefully I don't regret just letting this happen naturally, especially since your fame will likely explode into the stratosphere as soon as your album is released, but I'd rather take it slow."

I sighed. "I don't know how all the famous or not famous stuff will work out. To be honest, when I lost the competition, I was ready to give up my music career and go back to school. I'd all but decided to become a music teacher or something like that, but then I got the call from the record label and things turned back around. I'm guessing some things will change if I hit it big, but there's also no guarantee that'll happen. Most people don't make it even after getting a leg up from performing in front of millions on reality TV."

That seemed to put Chris at ease some and he sat on the stool next to me. As we both sipped our coffee, I thought about what I needed in our relationship. "Okay, I want something too. If this is going to work between us, whether just as friends or more, you need to let me be a normal person and not treat me any different because of my career or fame. I want to be treated just like any other guy. Deal?"

Chris extended his hand and we both shook. "Screw that, you said we could kiss," I said, and he laughed as I stood up and brought my lips down on his. Chris moaned as the kiss deepened, and even though I wanted to devour his lips a thousand times more than our breakfast, I pulled back.

"Whew, sealed with a kiss," he said almost in a whisper, causing me to laugh. "I think it's the only way we should make agreements from this point forward."

"Totally not going to get any argument out of me," I replied.

After breakfast, I helped him load the dishwasher and clean up, then we walked down to the library.

We'd straightened up the library the night before, so we had time before it opened to put together a couple bulletin boards and arrange a display of recently released books.

"This is the first time I've been able to do this sort of thing," Chris said proudly. "Usually, it's rush around like a chicken with his head cut off, then open and continue being in a frenzy all day."

"Glad to help. Now, how do you want me to help out the rest of the day? Should I hang out at the hotel and come back after you close?"

"If you're willing to help, I'd like you to stay. It doesn't do either of us any good with you hiding in the hotel all week. That said, if the press shows up here, I'd really like for you to take them outside, so it doesn't prevent our patrons from using the library. Not that Doc would mind a little free promotion of our services, I'm sure."

"I doubt any photographers or reporters will come here. At the moment, no one outside my family even knows I've got a record deal, because the label is planning to announce it closer to my album's release. Jake said that's to do with creating buzz and momentum at the right time. Anyway, I know other contestants who've gone back to their normal lives without much hoopla, and I don't see why that'd be any different for me right now."

"Hopefully," Chris replied contemplatively. "But, just in case, let's have a plan. The press stays outside, and if it gets insane, you switch back to mornings and evenings so as not to disturb the library? Is that okay?"

"Yeah, perfectly okay, and you're right, it's best to have a plan."

As I suspected, no press showed up and after the first couple of days volunteering, no one even seemed to think anything of me being there. I admit to feeling somewhat concerned that a well-meaning fan might ask about my career and what came next, since I didn't want to resort to lying, but no one did.

I ended up having to return to Nashville the following week for some final studio work and to meet with Jake about the PR involved in announcing my album release. I'd requested that we hold off until the last possible moment so I could enjoy my time in Crawford City without causing a huge scene.

Both Jake and the label agreed to hold off for now, but I thought that was mostly to maximize the shock factor and get as much media coverage as possible. Lettie had begun working with Jake to flesh out my commitments for promoting the album, and she occasionally texted me about my thoughts on this or that potential performance.

For the most part, I knew wherever they put me, I'd be freaking out with stage fright. The more Lettie asked me, the more unnerved I got thinking about singing in front of another live audience. I finally told her I didn't mind performing as long as they gave me a week or two off every so often so I could decompress.

Fortunately, Lettie knew all about my stage fright, and didn't need any further explanation than that. Knowing she'd fight to keep my schedule under control as much as possible while still fulfilling my obligations to the record label offered me a modicum of comfort. For now, I just wanted to continue living a normal life for as long as I could, and that meant returning to Crawford City and my cute librarian.

It was truly remarkable how quickly you could get into a routine with someone, especially someone as amazing as Chris. I didn't realize just how amazing he was until we were spending every day together. As much as I enjoyed helping out at the library, I loved spending non-work time with him, so after discovering he usually ran in the mornings, I asked, and he agreed to let me be his work-out partner.

We'd do an early morning run, then we'd split up and meet back at the library later to open up. He'd been facing pressure from the town council to open earlier in the day. He kept insisting the extra help—meaning me—he'd been receiving lately was temporary and that the library still needed to be able to function if and when volunteer availability dipped.

Of course, because he had a generous heart and loved the patrons who frequented the library, he was finally worn down into agreeing to certain days when he'd open early, but he announced them as special occasions. The townsfolk began calling those Roth Days, since Chris went to great lengths to tell everyone that my being there to help was the only reason we were having them.

He also began training a couple of the older volunteers who'd been schoolteachers before they'd retired with the intention of replacing me once I left. I had to hope that would help him out when the inevitable happened.

I tried not to think about that, though. I just wanted to enjoy what time we had together.

The summer months continued to get hotter, driving unsupervised schoolkids into the library for longer periods of time to escape the heat. Chris was prepared, though, and he and a handful of volunteers began planning activities to keep them engaged.

Since the unstable woman had let her kids run wild in the library, signs went up stating no child was to be left alone in the library. Luckily, most people obeyed the rules, but occasionally, a kid would show up on their own. When that happened, the volunteers, me included, would assign ourselves to the child to ensure they didn't get into trouble. As a result, I'd had a chance to meet most of the younger kids who'd arrived by themselves.

The teenagers were the hardest to entertain, but the majority were quiet and respectful and just needed a place to gather with their friends. Of course, they all knew me from TV, but after being momentarily starstruck wore off, mostly they liked to hang out and chat with me. I guessed that because of the competition, I was given honorary teen status, and they confided in me things they normally wouldn't other adults. Nothing concerning, just regular teen drama like who they liked, and what kind of music they preferred.

It also helped that Jesse's purchase of the condo went through, so I'd moved in with him for the summer instead of staying at the hotel. He mostly worked nights, and spent his days off with Jen when she was in town, so I didn't really see him all that often. The two of them would meet up with Chris and me for dinner at the café on occasion, though.

Thanks to Jen, Chris, and my volunteering at the library, by the time summer ended, I'd become fully entrenched in the little community. I knew most of the people in town by their first names, and more often than not, I'd be invited to lunch at the café with various people or groups.

I'd never felt like I belonged in a community before. When I was little, my grandmother moved around a lot, and even though my adopted family had deep roots in Nashville, I never really met our neighbors. The ones whose names I did know usually just yelled at us to stay off their property when we played outside, so it wasn't like they'd become family friends.

There was something special about Crawford City and the people here, something that went beyond just being neighborly. I could feel its community spirit, and the pride locals had in creating a welcoming and accepting place. In just a handful of months, this tiny town in the middle of nowhere had become home.

Right before Labor Day, Lettie showed up and told me my days of freedom were about to come to an end. The record label and Jake had scheduled me to perform on the opening night of the reality competition's new season, saying it would be the ideal venue to announce my new record.

Although the news didn't come as much of a surprise other than now having a fixed date, I was left with mixed emotions. I didn't want to lose the tether I'd established to this little community, and I hated the thought of not seeing Chris every day. At the same time, I was beyond excited to finally launch my career, even if it meant having to perform onstage.

I helped man the library booth at the town's annual Labor Day community potluck over the long weekend, and participated in several of the event's activities and competitions. I wanted to enjoy myself more, but my heart felt heavy. Needing to let Chris know my days in Crawford City were literally numbered loomed over me like a rain cloud. I dreaded that talk more than I could say.

I didn't know how Chris would take the news, or what would happen between us, if anything, once I left town. I just hoped I didn't lose the friendship that'd developed between us over these past months. My sweet librarian meant too much to me to let that happen.

SEVENTEEN

CHRIS

WHEN ROTH TOLD ME he was leaving, I knew it marked the end of what we'd been building together. I was not an idiot. It was a miracle I'd had him to myself as long as I did. Sure, I, my volunteers, and nearly everyone else in town had gotten used to having him around. He'd helped me get the library up and running, helped me train the few volunteers I had who took the job seriously, and charmed every person he met.

He'd certainly charmed me too, but our happy summer bubble had burst. Roth had a huge career ahead of him, with songs to sing, important people to meet, and adoring fans to entertain. The last thing I wanted to do was tie him down to this small-town life I'd built for myself. He deserved so much more than anything I could ever offer him here.

That night, we walked along the road between the library and the cabin. Doc and Amos had returned home from Oregon, so we lingered out on the huge porch until the wee hours of the morning.

"Do you think you'll miss me?" Roth asked shyly.

"I already miss you," I answered honestly. Just admitting that, even to myself, took more out of me than I felt I could stand.

"You know it's not forever, right?" he asked. "I'll call you next week. Hell, I'll probably call you at least once a day."

I rested my hand on his cheek. "You have to pursue your dreams, Roth. You're so talented. I don't want to hold you back."

Roth pulled me to him as we sat swinging on the porch. After a while, he cleared his throat. "I know this is stupid to say, now that we don't have more time to spend together, but I... I really... well, shit, Chris, I can't leave here without you knowing I'm over the moon for you."

That was more than my fragile composure could handle. Tears rolled down my face as I nestled into Roth's firm chest. "I feel the same," I admitted, and could already feel a gaping hole forming in my chest from having Roth ripped out of my life.

We swung on the porch for a while longer before Roth got up after kissing me goodbye. As I watched him walk toward his brother's condo, I knew things would be different from this point forward. Even if we could somehow work out a long-distance relationship, we'd never be this couple again.

EIGHTEEN

ROTH

"WELCOME, LADIES AND GENTLEMEN, to the seventeenth season of *Talented Citizens*," the host announced to the screaming crowd and millions more watching from home. "And to kick things off, please help me welcome back to our stage last season's runner-up and one of our all-time favorites, Roth Gallo!"

I tried my best to push through a wave of nausea rising up from my intense fear of performing in front of a national crowd. My stage fright didn't care that I'd done this several times before, on this very stage, and probably to many of the same faces in the crowd. Like all last season, this single performance had the potential to make or break the rest of my career, and I felt that crushing pressure from head to toe.

As I'd trained myself to do, I walked onstage practically on autopilot, waving to the crowd as the music to my first single, which would be released tomorrow, began to play. I grabbed the microphone, closed my eyes, and let myself get lost in the song.

"Two makes one, and one makes all..." The lyrics poured out of me, but instead of envisioning my granny as my safe place, as I always did when singing in public, I saw Chris. As I sang about how much my lover completed me, I drew to mind Chris and me walking down the lazy roads of Crawford City.

I thought of how we worked in tandem at the library. Mostly quietly, but sometimes I'd start to sing, and Chris's sweet tenor voice would tentatively join me.

As the song ended, instead of tears, I felt an ache in my chest. I'd told Chris I had feelings for him before leaving Crawford. Truthfully, I was in love with him, but I knew he was far from ready to hear that admission. I hoped he was listening tonight, because as I sang those lyrics, I meant every word for him.

As I took a bow and walked offstage, I knew the song would be a hit. The crowd was literally on their feet, screaming and chanting my name. It was a song I'd always equate with Chris and our summer together. That it could top the charts filled me with a secret pride, as if it immortalized our relationship in some way, even if only ever to me.

I had just reached my dressing room backstage, fully intending to call Chris, when my sister came bursting through the door behind me. "Come on, you've got an interview in thirty minutes!"

"What do you mean an interview?" I asked, totally caught off guard. "There's nothing more scheduled until tomorrow."

"*The Late Night Show* has a cancellation, and they'd like you to fill it. But we've gotta go now!"

I still wore a heavy layer of makeup that'd been plastered on and the stage clothes I'd performed in, which were sweaty now considering how nervous I'd been. But Lettie assured me it'd be fine. "Besides, being interviewed right after a huge performance is ideal," she said, sounding every bit the manager. "You're still pumped about it and that'll shine through during the chat."

I let her drag me down the back stairwell, out the rear entrance, and into a waiting car that whisked us off to the TV studio. Luckily, through all the hubbub, I didn't really have time to think about the interview and start fretting.

The host of the show was as funny in person as he was on TV, and after a few seconds, and a couple jokes about my beautiful makeup job, he'd put me at ease. He asked me about the competition last season, the new album, and the single I'd performed for the first time tonight.

They already had a clip of the performance cued up and played it while I sat there. "You look cool as a cucumber. Like you've been performing in front of crowds all your life. Is it true you still suffer from stage fright?" he asked me.

I nodded. "Yeah, very much so. I'm guessing it probably won't ever go away."

"How do you keep yourself so composed?" he probed.

I smiled, still feeling completely at ease. "I'm usually singing my songs to someone. That way, in my mind, I'm focused on that person and not the huge audience. I try to channel my energy, so the person I'm singing to knows how much I care about them, even if they're no longer here. I figure wherever they are, they'll still feel it somehow."

"So, considering you just performed a romantic ballad, who were you thinking of tonight?" the host asked with a sly grin.

For a split second, I considered being honest, but I couldn't do that to Chris. Our relationship was still too new, and besides that, I could see in my mind's eye throngs of people all but tearing down the door of the library in Crawford City trying to get at him, so I decided to deflect instead. "Oh, I think several people. I'm keeping my options open," I said with a playful wink I didn't feel.

I saw momentary disappointment in the host's face, like he'd lost out on some big scoop, but I was glad I hadn't exposed Chris or the town inadvertently.

"So," the host said, turning to the camera. "Roth Gallo's debut album comes out tomorrow online and at all major retailers. We'll be back with our next guest after a few messages from our sponsors." He held up a copy of the album's cover, something not even I had seen yet, before cutting to commercial.

Once we were off the air, the host stood with me and shook my hand. There wasn't much we could say since we still wore microphones and the studio audience sat watching our every move, but he leaned over my shoulder, and whispered, "You did sing to someone special tonight, didn't you?"

"Maybe," I whispered back.

"Next time you come on, I hope you're willing to share with us who that is."

I smiled at him and shrugged noncommittally before being whisked offstage and out the studio door.

Lettie sat waiting for me in the limo when I slid into the back beside her. "You did a great job," she said.

I smiled and side bumped her. "You're doing a great job, too, sis," I responded, and meant it. Lettie really was in her element. I was happy she'd agreed to take on my management.

"I know," she said matter-of-factly. "I'm good at this kind of thing."

"Conceited much?" I asked, causing her to chuckle.

"Not conceited, just self-aware," she announced, which made us both laugh. Lettie was not shy and didn't worry about being polite, which were advantages in this job.

By the time we reached the hotel, I was exhausted. With Lettie's help, I covered my face in some smelly stuff called Nauseous or something like that. Then I took a hot shower and happily scrubbed the stage makeup off my face.

I came back into my room and crashed face-first onto the bed.

The next morning, I woke at the crack of dawn thanks to my sister pounding on the door. "No time for sleep, baby brother," Lettie said when I complained about my lack of sleep. "You've got to be at the studio in just over an hour."

"What studio?"

"The one I told you about before we left, and the one I reminded you of yesterday."

"Let's skip this one," I said, my face still buried in the pillow.

Lettie chuckled. "Brother, no one stands up Miss King. Now get up!"

"Oh my god, I hate you right now!"

"No, you don't, you adore me. I'm going to get a pitcher of water if you're not out of bed when I come back."

She left and I sighed. The damn woman would do it too. Lettie did not make idle threats.

I managed to crawl into the shower, then throw some fresh clothes on before Lettie reappeared in my room. As soon as we arrived at the studio, a team of people rushed me to the makeup chair and began applying more stupid makeup and doing some weird shit with my hair. Of course, I was so tired, I didn't even care.

I managed to get several cups of coffee in me as the crew of two women and a guy, who all flirted with me shamelessly, primped and painted me.

By the time I sat in front of the morning show cast, I was at least coherent enough to communicate. They poked and prodded a bit about who I fancied these days, but that was easily pushed to the side by repeating my comment from the nighttime chat show about keeping my options open. In my mind, that seemed like the best way to keep people out of Chris's business.

I smiled as I thought about teasing him about how much he'd owe me for keeping the wolves at bay.

The rest of the month was pretty much the same as those first few days. The album was doing extremely well, and Lettie beamed whenever she relayed its chart status and sales figures.

I ping-ponged from coast to coast and visited countless cities in between, making TV appearances, playing the odd show here and there, and basically going wherever Lettie and Jake directed, as the weeks and months continued slipping away. I remained nervous about the prospect of performing onstage day in and day out, but the record label, Lettie, and Jake had all convinced me it was necessary if I wanted a career in this business. I couldn't really argue the point, and they were right, someday I'd regret having let stage fright stifle my career.

I had managed a few texts to Chris here and there, but texts that'd started long and full of details were now down to one-word responses or emojis. The handful of times I'd tried calling him had just gone to voicemail, and I could feel him pulling away. I'd felt powerless to stop it, until now.

After hitting all the circuits, as Lettie called them, I finally had a few days of respite before I was due to kick off my first North American tour. I wasn't about to waste the downtime sitting in some hotel room.

"Lettie, I need to visit Crawford City before I go on tour."

Lettie sighed. "I knew you'd want to, but seriously Roth, there's so much to do."

I put my hand up to stop her. "Lettie, I've surrendered my life to you and the label. I've not been home in ages, we both missed Thanksgiving, and now even Christmas is about to be snuffed out. I want one damned night to hopefully rekindle my relationship with Chris. That's non-negotiable."

Lettie smirked, looking pleased with herself. "I told them you'd say that. So, because I'm the best big-sister manager who's ever lived, I've already arranged for Christmas off and you'll have time enough to visit your librarian, but you've got to take the bodyguards with you."

I started to complain when Lettie shook her head. "That condition is non-negotiable with the record label, our family, and me as your sister and your manager. You are too popular right now to venture out without security."

I wanted to argue, but decided to let it rest. She was right. I'd heard way too many horror stories of rising stars being caught off guard. Even Ramona Letson, who'd won my competition and whose career was pretty much dead in the water right now, ended up in the news after some deranged fan attacked her a few months back.

"Okay, but we're going to eat at the café, and the bodyguards have to get their own food. They also have to sit at a different table so I can be alone with Chris."

Lettie grinned, seeming satisfied at getting her way. "Whatever you need, brother."

NINETEEN

CHRIS

"I'M KEEPING MY OPTIONS open."

Roth's go-to response to every interview question about his private life kept reverberating over and over in my head. I wasn't sure why. It wasn't like we'd agreed to be monogamous, or actually committed to anything at all. Friends who kissed, apparently, that's all we were, not that I could even claim him as a friend at this point.

Sure, we'd admitted to having feelings for each other before he split town, but maybe he just got caught up in the moment then. The problem was, I hadn't been. I liked Roth and cared for him more than I had any other man, to my own detriment. I'd known he'd only be here for a short time, but I let myself get attached anyway. Too attached.

Like a moth to the flame, I thought, I couldn't stop watching as his career took off, just like I'd known it would. One song of his after another climbed the charts, and although none had hit the top ten, it was just a matter of time before he cracked it.

Announcements of his upcoming tour were everywhere too. I'd seen magazine after magazine article about him. I guess that was my curse as a librarian, having his handsome face staring back at me from multiple covers as I picked up the library by myself each evening. Since Roth had gotten to know so many people during his months here, everyone that came into the library these days sought out the periodicals that featured him.

I knew Doc, Amos, Todd, and Ash felt sorry for me, and even though I heard about Roth day in and day out at work, none of them brought him up at home. At least I had a small sanctuary from all things Roth.

Right before Christmas, I got a call out of the blue from Lettie. "Hey, Roth has a break coming up and he wants to see you."

I was hesitant at first. I mean, we still texted one another occasionally, but I wouldn't even call them conversations. Why would he want to see me anyway? He was keeping his options open, right?

Before I could stop myself, though, I agreed. "When and where?" I asked.

"Just after Christmas. He wants to come there, of course. He's got an obsession with that little town and its café. He said something about fried chicken, but to be honest, I'd tuned him out at that point."

I chuckled. "He probably wants to eat there more than see me." I wasn't really jealous of the café. I ate there often enough myself. If I ever had to leave, it would definitely be one of the many things I'd miss about Crawford City.

"He said you specifically, I did pay attention to that part," Lettie replied, and I could tell by her tone she was trying to comfort me.

"Will he be staying with your brother while he's here?"

Lettie seemed to ponder that for a moment. "Yeah, probably. Now that Jesse and Jen are all but living together, Roth could stay in the condo and the bodyguards could stay at the hotel, then take turns watching him. That's a great idea, Chris," she said happily, as if I'd solved some problem.

"Glad to help," I replied, but didn't really feel that glad. After she hung up, I wondered to myself how I would manage being around Roth again after so long. On the one hand, I really did want to see him. I missed him so much, it caused my chest to ache if I thought on it too much. On the other, I didn't want to be a cog in his massive ego machine. Some small-town sidepiece to get his rocks off with whenever he was in the vicinity. Except I knew that was probably my hurt talking. Roth didn't seem like that kind of man at all, but then, perhaps I overestimated how well I actually knew him.

If nothing else than to distract myself, I went back to work shelving books and preparing for the library's Christmas party coming up the following week. We'd had a huge book drive, and I had tons of slightly used books that we could wrap up and give the kids for presents during the party.

Luckily, I had a plethora of volunteers who'd agreed to help with that project, so my only duties were to ensure the books that were donated were age-appropriate and in good enough condition to regift.

By the time I stumbled back home that evening, Amos and Doc were sitting in front of the fireplace in the huge living room, staring at a roaring fire.

"Hey, Chris," Doc yelled from his seat without getting up.

"Hey, guys. You look comfy."

I noticed then that the two older men were holding hands and that brought a smile to my face. Since moving in with them, I'd learned they had known each other their entire lives, but had only rekindled a relationship and gotten married within the last few years. They were so sweet to one another, even now. They gave my silly romantic heart hope that maybe someday, I'd have what they did.

I was just about to climb the stairs and go to bed, maybe read a bit from a new gay romance that'd just come into the library, when Amos told me dinner was in the microwave.

"Amos, I told you to stop feeding me so much. I swear I've gained twenty pounds since moving here."

"Son, if you've gained that much, it's muscle. Seriously, you aren't showing anything on that frame of yours that's of any concern. Now go eat!"

I chuckled. Amos was as much a mother hen about eating properly as my own mom. "Oh," I said, thinking of Mom and Dad. "Did you and my parents find anything yet?"

After hearing me praise the wonders of Crawford City probably too many times, my parents had finally been convinced to move here too, so Doc and Amos had been helping them look for a place. Dad and Amos had hit it off like long-lost friends, so much so that Amos hired Dad to work with his landscaping crew during fall cleanup season, and they wanted to keep him on full-time. Dad was ecstatic and Mom was thrilled too. She'd put feelers out after hearing from her friend Fran that several bus drivers were retiring from the local school district soon, and she got an immediate response. She'd since interviewed and been offered a bus route with the school district the following year.

"No luck finding a place yet," Doc said sadly. "There just isn't much for sale right now. What's on the market is in such a mess, your folks don't want to take it on."

"Could they hire Todd for renovations?" I asked.

"They want move-in ready," Doc said.

I sighed. Both my parents were being extremely picky about their move. Last time I talked to them, they'd said three times during our conversation that this would be their last move, so they needed to make it count.

I walked into the kitchen, zapped the beef stew and homemade bread Amos had made, and dug in. I'd been regularly visiting the gym at the hotel since Roth left, and Amos was mostly correct, I had gained some muscle. I'd never approach my father's build, but I had to admit that gaining some more strength made lugging around carts of books that much easier.

After finishing dinner, I washed and put my dishes in the dishwasher. "I'm headed up to read," I told Doc and Amos and they just waved.

I'd come to think of those two as family since moving in with them. I guessed they thought of me that way too. Last week, when we decorated the cabin for the holidays, they waited for me to get home. The triplets were over-the-top excited about decorating, and it was so cute watching them hang ornaments on the tree. Of course, precautions were taken to put the more delicate ones on the upper branches. The lowest branches were reserved for the wooden and plastic ornaments that were less likely to be broken by exploring hands.

I knew I needed to find my own place, and I made enough money to support myself, but I loved this family. I loved this part of town, and rarely even used my car anymore. Everywhere I typically visited on a daily basis—the library, the hotel to work out, the café for lunch, the donut shop for a quick coffee—were short walks from the cabin. I didn't want to move too far out of town, if at all. I'd gone out with my parents a few times to check out real estate, but Doc was right, there was nothing on the local market.

Well, almost nothing. I hardly let myself think about it, but two doors down from where the other doctor in town lived was an old mansion that'd burned sometime in the late nineteen nineties. Part of the place remained intact, the rest was charred and in disarray.

You couldn't see the large house from the road, as it was hidden behind a huge copse of trees. A tall fence surrounded the property, and the gate was padlocked. The only reason I knew much about it was because we had a local history reference section in the library. Being the default reference librarian, I had devoured all of the regional books I could get my hands on after dishing out far too many "I don't know" answers to patrons' questions.

I'd also learned that sometime in the past few years, the town had hired a kid to use his drone to take videos of the historic properties in town. I watched the one for the old mansion over and over, intrigued by how amazing the property looked.

Secretly, I wanted to buy it and hire Todd to fix it up. But the thought was preposterous. I made a decent living, but nowhere near enough to bankroll that kind of job. From a look at the fire damage, I wouldn't be able to afford the demolition and internal stabilization, much less the cost of the property and the refurbishment.

Even if I couldn't be the one to save it, I could still fight on its behalf. Maybe Jake knew some famous person he could convince to renovate it and turn it into a nice place again. I made a mental note to talk to him about it. I was sure most local people had completely forgotten the place still existed.

I ended up falling asleep reading my romance novel. I reached the part where the two men had overcome the odds and were kissing for the first time. My thoughts strayed to kissing Roth just as I drifted off, leading to one of the most vivid dreams of my life.

We were sitting on the porch, rocking in the old swing like we had the night he'd left. We went from listening to the screech of the hinges to Roth singing along with music drifting out of the house. The sound of his voice felt so soothing.

Within moments, the scene changed. Roth was now up on stage and a mass of people separated us. The crowd cheered so loudly I couldn't hear him. Then all of a sudden, I couldn't see him either. I stood up to get a better look, but the crowd kept pushing me further and further back. Before I knew it, I was having to fight the crowd to even stay standing.

"He don't like you no more," I heard someone say next to me.

"Why do you think a man like him would want a man like you?" another asked.

I kept pushing harder and harder until I stood at the front of the crowd. Roth had just finished the song about two lovers coming together for life when he turned toward a man I'd never seen before and took him in his arms.

He looked at me and shrugged. "I'm keeping my options open," he said, then turned back toward the stranger and kissed him.

I woke with a start. "Damn," I said as I wiped the sweat off my face.

I checked the time, and even though it was an hour earlier than I usually got up, I didn't want to risk having another unsettling dream.

I dressed warmly and despite the cold snap that'd just hit this part of the state, I jogged down to the hotel to use the gym. After a long hard work out, I stopped by the donut shop, ordered a Long John and coffee, and sat staring out the window as the sun slowly began to rise.

Jamie, the shop owner, came over and sat across from me with his coffee. "You're up early," he said.

"Yeah, had a nightmare and couldn't go back to sleep."

Jamie shook his head. "Yeah, I hate those. Well, I don't get them now, 'cause chasing the little ones keeps me tired enough I don't have time to have nightmares."

I chuckled. Jamie and his wife had just had another child less than three months ago. I didn't have much experience with babies, but I'd had enough exposure to Todd and Ash's toddlers and heard enough from friends who had kids, that life could be pretty stressful and tiring with a newborn.

"Wanna talk about it?" Jamie asked.

"Nah, nothing that important." I finished off the Long John, then tipped back the coffee. "I'm gonna run and hopefully get to the library early enough to get some extra work done. Thanks for the company," I said as I exited the shop.

Instead of going home, though, I jogged in the opposite direction to where the burned mansion stood. I looked past the giant fence, trying to see any sign of the building, but the trees obscured my view. I knew I was being silly. I had no idea why I felt so obsessed about the property, but something about it had gotten ahold of me.

I turned around, jogged back to the cabin, and got ready for work. Rather than head straight to the library, I decided to walk to the café. I wasn't hungry after my morning donut, but I hoped to catch Jake there to chat with him about the mansion. I possessed just the right amount of Southern mysticism to believe that maybe the old place was reaching out to me to help her find her next owner and I had no doubt Jake would be the one to help me do so.

As luck would have it, Jake was holding court in the far corner of the café with a group that included Ash, Todd, and Jake's husband Lance. I walked in and they all made room for me without asking if I wanted to join them. That's just what things were like here in Crawford City. You were just accepted into the group.

I sat down and ordered a coffee, telling Mrs. Cole I'd already eaten. When the group conversation hit a lull, I asked, "So, y'all tell me about the old mansion up by the McCartney place. The one nearly toasted to a crisp."

Todd and Ash both shook their heads. "That's a sad story."

We all turned toward them in anticipation, and Ash cleared his throat. "Well, when Dad was young, that place burned. It was one of the first homes in the town. The family that built it weren't popular here. They were Quakers that'd moved here from the Northeast. They'd come to be with extended family that'd moved here when this part of the world opened up. During the Civil War, the father and two of the sons were taken out and hung in the town square. Quakers, you know, are abolitionists."

"Wow, that's sad, but what's it got to do with the mansion itself? I read in one of the local history books that it'd burned only a few decades ago."

Ash shook his head. "Well, that home has been handed down through the generations. It's one of the few in this town that remained within its original family. But none of the descendants lived there full-time, so even though they kept it up, it mostly stayed empty."

Judging by how everyone had stopped eating their breakfast and sat hanging on Ash's every word, we were all clearly intrigued by his story. None of what he'd said had been documented in the books I'd read at the library.

"Well, when the place burned, the owner's son was there. He got out alive, but he was burned over seventy percent of his body. We've not seen hide nor hair of anyone in that family since then."

"I heard that some years after the fire," Todd added, "...the injured son inherited the estate, but he's still in bad shape after all this time. I'm guessing once he dies, it'll be sold and torn down. Even if it passed to his extended family, I doubt anyone would want to take on this place, especially if they had no intention of ever living here."

"I'm surprised the city doesn't force him to tear it down," I said with a sigh.

"Not how things really work here. It's safely secured behind its fencing and most people have no idea it's there anyway," Todd said.

"Do you think I could get in to take some pictures of it?" I asked, looking over at Jake.

"Why is everyone looking at me?" he asked.

"'Cause you're the one who knows how to find and bend people to your will," Lance said, causing us all to laugh. Jake must've taken that as a compliment, because he practically beamed at his husband.

"I guess I could make some calls. But you're just wanting pictures for the archives?" he asked, then winked at me.

"Yes, for the library archives. Definitely, not for curiosity purposes."

When Jake smirked at me, I knew he'd help make it happen.

TWENTY

ROTH

"**E**XHAUSTED," I SAID AS I fell on my parents' couch. Mom rubbed my head and put a glass of iced tea on the coffee table in front of me before disappearing into the kitchen. "Lettie is a freaking taskmaster."

Dad chuckled from where he sat in his easy chair. "This is news?" he asked.

"Hey," Lettie complained as she walked in from the kitchen, eating something I was sure Mom had set out for dinner.

"Listen," I said, looking at my sister. "You have to accept that about yourself. I swear if Christmas hadn't happened, you'd have forced me to start preparing for the tour without a break or even eight full hours of sleep."

"Oh, you baby. I'm up the same time as you every single day. Actually, before you, since I'm the one who has to drag your bones out of bed each morning. It's not like you're the only person having to work."

"Humph," I mumbled, but didn't have the energy to argue with her. I really was wiped out.

"As soon as your brothers get here, it'll be time to eat," Dad said, and I lay back and closed my eyes while we waited. It'd been so long since we'd all been together, I didn't even know how to act around everyone.

"You two be nice," Mom said as she came out of the kitchen. "Jesse is bringing Jen and he doesn't need you two acting like bickering children."

I shook my head. "Lettie started it."

My sister, who was sitting in the rocking chair next to the couch, whacked my arm with her foot, not bothering to get up. "I would never embarrass Jesse like that, not intentionally anyway. I love Jen. Have I told you she and I have been texting since last spring?"

"No, but the two of you were like peas in a pod when you first met. I'm not surprised," I said, and got another tap with her foot. "Ugh, keep your stinky feet off me!" I grumbled.

Dad had the game on, and now that Lettie was done thumping me, I actually fell asleep. I must've slept harder than I thought because when Lettie shook me awake, everyone was already sitting at the dining table.

"Wow, I've never slept that hard," I said as I took my seat.

"You have lately," Lettie said.

I ignored her and waved at my eldest brother and sister-in-law, who was holding little Jeffrey, my nephew, in her arms. I also waved at Jen, who was sitting next to Jesse on the other side of the table, and I realized just how cute they were together. Somehow Jesse, a nerdy doctor, and Jen, a drop-dead gorgeous model, seemed to fit each other.

"I'm famished," I said as I began filling my plate. The comfort of my family and the buzz that happened when we're together warmed me inside and gave me energy. I might be climbing the charts, but to these folks, I was just their son, their brother.

Partway through the meal, I glanced at Jen and could tell she'd become a little overwhelmed by the noise, and I winked at her. Then I leaned over my plate so she could hear me without having to yell, and said, "The only way to survive is to lean into it."

She smiled and seemed to relax a bit after that. I knew Jen had been an only child, and so had I until joining this family, and I remembered that same overwhelming feeling when I'd first arrived. Jen was funny and silly and all sorts of fun, so I had no doubt she, like me, would eventually find her place among us.

I couldn't help but wonder whether Chris would fit in like she did. I knew it was too early to consider him in that way, but my thoughts seemed to drift to my cute librarian all the time lately. Picturing him here, sitting beside me as we gathered with my loved ones for a holiday dinner, made sense in my mind.

I spent the rest of the meal watching my family and laughing at their usual antics. Being here with them, just catching up and enjoying each other's company, held so much more value than a number one hit ever could. Not that I'd snub it if that happened, though.

TWENTY-ONE

CHRIS

I SPENT CHRISTMAS EVE at the Crawford City Café. Mrs. Cole had invited me and my family, as well as several others, to join her and her husband for a holiday dinner there. Since the restaurant was closed, most of us brought potluck food along, which made for an eclectic but delicious meal.

When Mrs. Cole extended the invitation, she'd said she and her husband didn't want to spend the holiday alone since her stepdaughter would be spending it with her boyfriend's family. Everyone in town knew that Jen Cole and Roth's brother Jesse were an item, which meant Jen might be spending Christmas with Roth too. I tried not to think of that too much, lest I become either jealous or sad, so I focused on the positives of the day—food, friends, and family.

Dad and Mom appeared so at home here. I hadn't really noticed just how much they'd settled in, but seeing them mingling among the townsfolk, it was clear they considered themselves a part of the community. It made me happy to think they'd be moving here, hopefully soon.

I chuckled at how I'd become one of those kids who couldn't go far from the nest. Oh well, things could be worse. My parents had become as much my friends these past few years as they were family, and I looked forward to our spending more time together like we used to before I moved.

"Here's a toast," I heard someone behind me say. "To the newcomers to Crawford City."

Mr. Cole, Jen's father, was making the toast. I could tell he'd already made a couple toasts on his own, and smiled as the older man held onto his wife for balance.

As we finished our meal, I wondered for the umpteenth time if Roth was at his family's house in Nashville for the holiday. We didn't communicate much, and I hadn't texted him since my awful dream, taking it as an omen that it was time to let him go.

Sure, we had a date here at the café next week that Lettie had arranged, but I was sure that would be his final goodbye. Roth was a good man. I couldn't help but guess he wanted to do the right thing and let me go before things got any more complicated in his life. I had to respect him for that.

"Honey," Mom said. "Where are you? You've barely said a word all night."

I smiled. "Sorry, Mom, just the same old same old. Thinking about work and all."

"Don't you thinking mean a certain up-and-coming music star?" Dad asked.

"Oh, I don't think that's going much further." When I saw the sad and confused expressions on my parents' faces, I smiled. It helped to know they cared about me so much. "Listen, it's Christmas, not time to be worrying about my doomed relationships. Tell me, did you get the hotel room decorated for tomorrow?"

Both my parents smiled brightly. "Yes, it's gorgeous and Catherine lent us the decorations she had left over after decorating the hotel. We'll open presents when you come over tomorrow."

Opening presents on Christmas morning became our tradition after my grandparents died when I was still a pre-teen. We'd spent every holiday with them, but once we were a family of three instead of five, we spent our Christmases at home and were up at the crack of dawn to open everything. When I turned sixteen, I started sneaking Mom and Dad's gifts under the tree after they went to bed and put Santa's name on them. Seeing their surprise and amusement the first time I did it remains one of my favorite holiday memories.

We helped clean up the café while Mr. Cole ran the dishes through the commercial dishwasher. By the time we finished, the place was ready for the morning crew to reopen the day after Christmas.

I hugged my parents goodnight, grabbed the leftovers Mrs. Cole insisted that I take, and walked back toward the cabin to spend the rest of Christmas Eve alone. When my phone buzzed, I didn't pay much attention. Lately, I'd been getting a lot of spam texts, which I'd been working to block at every chance.

Amos and Doc had flown to Oregon with Todd, Ash, and the triplets to spend the holidays with their daughter and her family. They'd tried to convince my mom and dad to stay at the cabin with me, but my parents wouldn't hear of it. "It feels like an imposition," my mom kept saying. At least they'd agreed to stay at the hotel tonight instead of driving back home.

I had agreed to keep an eye on Todd and Ash's place while they were gone, so after depositing the food in the refrigerator, I went next door and did a quick check to make sure the house was still standing.

When I returned to the cabin and was just about to tuck into bed, I remembered to charge my phone. I noticed the unread message then. Roth had sent it.

Roth: *Merry Christmas. I hope you're enjoying time with your family.*

I didn't put much thought into the message I texted back.

Me: *We were at the café, quite a spread.*

When he didn't text back right away, I plugged the phone in and finished getting ready for bed. Before my head hit the pillow, I checked the phone again, but still nothing. Maybe he'd gone to bed too. At least he remembered to text me about the holiday.

I tossed and turned for a while, second-guessing the text I'd sent him. Maybe I should've asked about his family. Or if he was even spending Christmas with them.

There were a lot of things I could've said to him, but it was silly to dwell. I was sure he wasn't overthinking the benign text he'd sent me. Remembering the dream, I couldn't help but think maybe I should *keep my options open* too.

TWENTY-TWO

ROTH

I RODE TO CRAWFORD City with Jen and Jesse and allowed my bodyguards to follow behind in my rental car. I hated having bodyguards, but it seemed that was just par for the course in this profession. I could hardly believe it'd been nearly four months since I'd been in town. Labor Day weekend, in fact.

I felt strangely nervous about seeing Chris again, and was glad to have the backseat to myself as I thought about how today might go. I could feel my anxiety rising as my overactive imagination began picturing negative scenarios of him dumping me, or telling me he couldn't handle my fame.

"So, how are you enjoying the spotlight?" Jen asked.

Relieved she'd pulled me out of my downward spiral, I smiled. "It's a learning curve, but mostly I just go where people tell me. And by people, I mean Lettie."

Both Jen and Jesse laughed. "What made you pick her as your manager?" Jesse asked.

I smiled. "'Cause she's a taskmaster, and she can handle all the pompous people I have to deal with on a daily basis. If it wasn't for her, they'd run right over me."

Jen nodded. "You have to be tough and develop a thick skin, but if you are too demanding, you risk developing a reputation and can lose work. It's a balancing act. You're smart to have Lettie playing bad cop to your good."

"Hey, Jen, who do you use for your day-to-day management?"

She turned around in her seat to face me. "I have an agent who handles most of my stuff. My schedule was a lot more hectic when I first started out, since I didn't have my choice of gigs. Different industry than the music business, though. I once dated Olman Paul and his schedule was so intense, it finally broke us up."

Jen turned toward Jesse then, and I could tell she felt uncomfortable having brought up an ex. Although if the press was correct about only a fraction of the men she'd dated, there was no avoiding the subject forever.

Jesse glanced at her and winked. "You dated Olman Paul then?"

"He was a dweeb, no reason to be jealous."

"Never jealous," Jesse said. "Dating small-town doctors over the likes of Olman Paul is rather curious, though."

Jen was all spunk and energy when appearing on TV and even the first time we'd met, but she had more of a serene, almost shy, quality about her when around

Jesse. "I'm only interested in *one* small-town doctor," she replied so quietly I could barely hear her. My brother took one hand off the wheel to hold hers, and I felt as if I was intruding on an intimate moment between them.

To remind them I was still in the back, I said, "I wish Lettie was here. She'd tell y'all to get a room or something. I mean, seriously, it's getting deep up front there and I'm not able to get away!"

Both of them laughed before Jen went back to sharing stories about being in the spotlight all the time.

The two didn't waste any time ditching me once we reached town. Jesse gave me the key to his condo since he'd be staying at Jen's, and I ordered pizza delivery for my bodyguards. I texted Chris that I was excited to see him, but fell asleep still waiting for a response.

The next morning, I got up early and went for a run through downtown. I left my bodyguard sound asleep in Jesse's recliner. The streets of Crawford City remained decorated for the holidays, with Christmas lights outlining shop windows, wreaths tied to light poles, and a giant Christmas tree in the town square. I felt safe here, and figured I had a hundred bodyguards all around me since just about everyone in town would come to my aid if I needed them.

Just to be safe, though, I put on my knitted hat, a scarf and gloves, before hitting the street.

When I reached Doc and Amos's house, I saw the lights were on, so I ran up to the porch and knocked. Sure enough, Amos opened the door moments later.

"Happy holidays!" I exclaimed, feeling genuinely cheery for the first time in ages.

Within seconds, I was pulled into a bear hug. First by Amos, then by Doc. They ushered me inside while peppering me with questions. I couldn't help but feel like I'd come to my second home. I loved Crawford City and the friends I'd made here.

As I answered their questions, they led me back to the kitchen and, without asking, poured me a cup of coffee. When the conversation lulled, I asked, "Is Chris not here?"

Both Amos and Doc chuckled. "He's here, but he overdid it a bit at the winery's holiday party. We flew home just for that, and good thing 'cause we had to literally tuck the boy into his bed."

I chuckled at the thought of the very well put together Christopher Asbell ever overindulging with alcohol or, quite frankly, anything.

"Well, I'm gonna jog back to Jesse's place, but if you don't mind, tell Chris I'm here."

"Tell Chris what?" I heard a voice mumble from the kitchen doorway. I turned around and saw the most handsome man to walk the planet. His hair was sticking up all over his head and he had one eye shut while his hand shielded the other from the light.

"Um, hangover much?" I asked, causing him to cringe.

"Apparently. What did they spike that wine with? Everclear?"

Doc and Amos snickered. "No need to spike it when you drank half a barrel."

"Ugh," Chris groaned. "It was so delicious that I couldn't help myself. I never drink. Someone should've stopped me."

I walked over to where the man was miserably trying to stay upright and kissed his cheek. "Hi, honey. I'm home."

He gave me a small smile, then winced. "Let me get some coffee and Tylenol in me, then we can talk. My head hurts too much to do anything but be a blob right now."

I helped him to a stool at the kitchen island and let Doc and Amos ply him with medication and coffee. Doc also instructed him to drink several glasses of water. "That'll help you more than anything else."

Chris just waved at him, and began slamming down the coffee as if it were a hangover elixir.

I sat back down and waited for him to feel some relief. The moment my butt hit the stool, though, I got a phone call. Chris cringed at the sound of my ringtone, and I had to struggle to hide my smirk.

I groaned when I saw my bodyguard Riff's number pop up. "Hey, Riff," I answered, trying to sound friendly.

I had to pull the phone from my ear as he yelled at me. "Where are you?" he demanded.

"Um, I went for a run. I'm at a friend's house in town."

After listening to the usual rant about not keeping bodyguards with me at all times and blah, blah, blah, I sighed. "Riff, man, you were asleep. So was all of Crawford City. No one saw me."

That must not have been the right thing to say because another blast of anger surged through the phone. "Okay, I'm at Doc and Amos's place," I admitted, hoping they wouldn't show up here. "Doc is the freaking mayor, so nobody's going to try anything. I'll call you before I jog back."

"You aren't jogging!" he said. "It's too dangerous. We'll be there..."

I clicked off before he had a chance to finish, but texted him the address. I'd had more than one argument with Riff and Doug about what they thought I could and couldn't do. My two bodyguards would keep me in a padded room if they had their way. I knew I needed to be careful, but I also needed to have some sort of life. Doug was more laid-back than Riff, but they were still both total control freaks.

"Trouble?" Doc asked.

"Always. I swear I have another set of parents with those two."

Doc chuckled. "Probably best, though. I'd imagine even well-meaning fans might get too close for comfort on occasion."

"I guess, but now they've demanded I stay inside until they get here to umbrella parent me."

Chris's complexion was looking better, and he smiled before saying, "Trust me, I have the same thing going on here. I swear Mom and Dad have weekly meetings with these two to dictate my life."

"You don't have a life, honey," Doc said, deadpan. Even Chris laughed, because unless something huge had happened that I didn't yet know about, his dedication to his job certainly made that true.

I leaned over and kissed Chris's cheek again, and wished we didn't have an audience so I could kiss more than his cheek. "I know we didn't plan to meet until tonight, but if you aren't busy, I'd like to spend the day with you. Do you have plans? Can I help you at the library?"

He shook his head. "No, I finally got a new assistant librarian, so she's taking today while I use up some of my comp time. Jake has arranged for a group of us to tour a historic property here in town. You're welcome to join us."

I was thrilled. "Yes, I want to join you. I've missed you... all of you," I quickly added. "So much."

Amos and Doc grinned knowingly. I wasn't doing a very good job of hiding my emotions, but that hardly mattered since I was among friends. I felt relieved that Chris and I seemed to just pick up where we'd left off as if I hadn't been away for several months. I vowed to myself to do a much better job at staying in close contact with him when I had to leave again. We both deserved as much.

TWENTY-THREE

CHRIS

The tour of the old mansion ended up being a well-attended one. Initially, Jake had invited Ash and Todd, Doc and Amos, and me. Then our party expanded to include Jake's husband Lance as well as Lance's brother and brother-in-law, Allen and Gib McCartney. When I invited Roth to join us, it meant both of his bodyguards came along as well.

As I'd expected, the property had not been maintained at all. Luckily for us, a paved driveway led to the house, so we didn't have to contend with cutting across the property. Even in winter, the overgrown vegetation remained thick and impassable. If it had been summer, the risk of a snakebite would have been significantly higher too.

It was strange to have Roth with us again, as if he hadn't spent any time away. He stuck to me like he'd never done before, which I had to admit was beginning to melt some of the ice that had formed around my heart ever since he'd said on TV he was "keeping his options open."

We walked quite a way into the property before the mansion finally came into view. As we passed by a large section of yard that I assumed used to be a beautiful garden, I couldn't help but wonder if my dad could restore it, given the chance.

"Wow," I said, and took my phone out to begin taking pictures. I lost track of the rest of the group as I snapped pics of the ruined garden in contrast to the huge home, though Roth stayed close, as did his bodyguards. Once I had my fill of photos, we continued walking toward the house and the destroyed section came into full view.

The building had two wings, one on either side, which honestly made it look a little strange. Clearly, those had been added well after the original build. The wing on the right was merely a shell, having been completely destroyed by fire, and the remaining two-thirds of the roof sagged into the void.

To my secret delight, though, the rest of the building looked to be in fairly good shape, particularly for a place that'd been empty for a very long time.

As we walked around, Lance, who was an architect, began telling us that the original building was Georgian style. He noted the wings had been added later and reflected the antebellum period more.

"And this home was never a plantation?" I asked, intrigued by its unique history.

"No, I don't think so," Doc said. "It's always been owned by the Crawford family, and they were Quakers."

"Why is it so huge then?" I asked.

"They were plentiful," Doc added, then laughed. "They had and probably still have multiple homes. Most of the family live in Pennsylvania. Until the last generation, the families who'd inherited this property were huge."

"Have you met the current owner?" Jake asked Doc.

"Amos has," Doc said, and shot Amos a look that was not at all warm.

"He and I were... well..." Amos began, clearly uncomfortable.

"Amos dated the younger Rutherford Crawford, before the fire."

"Rutherford's older cousin Farlow... and we didn't date. Mostly, when I'd come up to help my dad on construction project one summer, Farlow and I hid behind the house and kissed." Amos looked over at his husband and shook his head. "He and I were both closeted, so nothing more came of it. He's was a good guy though, and it's terrible what happened to his cousin Rutherford."

Amos was still clearly walking on thin ice with his husband around the topic, although Doc's expression softened a bit. I knew Doc and Amos had been childhood sweethearts, and despite both going on to marry and have families, Amos's encounter with Rutherford Crawford clearly still didn't sit well with Doc. Deciding to take pity on Amos, I changed the subject.

"So, how much damage is there? Is there any hope the place might be saved?"

"I doubt it, at least not without a huge amount of money," Todd said. "The fire damage is bad enough, but add to that the cost of restoring property that's been neglected for decades, and you're looking at millions of dollars to make this place habitable again."

That's not what I'd hoped to hear, and I couldn't help but frown. "That's sad. I mean, I did quite a bit of research on the place. It's not the first Georgian style home built in Tennessee, but it's one of the first, and it's especially significant considering the residents were Quaker. Not to mention the Crawford family founded this town."

"The home has ties to the Quakers in Friendsville too. They're rumored to have been involved in the Underground Railroad," Doc added.

"I read the home was used by the Southern troops as a hospital and headquarters for a while," I said.

"That's correct too," Doc said. "It's one of the most historically important homes in the area."

I snapped what must've been a thousand more pictures as we walked around the building. Jake said the owner had given explicit instructions not to go inside the building because of liability reasons, but I was able to hold my phone up to the windows and get pretty good shots of the interior.

Our tour ended abruptly soon after that as gray clouds rolled in, looking like it could snow. We all rushed down to the café, ordered coffees, and warmed up with Mrs. Cole's delicious lunch buffet.

"You seem to have really enjoyed that," Roth said when he set his plate down next to mine.

"I love history, local history especially. Probably because I'm such a huge reader, I can almost see the family wandering around the huge estate all those years ago. It really should be saved."

"Doc, isn't there government money available for that kind of restoration?" I asked when he and Amos sat down across from us.

Doc shook his head, looking disappointed. "No, son, there's been monies come and go over the years, but that type of funding has largely run dry as of late. Besides, someone would have to convince the family to sell first and that's a tall order."

"Actually, I got the impression that's an option," Jake said from the end of the table. "I spoke to Mr. Crawford's financial advisor, who got us permission to tour and sent me the gate key, and the man almost sounded pleased that anyone even wanted to see the place."

"Well, if nothing else, it would be nice to have the property in the hands of someone who'd manage it. Even if they tore the home down and cleared the overgrown forest the grounds have turned into, it'd be an improvement," Doc said on a sigh.

A lump instantly formed in my throat. The thought of losing that amazing home stabbed me in the heart. I turned to Doc, and said, "If it comes to that, promise me you'll have someone go in and document the property first. I'll even do it myself, for the library archive. That building is too important and magnificent, even as a shell of its former self, not to chronicle it as thoroughly as possible."

I'd rarely, if ever, felt this passionate about a cause, but the old place needed someone fighting for it. Even if that fight only helped ensure it wasn't entirely forgotten.

Doc nodded, but I could tell he didn't have a lot of faith in my suggestion ever happening, probably because it was unlikely the owner would ever consider selling it, even though he'd abandoned the place decades ago. Not that I couldn't understand his dilemma. Hell, if it had come down my family line for generations, I sure as heck wouldn't sell either.

Roth patted my hand under the table. It felt good thinking he could sense my inner turmoil about the whole thing. I was sure most everyone thought I was being silly. Well, maybe not Doc, since he was as into Crawford City's history as me. I was sure if Lance was asked, he'd have a few opinions on the matter as well, but I could tell I was the only one in our group who felt an intense desire to save the old property. For me, knowing I'd never have the money to do it just made it that much more of a loss.

If it hadn't been for Roth, I probably would've spent the rest of the day organizing the pictures I'd taken and digging through the library archive for more details about property. Instead, after we'd eaten, Roth whisked me off in Jesse's car while his bodyguards followed be-hind. It was too cold to hike, and it had started snowing a little, so we drove around the backroads and just enjoyed spending time together.

I was still put off by him "keeping his options open," but Roth was so sweet and charismatic when we were together, I couldn't help but warm to him. Although, he must've figured out I was holding back, because as we pulled into the parking lot near the winery's chapel, he asked what was wrong.

At first, I almost blew it off, but then I figured, what did I have to lose? I should just be upfront.

I looked over at Roth, and said, "I know we're not official. I mean, you and I haven't even seen each other for months." He stared at me intently, waiting for me to finish, and I could feel my face getting hot. This was harder than I meant it to be.

Roth took my hand. "I don't understand, Chris," he said. "Are you breaking up with me?"

I barked out a laugh. "We aren't together enough to break up. Dang, Roth, you yourself told the press that you were keeping your options open. How does that translate to us being a couple?"

There it was. I had spilled it. I assumed this would be when he told me he was indeed seeing other people. That he and I had been a summer fling as he waited for his life to start.

"Chris, the only reason we aren't more is because you wanted to go slow. I said what I did to the press to keep them off your trail. If they catch wind of us dating, they'll track you down here and swarm you like bees, only their stingers are worse. Seriously, you don't need that kind of unwanted attention."

"So, you aren't dating other people?" I asked sheepishly.

Roth let out a heavy sigh, sounding relieved, then kissed my knuckles. "Chris, you beautiful man, you are the only person I even want to date. And in case you haven't noticed, we're on one right now," he said, chuckling. "Besides, Lettie keeps all the wannabe hookups well away from me. She considers it part of her job, as my manager and big sister. I couldn't be any more chaste at the moment if I wore a chastity belt."

"Really?" My lips quirked a little at that visual, but I couldn't laugh, not yet. I needed to know where we stood. "So, you're saying you aren't seeing other people?"

"I am *not* seeing anyone else, and I don't want to. Chris, I want to get to know you better. I want to see where this goes. I don't have a lot of experience with other guys. I've never been into dating, but it's all different with you. I've wanted to get to know you better since the first time I laid eyes on you."

I wasn't expecting the emotions that hit me hard from Roth's heartfelt words. Tears sprang from my eyes, and I put my hands over them to hide my mortifying response.

"Oh, baby," Roth said, gently pulling my hands away from my face. "If you were afraid I was running around on you, why didn't you just ask me?"

I shrugged. "I don't know, we didn't have a commitment and you're famous, and..."

"Shh, it doesn't matter whether I'm famous or not. That doesn't change who I am, and I would never do that to you."

"Doesn't it change things, though?" I asked. "You can't say men haven't flung themselves at you since last summer. I see it on entertainment news shows and on social media, Roth. The press loves to show you flirting with men and women."

He chuckled. "I'm not flirting. Most of the time, those pictures are taken way out of context. I can't brush off everyone who winks at me or wants me to autograph a body part. It's a dance I have to do, but they're just enthusiastic fans, that's all."

"And what about times you've been photographed with other celebrities? Going to events together, going out to eat together?" I asked, unable to avoid asking what I felt I needed to know.

"That's all set up, it's a PR thing. They parade someone in front of me who needs exposure or a moment in the spotlight. I don't know any of them and the ones I said more than two sentences to are as busy as I am. I've actually made a few friends out of it, but that's all they are, Chris."

I sighed and wiped at the tears. "I'm sorry, Roth, but I can't go on waiting and wondering, while you pretend to the world that you're playing the field. I honestly think we should let the sun set on whatever we had going this summer, then you can do the famous bachelor thing without any strings."

Roth lifted my hand to his lips again, and I swallowed around the lump in my throat. "Baby, I don't want to do the bachelor thing. I don't do one-night stands. I hate dating. That's why when you slowed us down and wanted to be friends first, I went along with it. That doesn't mean I was any less attracted to you then. In fact, the more I get to know you, the more I want you to be mine. Can't you see that?"

I shrugged and realized I was pouting a little. "Okay, but you stopped texting me and I just figured you weren't interested any longer. So, if we're going to really make this work, you've got to do more than one-liners and emojis."

"Same to you," he said. "I thought you were losing interest too."

"God, no," I admitted with a nervous laugh. "I adore you. Way more than I ever meant to."

The smile on Roth's face could've lit up the darkest night. He leaned across the console and kissed me deeply.

"I've missed you," I admitted quietly as we parted, and he rested his forehead against mine.

"I've missed you too. Now, let's talk about how you and I can spend some quality time together while I'm on tour."

Twenty-Four

Roth

"I'M AN IDIOT," I admitted to my sister, who just nodded distractedly. "Lettie, I'm pouring my heart out over here and you're texting someone, come on!"

She looked up from her phone and sighed. "Roth, I've got five things happening all at once. Your tour begins in a matter of weeks. Not all our accommodations are set up, and the recording studio is being obstinate just for the hell of it. Seriously, can I hear about your love life later?"

"No, I need to talk to my sister right now, not my manager. Put your damned phone down, come over here, and sit."

I didn't usually stand up to Lettie, or anyone for that matter, so I thought the shock caused her to comply. "I don't know what's going on with you, but you're working

203

every waking hour," I told her. "Are you sure this isn't overwhelming you?"

She let out a sigh as she sank deeper into our parents' oversized couch. "It's a lot of work managing your life, little brother. I'm afraid if I let my guard down, someone's going to take advantage of you."

"Wait, stop. So, all this time, you've been overworking yourself because you're afraid for me? Why haven't you hired someone to help you, like a personal assistant or something?"

Lettie chuckled. "I'm the hired help, Roth. You don't hire help to help the hired... help. Geez, you know what I mean."

"Lettie, I swear, hire someone to help you. You can't be working twenty-four seven. You aren't just the freaking hired help, you're my sister and you're my best friend, and I need to be able to talk to you sometimes."

Mom walked around the corner just as I finished my rant. "He's right, you know," she said in passing.

"Oh no, you did not just get Mom in on this."

I laughed. When we were growing up, Mom seldom took sides, usually acting more as a referee.

"I'm on no one's side, Lettie, but if you keep working this hard you're going to burn out. Listen to your brother." She walked past us toward the back of the house and as she disappeared out of sight, she hollered, "...*especially* since he's your boss too!"

Lettie's eyes immediately shrank to half their size as she stared a hole through me. "You aren't the boss of me," she said, which technically wasn't true, but God help me if I was going to correct her. "Okay, okay. I know someone. In fact, I was already trying to find her work. Do you remember Zania, my friend from Holland?"

"Vaguely," I admitted, an image of a tall, thin woman with long, straight, auburn hair flashing to mind. "I thought she was working for Octavia Hayes as the nanny for her and Jaydon's kids."

"She was, but remember when Octavia went batshit crazy and thought Jaydon wanted every White woman who ever lived? Zania was one of the women she accused, and because of that, it's been difficult for her to find work."

"Would she be a good assistant?" I asked, thinking about the last time I'd seen her. She'd been literally passed out drunk on a couch at one of the artsy parties Lettie had dragged me to.

"She's the best. Smart, easy-going, knows when to put her foot down, and even when she lost her job for doing so, she chose to tell the truth instead of lying about Jaydon."

I smiled. "You're the boss on this one, Lettie. I'll let you hire whoever you believe is best, but I want my freaking sister back, at least some. That's all I ask."

Lettie spontaneously hugged me. "I love you, too, little brother. And to answer your question earlier, yes, you're an idiot. Make sure that cute little librarian knows exactly how you feel at all times. Things are going to get really crazy once the tour starts. I have you lined up for dates with various eligible celebrities just to make you look more interesting. My god, you're as dull as a rusty old knife, so we've got to do something to spice you up publicly. You make sure he knows it's all for show. Now, some of us have to work around here so let me get back to it."

I flipped her off, but took note of her advice.

I quickly texted Chris.

Me: *You free for a moment to talk?*

Chris: *No. At library. Buried!*

I chuckled. I imagined that was true. It was the first day the library had been open since the Christmas holiday and with New Year's just around the corner, they'd be closed again soon. It made sense they'd be slammed the few days they were open in between.

Me: *No problem, we'll talk this weekend. Wanted to invite you to a New Year's thing with me and Lettie. Very low-key.*

Chris: *No, can't. Got plans in Crawford. But you can come here!*

I thought about it. Lettie wanted me out on the town in Nashville for New Year's Eve, but she apparently already had plans for me to fake date all the people I would be meeting that night anyway. It all seemed like overkill. Not to mention, I'd much rather ring in the new year with my cute librarian.

Me: *Okay, I'm in. Where we going?*

Chris: *I'll call you later after we close!*

"Lettie, I'm going to Crawford City for New Year's Eve, get over it!" I hollered toward the kitchen where she'd gone. Then I ran toward my bedroom and locked the door so she couldn't come after me.

I ignored her like I had so many times growing up when we were in a fight and she'd yelled at my door to try and get the last word. Regardless, I usually won those fights because she was never patient enough to wait me out, just like I won this one.

After she predictably left, giving up on the argument, I lay back on my old bed, closed my eyes, and dreamed of dancing the night away with the handsome Christopher Asbell.

TWENTY-FIVE

CHRIS

"T HIS IS IT?" ROTH asked, when he cornered me in the kitchen of Ash and Todd's place.

"Yep, I told you it'd be a small get-together with friends."

Roth tipped his head back and laughed. "It's just not quite what I envisioned. I had no idea you meant card night with a couple with triplets and their friends.

"I'm sorry, Roth, I should've mentioned that. I'm sure if you go now, though, you can still get to the big event Lettie had planned for you."

I scooped Chris into my arms, kissing him hard on the mouth. "No way," I said when I pulled back. "This is the best New Year's Eve party I've ever been to." Then I leaned in close and whispered in his ear, "Because I'm spending it with you."

I took the opportunity to give his neck a kiss, and he laughed before bringing his lips to mine.

"Hey, that's not till midnight," Ash said as he came into the kitchen.

"Speak for yourself, old man," Todd said as he came in behind his husband and wrapped his arms around Ash. "I, like Chris and Roth, think kissing is appropriate anytime."

"Is that so?" Ash asked, and turned in Todd's arms to face him. "Now, guys, carry on, while we join you."

The night was like that from that point forward. The little ones were happy, being bounced from parents, grandparents, aunts, and friends. At one point, as the card game became particularly eventful, I looked over to where the three were conked out on the large sectional in the back of the room, and wondered how they could sleep through the noise.

Around ten, the little ones were taken up to the nursery, and put to bed.

We switched to stronger beverages then, with only Ash holding back from the eventual inebriation. The party grew and waned throughout the night as people stopped by to wish us all a happy New Year, but then left shortly after.

This really was the friendliest and most welcoming community, and I loved being a part of it. Mom and Dad were spending the night in Doc and Amos's guest room. Lisa, Doc's daughter, and her three kids were flying in on the second to spend a week with the family, and so my parents were leaving tomorrow, but it was fun to have them here now.

Mom and Dad visited often, Amos finally putting his foot down and saying they'd be staying with them from then on, whether they liked it or not. That'd helped increase their visits, but I couldn't help but look forward to when they finally moved closer. But if they were any pickier, they might never find a house here.

By eleven, I was pretty much done, so Roth and I snuggled on the sectional vacated by the triplets. Between the fact that I tended to go to bed early, so I could get up to run the library, and the significant amount of alcohol I'd consumed, I must've fallen asleep because just before midnight, Roth whispered in my ear, "It's almost time, baby. Wake up and welcome the New Year in with me."

I yawned and turned toward him, admiring his beautiful full lips and handsome smile just as the group began counting down. We didn't make it to zero before I had my lips on Roth's mouth. We kissed much longer than the quick peck of most other people, and didn't pull apart until the group had almost completely finished the first stanza of "Auld Lang Syne."

"You know what?" I whispered as the song ended.

"What?" Roth whispered back.

"I'm fairly taken with a very handsome and talented musician."

Roth chuckled. "I'm fairly taken with an utterly adorable and dedicated librarian. Does that mean I can finally call you my boyfriend?" he asked.

I nodded and smiled. "I'd like that. Know what else?" I asked. Roth shook his head. "No more keeping your options open, got it?"

He grinned and kissed me again before putting his lips next to my ear. "Baby, you've been the only option I've wanted for a long time."

TWENTY-SIX

ROTH

T OURING. OTHERWISE KNOWN AS a surefire way to obliterate stage fright. It hit me my first several shows, but my band had my back and helped me work through it before we'd go onstage. I still had to psych myself up before each concert, but my general anxiety about performing gradually seemed to disappear altogether.

Once we hit the road, it became obvious that devising our touring schedule had involved booking as many shows within the shortest amount of time as humanly possible. I barely had time to fall asleep before being woken up by Lettie or her new demon recruit, Zania, to begin it all again.

Not to complain, since I was living my dream of being a professional musician, but I seriously felt like I got no rest. When I wasn't rehearsing with the band, I was in dance classes, or making appearances, or listening to demos for my next album. Interestingly enough, my only real respite came from actually performing onstage, until the adrenaline crash afterward anyway.

As promised, Lettie had arranged multiple dates for me with people I'd only seen on TV or the covers of magazines. To be honest, they often looked as tired as I felt, and besides the moments where we'd sit alone at a restaurant as people took our pictures, I didn't get to know any of them well.

I got to where I'd text Chris before each date, telling him who I was meeting and where we'd be going, and then afterward once I returned to my hotel room or tour bus. When I didn't just fall asleep from exhaustion, I'd call him, and we'd laugh about whatever awkward things had happened on my fake date.

The first leg of my tour, which crisscrossed the country and crossed into Canada several times, ended right before Memorial Day. I had a month off before the second leg, which would take me overseas. Wanting to spend as much time with Chris as I could, I moved my stuff to Jesse's condo, which was now, incidentally, completely empty, because he and Jen had officially moved in together.

The townsfolk quickly got used to seeing me around Crawford City again, although now I had full-time bodyguards tailing me everywhere. At least they were very good at staying in the background, most of the time anyway. A majority of the single women in town seemed to find my muscle-bound bodyguards appealing, but to the best of my knowledge, the only buffet Riff and Doug partook in involved the café.

Chris and I spent a lot of time touring Tennessee's state parks that month. We also loved visiting the winery, and spent time there hiking the many new trails Matt and Logan had created on the estate.

Nights were usually spent curled up in front of the firepit Todd had built between his parents' cabin and his home. Sometimes they'd join us, but usually it was just Chris and me.

I was happy that Doc and Amos weren't leaving for Oregon until June so I could spend time with them too. I'd become rather close to the older couple since Chris and I officially began dating.

"Are you looking forward to getting back on tour?" Chris asked me a couple nights before I was scheduled to leave.

"Yes and no. All the back-to-back performances are physically draining, but I sort of love performing now. Doing it so much has really helped me overcome my stage fright. I mean, I still get nervous, but it's more like a nervous energy rather than being flat-out terrified."

Chris snuggled back into me, and I kissed his head. "These quiet nights spent with you, they've healed me and filled my energy tanks up again. To be honest, I think I'm going to miss that more than anything else," I admitted.

During my final week there, Chris took a couple days off work, and we rented a lakeside cabin at Fall Creek Falls.

"Are you sure you don't want to have an open relationship?" Chris asked sheepishly the night before I was scheduled to go back on tour.

His question caught me totally off guard. "What do you mean? Are you wanting to see other people?"

We'd been sitting in Adirondack chairs on the back deck, looking out over the lake, and I turned to face him. He didn't meet my eyes. "No, not me. It's just you're going on the road, and I'd rather us have an open relationship than learn from the press that you're sleeping with other people."

"I don't want to sleep with other people. Besides, Lettie watches my every move. Trust me, if the idea even crossed my mind, she would quash it."

Chris looked concerned. "I know, forget it," he said.

I took his chin in my hand and tilted his head up to look at me. "Baby, we agreed to be forthcoming. What's bothering you?"

"I really care about you, Roth, and I'm not a cheater. I'm a one-man man. I need to know if you're going to be out there, that you're upfront with me."

"Why wouldn't you trust me?" I asked, feeling confused. My thoughts raced through the past year that I'd known Chris, trying to think of a time I'd given him reason to doubt me, but nothing came to mind.

"Because I've been lied to before," he admitted.

"Well, that's not me. I'm not perfect, but I'm honest and I'd never lie to you."

Chris sighed. "I'm sorry, Roth, It's just hard when we're apart for such long periods of time."

"That's why I asked Lettie and Zania to build some time off into my schedule to spend with you. If you can meet me on the road, I'll fly you there. If you can't get off, I'll fly back here."

Chris looked at me with unblinking eyes. "When were you going to tell me all this?"

"I planned on surprising you, but now I'd rather you know I'm thinking about doing what I can to strengthen our relationship. You mean too much to me not to try."

Chris smiled his adorable smile at me. "I love you, Roth Gallo, so much it hurts sometimes."

The admission should've shocked me, but he'd just given voice to how I already knew I felt. Happiness bubbled up inside me and I could feel my face flush.

"Good," I said, leaning over the arms of our chairs and kissing him long and hard, "'cause I love you so much it hurts too."

Chris stood and extended his hand to me, pulling me out of my chair, and led me inside our cabin.

TWENTY-SEVEN

CHRIS

I HADN'T PLANNED ON confessing my love to Roth, and certainly not when I'd been trying to hedge my bets against heartache by agreeing to an open relationship, but the words just flowed out of me. He didn't even blink before telling me he felt the same.

As I knew it would, I felt his absence after he left on tour. I'd taken to marking days off the calendar in counting down to when we'd see each other again. Eight weeks, then seven weeks... I just had to survive a few more weeks and I'd be joining him in London. He'd already promised to show me the historical sites of the city, and he'd scheduled for us to go see Stonehenge.

I was floating as I thought about the vacation and seeing Roth again. I'd been happily distracted with that while doing busy work at the circulation desk when Lorna Bailey, the woman who'd left her kids unattended at the library last year, showed up out of the blue and began yelling at me.

"You shoved my son into that shelf, now they're blaming me. They took my kids away and gave them to my sorry excuse for a husband because of you!" she screamed.

I was shocked at her yelling more than I was afraid of her. I stood and, in a measured but firm tone, said, "Ma'am, you need to leave the library before I call the sheriff and have you arrested for disturbing the peace."

"Screw you!" she yelled, and flipped me off as she walked back out the door in a huff. A few moments later, the sheriff and one of her deputies arrived. I looked outside and saw the deputy talking to Lorna, clearly attempting to calm her down, while the sheriff was heading my way.

"So, she's back," Sheriff Cross said as we stepped into my office behind the circulation desk.

"Apparently. What's her problem? I mean, all that business with her abandoning her kids at the library happened last summer. Has she spent the past year blaming me for everything wrong in her life or what?"

"We've been keeping an eye on her since she threw the bottle at you and Roth Gallo. I didn't want to take a chance in case she escalated, or made Roth more of a target given his success. She had family court today and I'm guessing she lost custody, so that likely triggered what just happened."

"She lost her kids because her son got hurt in the library?" I asked, confused. "Everyone knows his running into the bookshelf was an accident, and we all gave statements about it."

"Nothing like that. I wasn't in family court today, so I don't know all of the strikes against her, but I do know she's got a Meth habit and the children were not safe in that home," she said. "Anyway, my deputy recognized her as we were coming out of the café across the street, and we came over as quickly as we could."

I sighed. "That woman is like a bad penny. I'd all but forgotten about her until she came in and started screaming in my face."

"Well, she clearly hasn't forgotten you. We're going to escort her off the premises and have a conversation about her behavior today, but you still need to watch out for her. She's not a good person."

"Do you think she's a serious threat?" I asked, feeling concerned about my safety and those around me. "Do I need a restraining order or something?"

The sheriff shrugged. "We'll do what we can to keep her away from you, regardless. I'm not trying to scare you, Chris, but we can't predict her behavior, and we can't be around you twenty-four seven. Just please look out for yourself."

"I will. Thanks, Sheriff," I said, then walked her to the entrance.

I watched out the window while they spoke with Lorna, and the woman seemed to regain her composure the longer they talked. By the time the sheriff and deputy got in their patrol car and left, the entire library was full of people watching me. I smiled at everyone, but hightailed it back to my office to distract myself from the situation and hopefully get some work done while the drama settled down a bit.

Lettie called after the library closed, which surprised me. Roth had given me her number before he left for the second leg of his tour so she could get in touch. He said she'd be the one in charge of setting up a time for us to meet up whenever he had a break in his schedule.

"Hey," I answered. "How are you, Lettie?"

"I'm good, cutie pie. What're your plans for next weekend? Can you take Friday and Monday off?"

"Um, I don't know. I'd have to see if I can get someone to take my shift on short notice. Why?"

"Roth was supposed to be in Japan to film a special segment with a Japanese version of the competition, but they canceled last minute. He'd like for you to meet him in Amsterdam, if we can swing it. He's chomping at the bit to see you."

"Like a horse?"

She cackled. "Yeah, don't take me literal now, although he can be a horse's ass, if that counts. Anyway, call me back when you know."

She hung up before I had a chance to say goodbye. She seemed just as insanely busy as Roth, if not more so. Lettie really was made for that job.

Despite the late hour, I quickly called Mrs. Elliot, who was still my boss, and asked if someone could cover for me and she immediately volunteered. "One seldom gets the chance to be whisked off to Europe for a romantic rendezvous with their sweetie," she said.

I chuckled. As I'd gotten to know her more as a colleague over the past year, it'd become clear that she was a romantic at heart. "Thank you, Mrs. Elliot. I'm happy to make it up to you whenever you need coverage too."

"Like you'll ever be able to leave Crawford City. I swear that little library is the busiest one in our entire system. Anyway, I was hoping to get over there to spend some time checking out some of your innovative programs. This is the perfect opportunity."

"You mean you're coming to check up on me."

"Of course, that's my job, but I also want to see for myself all of the ways you've made your library a hub of the town. I've received such wonderful feedback about it. You really have done an excellent job, Mr. Asbell."

I couldn't deny feeling elated that Mrs. Elliot had such glowing things to say about my work. Too often, I'd wondered if anyone even took note of all the extra hours and effort I'd put in over the past year. Apparently, it hadn't gone unnoticed.

I also wondered why she'd addressed me so formally all of a sudden. She usually called me Chris, and I thought perhaps she'd begun to think of me more as a colleague, too, than a subordinate. I decided to just take it as a compliment, though.

I quickly called Lettie back and confirmed I could make the trip. "Can you send me the details of where and all that? I'll try to schedule a flight..."

"You'll do no such thing," she interrupted. "You are our guest, well, you're Roth's very special guest. You'll sit back and enjoy our hospitality. I'll send a car to pick you up for your flight Thursday night, after the library closes. You'll have a couple of layovers, one in New York and one in London, but they should be fairly short."

"Thank you, Lettie. I'm looking forward to seeing you too."

"Psst, you won't even notice I'm there, but thanks for pretending. I'll email you all the details."

She hung up and as I was locking up the library, an email notification dinged on my phone. She'd already sent all the travel information. "Wow," I said out loud. "The woman does work fast."

Twenty-Eight

Roth

Somewhere between Madrid and Amsterdam, I'd caught my second wind and was sailing through the countless interviews, appearances, and performances like I was in a dream.

When Lettie told me my Japanese TV cameo had been canceled, so I had a long weekend before my sold-out concerts in Tokyo, I'd immediately wanted to fly home, but she quashed it.

"No, you're just now getting your momentum back. If you fly all the way to Nashville, then to Tokyo, you're going to be exhausted again," she'd said, sounding every bit my no-nonsense manager. "It's better to stay here in Amsterdam and have Chris come to you. Don't worry, I'll set it all up."

After giving my final performance in Amsterdam, I planned to crash for a few hours to relax before Chris was due to arrive. I was so freaking excited. I had an entire floor in the hotel to myself, since my presidential suite took up that much space. The hotel staff had told me the rooms on this floor were tiny, so Lettie and the band wouldn't like them and were therefore put in rooms on the floor below.

The whole thing was strange, but whatever. After the last concert, though, the band partied a lot harder and longer than I'd planned. The arena that held it had been so kind to us, though, that it seemed rude not to just enjoy hanging out with the event staff for a while to thank everyone, have some drinks, take pictures, and sign autographs. I ended up crawling into bed in the wee hours of the morning.

I woke up in my hotel room tired and hungover. The all-Dutch crew assigned to us had been so determined to show us a good time, which they succeeded in doing, but thank God not many other venues went at it so hardcore. When I opened my eyes, I immediately wanted to leap out of bed, but my body did more of a slow-roll.

"What the fuck!" I yelled when I saw a naked man and woman sprawled out on my king-size bed.

"Who the hell are you?" I demanded.

The two barely heard me and only groaned a bit, so I quickly threw on clothes and grabbed my phone as I darted out of the hotel room. In a panic, I dialed Lettie and paced the empty hallway while waiting for her to pick up.

She answered groggily on the fourth ring, indicating she'd just woken up as well. "You need to get your ass up here 'cause there are two naked strangers in my bed, and I sure as hell don't know how they got there."

"Wha... what?" Lettie said, and I could hear the sleep clearing from her voice.

"You heard me. Some naked couple I don't know is in my bed. Lettie, if this is a setup, I swear to God!"

"Shut up and calm down. Where are your body-guards?"

I'd forgotten about them. Looking up and down the hallway, they weren't anywhere to be seen. "I have no fucking idea. Usually, one of them is asleep on the couch. Let me look in the guest bedroom."

I darted back into the suite and peeked into the little room off of my bedroom, but the twin bed hadn't been slept in. Not for the first time, I lamented not bringing my personal bodyguards Riff and Doug on tour, but the record label had insisted we use an international security team while overseas.

I stepped inside the room and locked the door. "Lettie, call security and have these people removed from my suite. Then call and find out where my damned bodyguards disappeared to."

She hung up without saying anything. I moved the dresser in front of the door, not at all sure what the hell was happening. I had been buzzed from the partying, but I knew I'd gone to bed alone. How a couple of strangers had gotten into my suite, let alone my bed, was a mystery to me. My mind raced, replaying the events of last night in a futile attempt to remember something I remained convinced never happened.

Lettie called back a moment later. "The bodyguards were found unconscious in the green room at the arena last night. Looks like someone roofied them. They're okay, though. We must've been so drunk when we came back that we didn't even notice they weren't with us."

"Well, I'm noticing now," I said, feeling more freaked out by the minute. "That still doesn't explain who the hell these two naked people are, though."

"Yeah, sit tight. Hotel security is coming up now. I'm on my way as well."

I sat on the phone as I listened to Lettie talking to hotel security in the elevator. She began cussing the moment the elevator door dinged. "What is going on here?" she yelled, and I heard cameras snapping. "Damn, paparazzi," I said on the other end of the line.

"Can you get rid of these people?" Lettie yelled, I assumed to the security guards.

I heard someone yelling in Dutch mixed with some English, telling people to get out before the authorities were called. Then I heard the front door of the suite open and a second later, the guest bedroom doorknob rattled.

"Mr. Gallo, are you in there?" I didn't answer them. Instead, I whispered into the phone, "Someone's trying to come through the door."

"Don't say a word, it's the freaking paps. They somehow gained access through the damn stairwell," Lettie said. The next thing I heard was her coming into the suite and yelling at whoever stood outside my door. "Get the fuck out of here before I whack you with that camera, you sorry piece of dog poop!" she shouted. I heard scuffling, then what sounded like a flurry of activity before things got quiet.

Still on the phone, Lettie whispered, "Stay put! I'll let you know when it's safe to come out."

I heard more shouting and assumed the naked people were being escorted out of the suite, hopefully wearing clothing. As I sat on the bed, waiting for the hubbub to settle down, I remained completely dumbfounded. Who had drugged my bodyguards? And for what reason? Had this all been some kind of setup?

A few minutes later, Lettie knocked on my door, telling me the coast was clear.

"What the fuck, Lettie?" I asked the moment I saw her.

"No idea, but I'm working on it now. The authorities are investigating what happened to your bodyguards, and I've got the hotel security team looking into how those two people got into your bedroom."

With Lettie assuring me she'd stand guard and keep an eye on things, I was just about to go take a shower when we heard a knock at the door. "Go away," Lettie said to the door. "We're not taking visitors at the moment unless it's hotel security and I have them on speed dial so don't try anything."

"Lettie, it's me, Zania," the woman said, and I could hear her confusion. "I've got Chris with me."

I felt my heart drop into my stomach and my blood ran cold. Had he witnessed any of this? What must he be thinking? I couldn't imagine, since I didn't even know what to think of it at this point.

Lettie told me to get out of sight, but I refused. Instead, I jerked the door open and looked into the pained eyes of the man I loved. "Chris, did you see all this?" I asked.

Before he could respond, a paparazzo rushed out from around the corner and began snapping pictures of Chris and me. I grabbed Chris's hand and pulled him into the room, all but slamming the door in Zania's face.

I could hear her trying her best to remove the vulture from the hallway.

"Chris," I said, my hand still clasping his.

"Why didn't you just accept my offer of an open relationship?" he said, sounding on the verge of tears.

Chris tugged his hand away and wrapped his arms around himself, as if closing himself off from me. Without another word, he turned, opened the door, and walked out of the suite.

"Wait!" I yelled but Chris was already halfway down the hall, sprinting past Zania and the paparazzo toward the stairwell.

I was about to run after him when Lettie grabbed my arm. "No, it's not safe, not without your bodyguards," she said. I almost ignored her, but she was gripping me with all her strength, and I could see fear in her eyes. That wasn't something I saw very often, not from my sister.

"Someone set this up, Roth. I'm not sure who or why, but it's not safe for you. I'll find someone to track Chris down, but you can't leave."

I collapsed onto the couch and let the tears flow. The morning had been an emotional shitshow, and that was before Chris had even arrived. Not only did I wake up to strangers in my bed, but my bodyguards had been drugged, the paparazzi had descended like vultures, and my boyfriend had walked right into all of it.

I knew my sister would make it her new mission in life to get to the bottom of this mess and hold the responsible people accountable. My focus was squarely on Chris. He'd already admitted he had trust issues. Given the way he literally just ran away from me left no doubt the thin thread of trust he'd extended to me had snapped, even though none of it had been my fault.

Lettie was right, this was all a setup. The only question that kept revolving in my mind was how I could convince Chris this hadn't been the type of setup he thought it was.

TWENTY-NINE

CHRIS

I'D FLOWN ALL THE way to Amsterdam for that? To be humiliated. Devastated. Made to feel the fool I clearly had been all this time. *This is why you don't date famous people*, I kept chastising myself. After wandering along the canals and crossing the narrow bridges the city was known for, tormenting myself with thoughts of how amazing it would've been to see with Roth, I came across a little café where the servers spoke English. I ordered a coffee, then sat in a corner, wiping away the tears as they flowed and thanking the universe that I was the only patron in the place.

I wasn't sure how long I sat there, but the poor server kept refilling my coffee until I got ahold of myself well enough to book a flight back to the US and Nashville.

I grabbed a taxi, not even worrying about my luggage, which was still with Zania. Thankfully, I'd kept my passport on me. A couple of hours later, I boarded a flight from Schiphol Airport to New York, going right back the way I'd come.

I flew coach instead of first-class as I had on the way there, but that hardly mattered. Luckily, I was in the back of the airplane and only had one other passenger sitting near me. I slept most of the way and when I wasn't asleep, I was crying. The man two seats away just ignored me, which I preferred.

I caught a connecting flight to Nashville three hours after landing in New York and by the time I got to Crawford City, I was completely wiped out. Doc and Amos weren't home when I arrived, so I texted them saying I was back and that I needed to sleep for a while after all my travels.

I anticipated a lot of questions, but at that moment, I just needed rest and to be alone to process the betrayal and deceit. *I'm such an idiot. A total and completely foolish, gullible idiot.*

I finally fell asleep after tossing and turning for a while, and didn't wake up for several hours.

When I woke and couldn't get back to sleep, I went downstairs and into the embrace of Doc and Amos. They group hugged me, sat me down, and began plying me with comfort food. Neither of them asked what had happened. I guessed that flying all the way to Europe just to come right back must've been enough information to know things hadn't gone well. Well, that and my eyes were still red and puffy from all of the crying.

Within what seemed like minutes, Mom and Dad showed up. My parents had moved to Crawford City over the summer, not too far from Doc and Amos's place. They still hadn't found a home to their particular liking to purchase, so they decided to rent a house for the time being since Mom was due to begin her new bus-driving job for the school district in the fall.

With everyone's eyes on me as we sat gathered around the table, I realized my time of sitting quietly was over. My mother wouldn't tolerate me not being forthcoming, not with something important. So, I sat across from Mom, Dad, Amos and Doc and relayed everything I'd seen since stepping off the hotel elevator. I rambled my way through it, sniffling and hiccupping as I spoke, but no one said a word while they listened.

"Roth's assistant met me as I arrived and told me how excited Roth was to see me. I was just as excited, but you all already knew that. When we got to his hotel suite, the entire hallway was full of people with cameras aimed at his door, snapping away. A few moments later, Lettie showed up shouting about everyone needing to leave and hotel security began escorting people down the stairwell. Zania flashed them her ID and they let us linger as they cleared the floor. We were about to knock on the door when two half-dressed people came out, both high as a kite and smiling from ear to ear. I heard the woman say, 'That was so good,' and the man laughed. Then security forced another man out of the room who was clearly one of the paparazzi and as he walked past us, he winked and said, 'Ménage à trois.' I thought it was a setup until I heard one of the guards say something about the half-naked people being prostitutes and that famous people hire them all the time."

I took a deep, shaky breath as tears streamed down my face. Mom handed me a tissue. "When Roth opened the door and pulled me inside the room, and I saw he was half-dressed himself, I knew. I knew he'd been with them, the prostitutes. I said something but I don't even remember what and didn't give him the chance to make excuses. I didn't want to hear any of his lies so I didn't wait, I ran out of there and caught the first flight I could back home."

Mom put her hands over mine, and I saw the sadness in her eyes. "Of course, you did, honey. Of course, you did."

"How did you know I was home?" I asked.

I glanced at Amos, who had a guilty look on his face, and I knew who'd told her. I reached over and patted the older man's hand. "Thanks, Amos."

"Let me fix you some dinner," he said, and I shook my head. "I need to be alone for a while. Thanks for listening, though. I needed that too."

All four of them nodded and I escaped back upstairs to what I thought of as my sanctuary. I hadn't known that a person could go from being the happiest human in the world to the saddest in a matter of minutes. Not until today.

Thirty

Roth

"**D**EAR GOD, LETTIE, IT'S a mess! How did this happen?" I asked after the police left my hotel room.

She shrugged, but appeared just as frustrated. "Sounds like it's an ongoing problem. Someone at the hotel set it all up. You being on a different floor than us, your bodyguards not here, you being too drunk or, more likely, drugged to know what's happening, two prostitutes sleep in your bed and paparazzi show up out of nowhere. The staff have strict instructions to keep the paps out of the hotel, and hell, it takes a special key to access this floor whether by elevator or the stairs! This had to be an inside job."

"You're going to try to keep this under wraps, aren't you?"

"I mean, I've spoken to the record label execs, and they want it kept quiet. Jake advised as much too. They don't want your name smeared with prostitutes."

"Fuck that, Lettie. I want to hold these idiots accountable. Who knows what could've happened or what might happen to the next guy."

She sighed. "Well, it should be your call, but know the press will have a field day with this. Truth doesn't matter, only how they spin it, and this shitstorm is going to spin like a damn tornado."

The thought that my career could tank based on bullshit and lies sickened me, but not as much as what my boyfriend was likely going through. At least, I hoped Chris was still my boyfriend.

"Have you heard from Chris?"

She shook her head. "No. Zania said he changed his return ticket and caught a flight back to the States that same day, and he hasn't returned any of our calls."

"Shit. Lettie, I don't know how to fix this."

"Me neither, sweetie. But we'll try."

"I want to fly back and talk to him, but I have to be in Japan next week and don't have a break for several weeks after that."

"Do you want me to go talk to him?" she asked.

"Yes, that's the best way to handle this. I mean, he won't talk to me anyway. Not that he'll want to see you either, but Lettie, I can't lose him over this."

We sat quietly on the couch, staring into the void, unsure of how to move forward, when it hit me. "You know, if I fight this publicly, at least he'll see that I'm not lying, right?"

Lettie shook her head. "Or it could just make it worse, and you could be seen as a whoremonger who got caught and is now trying to spin things to your advantage."

"Well, I'm gonna fight anyway. I want other people to know not to trust this hotel, and if the event staff at the venue were involved, I want them held accountable too. This is ridiculous!"

Lettie found our crew another hotel to relocate to by the end of the day, and Jake hooked us up with some top-notch attorneys, who wasted no time contacting the venue and hotel. After some heavy negotiation with the record label, they agreed to pay for the attorneys and hire a private investigator to hopefully uncover additional details about that horrible night.

By the time I left for Tokyo, I was scheduled to do an interview with the BBC when in London about what'd happened and the aftermath.

After getting me set up in Tokyo and putting Zania in the adjoining room in my hotel suite to ensure nothing like Amsterdam happened again, not to mention hiring a different security service that wouldn't let the ball drop like the last one had, Lettie flew back to Tennessee.

My stomach twisted itself in knots as I thought about the past several days. I hadn't felt so lost and so alone since Grandma died. I'd been insulated from the ugly in the world since finding my place with the Ramirezes. I rubbed my upset stomach, hoping to lessen some of my anxiety, and hoped my determined sister would be able to at least get Chris to listen to her.

I needed a chance to explain the truth to him, even if it was through Lettie, and even if it was too late to save our relationship. He needed to know I would never betray him like that. He needed to know that him even thinking me capable of it was tearing me up inside.

I performed in Tokyo twice before Lettie returned, and I knew the moment I saw her face she hadn't had any luck getting through to him.

"Chris wouldn't even see me," Lettie explained. "I even tried intercepting him at the library, but the entire volunteer staff stood between me and his office. They literally blocked my way. Even Jesse is being kept at arm's length. I'm sorry, Roth. Maybe he just needs some time."

I wanted to cry. I felt so dejected. I knew I'd probably blown it, but what more could I do?

After my performance that night, I couldn't sleep. So as not to disturb Zania in the guestroom or my new bodyguard sleeping on the couch, I stayed in my room and began strumming my guitar.

I didn't claim to be a songwriter. I never even tried to be, if I was honest, but the words came pouring out of me as I sat in bed.

"I wish I could explain all the things I cannot say. I wish I could show you all the ways you make me feel..." I sang quietly.

I kept at it until I strummed the final chord. I hit record on my phone, played the song in full, and texted the video to Lettie.

Maybe if Chris heard this, a song that'd come from my heart, maybe he'd consider at least giving me a chance to explain.

I texted Lettie again, telling her I was going to sleep in since I hadn't slept all night. She told me later that day that she loved the song and had sent it to the record label.

I finished my stint in Tokyo and then flew to London, where I was scheduled to perform at a music festival. I'd been looking forward to the festival since so many famous musicians had performed at it over the years, but with the BBC interview looming over me, I was feeling reticent.

The interviewer, a woman about my age, sat across from me. Lettie had assured me she'd placed limits on what could be asked, and she stood just off camera behind me, prepared to pull me out of the interview if they didn't follow the agreement.

I didn't really care. The woman could ask whatever she wanted. If I didn't want to answer, I wouldn't.

"We are here today with Mr. Roth Gallo. Roth, thanks for being with us."

"Thank you, Julia," I responded, trying to sound pleasant, but still strike a serious tone.

"So, your latest single has been racing up the charts. Do you think it's going to hit number one?" she asked.

I chuckled, relieved she'd started with a softball question. "I think that's out of my hands, really. I do hope people like the song, though, and it has been fun to perform. The fans who've come out to see me on tour sing along to it."

"About the tour, you seem to be having fun."

I smiled. "I was, at least until a couple weeks ago."

"Yes, that has been quite a scandal. You were touring in Amsterdam at the time. Do you want to share with us what happened?"

I started from the beginning, from having a few drinks with event staff at the arena to waking up the next morning with two strangers in my hotel bed. "The toxicology report was inconclusive on me, but it did show that my bodyguards had been drugged. We assume whoever did this used the same drug on me."

The interviewer glanced at Lettie, and I knew she was about to ask something not agreed upon. I was prepared, though, so I waited for the question.

"There are rumors that you roofied your own bodyguards so you could hire the two prostitutes who were found in your room."

I heard Lettie moving behind me, ready to put the brakes on the interview, and I raised my hand slightly to stop her. I wanted to answer.

"This is not a judgement on sex workers or those who hire them, but I am not inclined to do so and never have been," I said. "The real story, and what I think has gotten lost in the media coverage about it, is that a crime has been committed here. Multiple crimes, actually, against me, against my bodyguards, and in a way, against everyone I care about who's being dragged through this with me."

"In a statement about the Amsterdam incident released by your PR agency, you allege someone set it all up so that you'd be caught in a compromising position. Elaborate on that."

I nodded. "I returned to the hotel that night with my manager and band, and I went to bed in my hotel room alone, which I remember very clearly. I woke up the next morning with two strangers in my bed, a man and a woman, both of whom were naked. I immediately contacted my sister, who is also my manager, and she arrived with security to find a hallway full of paparazzi on my floor. Clearly, someone had paid those two people to come into my room, then arranged for the paps to be there to document it."

"So, what's the latest on that? Is it being investigated?"

I nodded again. "Yes, we have a few leads, which I won't go into detail about since it'll end up in the Amsterdam courts. What I can share is that the two people who'd snuck into my hotel room have begun talking with authorities about what led up to that. The investigation is ongoing, so hopefully we'll get the full picture of what happened and why."

The interviewer nodded. "As you said, this has been very difficult on you and those around you."

I realized then that the spirit of the interview was changing. She was going for the victim approach versus the salacious scandal.

"It has, in fact, been extremely difficult on someone who means a lot to me."

"A girlfriend?" she asked, and I smiled.

"Yeah, something like that," I answered, not wanting to give much away. I still felt very protective of Chris and his privacy, and I suspected I always would. "Obviously, it's been a very difficult time for everyone in my life, and in ways I couldn't have ever imagined. My family, my friends, my fans, and my record label have all remained incredibly supportive."

I took a deep breath and let it out slowly, then looked directly into the camera lens. I hoped that somehow, Chris would watch this interview and know I was speaking directly to him. "I am in a relationship with an amazing person who has made me happier than I've been my entire life, and who has been hurt deeply by these lies. I won't stand for having my relationship, my name, or my career tarnished by gossip and vitriol," I said, turning back toward the interviewer. "That's one of the reasons I'm here talking with you today."

"Now, I know we've agreed not to discuss your sexuality, but you have to know your fans and people who follow your career also care about your life. Do you plan to come out as gay or straight anytime soon? Or perhaps you land elsewhere on the LGBTQ-plus rainbow?"

I laughed. "I didn't think that coming out was a requirement for straight people, but I haven't really thought about it and have no immediate plans to do so. If and when I decide to announce it publicly, you'll be my first call, Julia."

That caused her to laugh. "Okay, a promised scoop! That's good enough for now, and I'll hold you to it," she said, glancing at her notes, which signaled a welcome subject change. "You have a new song, and I'm told you don't mind if we share it with our listeners. It's my understanding you wrote this song yourself, following the Amsterdam incident."

"Yes, it's my first attempt at songwriting, so I only ask my fans not to be too harsh with me if it isn't that good. Luckily, I don't have to rely on my own writing skills to put out good music. Usually, other, more talented songwriters do that job for me."

"I don't know," the woman across from me said and I noticed her blush. "This song is pretty amazing. Let's play the clip and let our audience decide."

The clip was the phone recording I'd texted Lettie of me just sitting on my hotel bed and strumming the guitar while I sang. Raw, unfiltered and incredibly honest. I had to hold back my emotions as we listened to it together.

When the clip ended, the interviewer quickly dabbed a tear away, clearly touched. "That song really came from the heart, didn't it?" she asked.

I nodded but didn't reply.

"Do you plan to turn this into a single?" she asked.

"I think the label is working on setting up a time for me to get back into the studio to record it. But with the tour, that probably won't happen right away."

She nodded. "So it goes with a touring artist. That's about all the time we have. Thank you, Roth, for sharing your story and your new song with us. We look forward to seeing you perform at the festival this weekend."

"Thanks, Julia, it's been a pleasure."

Once given the all-clear we were off the air, the interviewer hugged me, then apologized. "After hearing your song, I felt like that was necessary. I'm so sorry about Amsterdam. What a load of crap."

I smiled. "Thanks, and thank you for helping me share with the world what really happened."

"No problem," she replied, just as one of the studio crew members pulled her away.

I hoped after the interview aired, maybe Chris would get in touch with me. I'd been informed several magazines would feature the interview, too, as a cover story. It gave me hope that even if he never watched the interview online or in pickup coverage back in the States, he'd read it in print. I figured he wouldn't be able to avoid it since he usually did the sprucing up of the magazine section of the library.

I waited a week, then two, but he continued to ignore my texts. I felt more and more depressed as time went on, and more convinced that I'd never hear from him again.

The week I'd planned to spend with Chris in Paris was on the horizon. Since he clearly wasn't coming, I decided to fly home to Nashville to record the song that'd begun to climb the charts, even in its rough form. The recording already had twenty-eight million YouTube views, and the label was desperate to capitalize on the momentum.

I was determined to get to Crawford City to visit Chris in person, but of course, Fate had other ideas and I couldn't get away. As it was, I barely had enough time to record my studio vocals before having to fly back overseas to finish my tour.

Gradually, I began to feel my heart scab over where the raw, deep wound had festered. I knew Lettie was worried about me and, quite frankly, I was worried about myself. I couldn't keep performing night after night in a hazy fog of heartbreak-driven depression. I had to either overcome it somehow or risk losing everything I'd worked so hard to achieve. As my granny used to say, "You gotta put your big girl panties on and get on with it."

As hard as it was, that's what I did. But not one night went by that I didn't think of my sweet, adorable librarian and the small town I already considered home.

When I got the phone call from Jake informing me the old Crawford property we'd gone to visit was for sale, I didn't hesitate. I jumped in with both feet. If Chris never wanted to see me again, I respected his choice, regardless of how much it gutted me. We could even avoid each other if it came to that, but I loved Crawford City, and his love of the historical property had been infectious and stayed with me all this time.

Jake agreed to ask Todd and Amos to look at the property and give me a bid to restore it. Lance, Jake's architect husband, was working with another local architect named Tom in planning how to preserve as much as the original design as possible while incorporating my request to include a couple of ground-level suites. One would be for my parents or Lettie to stay in, and the other for Chris's parents.

I knew it was stupid to be planning a future with a man who didn't even want to speak to me. When we'd toured the place, though, I couldn't help but dream about it not only being a home for the two of us, but also for the people in our lives that we cared about the most.

"Hey, Jake? I have a favor to ask," I said as I described my property ideas to him and Lance. "I prefer Chris not know I'll be the new owner. I mean, I'm sure he'll be excited and intrigued about the place being saved, and you guys can discuss the restoration plans with him, but please keep my name out of it. He sort of hates me right now, and I don't want him to be disappointed or angry about who's buying it."

Jake was hesitant, but finally agreed, as did Lance. "We can keep your ownership a secret, but not just to Chis. You know how close he is to Amos and Todd. If they learn you're buying the place, they'd tell him. If you truly don't want Chris to know, it's best that no one else in town does either."

I took a deep breath before I agreed. "Yeah, it's probably best to keep it a secret anyway. Otherwise, anyone could blast that information to the press too. The last thing I want is for reporters or worse, paparazzi, descending on this town."

As the months flowed by, Lance and I became close as he sent me updates on the planning. The old building was in a lot better shape than any of us imagined it would be given the fire and decades of neglect. Only a small section would have to be torn down, so most of the historical elements could be saved. Even the termite damage had been minimized because of previous treatments.

The sale finally closed in December, and we could begin the restoration process. Through Jake, Todd had provided all the estimates for the stabilization and repair, which he figured would take at least a year to complete.

I'd admit I about swallowed by tongue when I saw Todd's total cost projection, but I'd been socking away as much of my income as possible ever since my career took off. In any case, the price tag involved didn't sway my decision in the slightest. My desire to restore the Crawford property had never been about money.

The final leg of my tour, which spanned the Southern Hemisphere from Australia and New Zealand to Brazil, would end six months from now. That meant I'd be free to hang out in Crawford City all summer, hopefully while staying in Jesse's condo, while the last of the property work wrapped up. I'd loved spending the past year traveling the world on tour, but I couldn't wait to slow down and return to small-town life for a while.

Spending the summer in town also meant I could be on-site to help pick out the final finishes, which Todd had assured Jake was the only part the owner really needed to be involved in directly. I couldn't have timed it better than if I'd planned it all myself. I just hoped the big reveal of me being the property owner went over

well with Chris, Todd and Amos, and an entire town of
my soon-to-be neighbors.

247

THIRTY-ONE

CHRIS

LETTIE SHOWED UP IN Crawford City the week after I flew back from Amsterdam. I probably should've listened to what she had to say, but I just didn't trust her or her brother. So, I sent her on her way without even speaking to her. I knew it was rude, but I just couldn't help it. I felt so betrayed.

Fortunately, Doc and Amos didn't press me too hard on my early return. After telling them Roth and I were over, they didn't bring him up again. I knew that was hard on them since they considered Roth a friend, too. Their thoughtful silence was good for me at the time, if not a little heartbreaking.

Unfortunately, the other townsfolk didn't take the same approach. Every time Roth's name came up in the press, it seemed everyone in town would come into the library to talk to me about it. No matter how distant or disinterested I appeared, they kept on pushing it.

That's how I learned that the incident in Amsterdam was indeed a setup. Roth went on record denouncing it, and even wrote a song about how the aftermath had affected him. That beautiful, heart-wrenching song that I knew he'd written for me.

His poetic words had touched me deeply, and I felt relieved he hadn't lied to me after all, but I just couldn't bring myself to go back to him. That was the only guarantee I had of preserving what remained of my heart.

I just wished I could convince my heart it was the best thing for me and for Roth. I had daydreams of what it'd felt like for him to take my hand or sneak a kiss while we were tidying up the library after we closed. When I worked in the children's area, I'd remember him there too. It wasn't like he read to the kids every day, but he'd been so sweet with them, so theatrical in his reading, the memories still filled me with butterflies.

I couldn't escape thoughts of Roth entirely, but if I let myself think about him too much, I'd spiral down into a dark hole of depression. Sometimes it felt as though self-recrimination and doubt would strangle me, and I'd have to pry myself out of bed. Those were the worst days.

As had become my routine on Wednesdays, I rushed to the café to get my weekly cinnamon roll before I had to open the library for the day. I'd made a deal with Mrs. Cole that if she'd save me at least one, I'd open the library after-hours on Saturdays just for her, so she could get a new book to read on her one day off each week.

Of course, I'd have done that for the amazing woman anyway. She was like the mother of Crawford City. Not only did she know what was going on with all of us, but she made sure we ate a healthy meal every day, if we wanted.

When I'd begun playfully harassing her to save me a cinnamon roll before they ran out, which always happened very early, she proposed the deal. Now, I knew not only did I get that delicious morsel every Wednesday morning, but I got to spend Saturday evenings shooting the bull with her. Often, Mr. Cole and sometimes even Jen would stop by.

As much as I liked Jen, I had also come to dread seeing her. She and Jesse, Roth's older brother, were thick as thieves. Jen, unlike Amos and Doc, didn't hesitate to bring up my former boyfriend anytime she saw me. And she always had something new to share with me about him.

I had resorted to giving her the stink eye, which only caused her to go at it harder. I'd swear, the woman was as incorrigible as any human being I'd ever met.

I'd never had siblings, but if I did, I'd assume she would be what mine would act like. I'd certainly read enough young adult fiction to know siblings lived to harass each other, especially older sisters to their younger brothers.

Everything came to a head over Christmas. It seemed like every time I turned on the TV, I couldn't watch any damn show without seeing Roth, either giving an interview or performing. Magazines were no better with his face plastered on countless covers. Straightening up the magazine section of the library each night, I couldn't escape him.

I'd been invited to a huge potluck party Todd and Ash were throwing prior to the holidays. I arrived to it late, having to close up the library myself since my assistant was home with the flu that week.

Jen immediately called me over to where they were sitting with their significant others. She, Todd and Jake were clearly best friends with a long history. "Hey," I said to the group after putting my biscuit pudding on the table in the dining room. Mrs. Cole had made it for me to bring.

"Hey, yourself. So, have you heard about the old Crawford mansion?" Jen asked.

"No. Has something happened?" I asked, wondering why Jen was asking. She hadn't been with the rest of us when we'd toured the place.

Jake chimed in then. "Yes, someone bought it." For some reason, he gave Jen a pointed look before continuing. "They're going to restore it."

"Do you know the owner?" I asked, feeling suspicious all of a sudden.

"Yes, but they've asked to remain anonymous," Jake replied.

The way Jake looked to Jen, and the way she looked me in the eye with her usual *have you heard the latest about Roth* look gave me my answer.

"Well, that's good news. I'm glad the old lady won't be torn down. If you'll excuse me..." I started to say, ready to make a run for it.

"Oh no, don't leave," Jen said. "Jake was just telling us how we'd like you to help plan some of the designs, since you've studied the home's original style and all."

I'd indeed done a lot of research on the home and had put together a comprehensive file that we kept in the reference section of the library. Much of the information had been sent to me directly from the Crawford family.

I'd already thought about compiling the research into a local history book since the place was so obscure and unique compared to other historical structures and areas in Tennessee. The Quaker influence really had an impact on the home and the town.

"I'm sure you could find someone more qualified to help with the designs, like Lance," I said, and looked over to where he was sitting.

"Really?" Jen said, sounding disappointed. "I'd have thought you'd love to get your hands dirty and dig into the architecture. I mean, aren't you the one who got all this started?"

I sighed. I was just about to admit to having figured out the new owner and knowing what she was up to when the triplets came barreling into the room. "Uncle Kwis!" Jessica exclaimed at the top of her lungs.

The three had started calling me uncle a while back. Although I'd done nothing to encourage it, I did sort of like it.

"Hi, Crackerjack. What's up?"

"Can we go to the libwawy to see Santa?" she asked.

I chuckled, as did everyone within hearing distance. I'd made the mistake of telling the triplets Santa would be making a special visit to the library next week, and they'd harassed me since then to go see him. Of course, I didn't dare tell them that Santa was going to be their grandpa Amos, who'd been growing a beard for that very purpose.

When I noticed Amos grinning at his granddaughter, I couldn't help but smile too. "I'll tell you what," I said to Jessica. "I know Santa wants to see you too. I'll make sure you and your brother and sister have lots of time to talk to him, is that okay?"

She clapped her hands and squealed adorably, then waved goodbye before she was off again. She really was as cute as a bug's ear.

That'd been the bright spot of my evening so far. I didn't feel much like keeping up the charade of not knowing Roth had bought the Crawford property, so I stood and looked at Jen as I addressed her earlier question.

"If I can help in any way, I'm happy to, but I'm no building expert. This town has old Tom and Lance for that. But I did hire a photo restoration company in Nashville to create a 3D model of the mansion based on historical pictures. I'm planning to display it in the library as a way of promoting the local history books in our reference section. You're welcome to it in the meantime, if you want."

Lance seemed the most interested in seeing the model, which made sense. I slipped away after that, wanting to avoid more of Jen's probing questions. As I mingled with the crowd, I couldn't help but wonder what it'd be like to live in the same town as Roth. I mean, I doubted he'd be here very much overall since his career would still involve being on tour and recording songs in Nashville. Still, I didn't know how I'd handle randomly running into him even occasionally, be it at the café, grocery store, or a party like this one.

After Christmas, Mrs. Cole had taken my mom and dad's suggestion of turning the café into a karaoke bar on Friday nights. I wasn't sure how they managed to convince her, but I had a blast the first night I attended.

To maybe everyone's surprise, Crawford City was busting at the seams with vocal talent. Naturally, most of the karaoke songs were country music, and you could tell from the high caliber performances that this was music that had been honed in this area for generations.

Karaoke night gradually transitioned into general music night, and it became a highly popular event. By March, instead of using CDs and digital files, we had a full band that could basically play anything from old-time country to the most modern pop songs.

Since my parents and I had been singing karaoke together since my childhood and pulled me into the fray at a young age, I enjoyed performing myself. I gravitated toward eighties and nineties classic pop and even some of the country-pop crossover artists like Garth Brooks and Amelia Denton. I took song requests, too, and thankfully, no one ever requested that I sing one of Roth's songs. I didn't think I'd be able to get through one without choking up, even after all this time since our breakup, and even though I knew all the words to every song he'd recorded.

By the Fourth of July, the entire town had decided to take karaoke night to a whole new level. Soon we'd be holding the inaugural Crawford City Singing Carnival in the park downtown, located just down the street from the library.

Doc, ever the Crawford City promoter, and I volunteered to organize the event. The town council readily agreed to streamline the permitting process after being informed the carnival would serve as a fundraiser for the town budget, which would also increase my typically meager library budget. Thankfully, we already had at our disposal a large tent and stage typically used during the annual Labor Day community potluck, so our event expenses remained fairly low.

The high level of talent in our community continued to surprise me. It seemed like being onstage at karaoke nights had bolstered everyone's confidence that much more and so the event was a huge success. Being the carnival's co-organizer, I'd been running nonstop all day and was just about to sit down for a much-needed rest between performances when the crowd began chanting my name. "Chris sing Garth! Chris sing Garth!"

That was a pretty common occurrence on karaoke nights at the café, and I secretly loved it. "Okay, okay," I said as I climbed the stairs to the stage. "The Dance," I said to Claude, the lead guitarist in the band.

As I launched into the emotional song, several couples stood up and began to dance. That was also pretty common on karaoke nights. I never sang more than a couple songs at a time, and since my first choice usually resulted in slow dances breaking out, I usually tried to follow it with something a little more upbeat.

Just as I was coming to the end of the song, Roth stepped out of the shadows and stood directly in front of me below the stage. I could tell the heartfelt words were hitting him and as a result, I hiccupped on the final line.

Everyone listening heard me falter and looked to where I was staring. The moment they recognized Roth, the crowd descended on him. I was just about to dash off the stage, and hopefully get the hell out of the performance tent, when I heard Roth ask, "But is the dance over?"

That stopped me in my tracks, and I looked out to where the crowd had parted around him. "Is the dance over for us, Chris?" he asked again, referencing the song's heartbreaking message of love and loss.

"Did it ever really begin?" I asked, and blushed when I realized I'd just said that in public.

He looked suddenly unsure, like my question caught him off guard, and he shrugged. That was when it hit me, two could play at this game. "Play 'Here You Come Again,'" I whispered to Claude.

As soon as the music started, I walked down the stairs, never taking my eyes off Roth as I began singing about an ex seeing their old flame. The man shocked me when he took the microphone from my hand to sing the second verse. We continued like that, matching each other verse for verse, until the end when we sang the last two lines together.

We sang in such harmony that it sounded as if we'd practiced it as a duet.

We stood staring at each other as the crowd around us erupted in cheers. Roth tossed the microphone to Claude onstage, then grabbed my hand and pulled me out of the tent.

"I'm sorry to sneak up on you like this," he said, not letting go of my hand as we walked.

"I knew it was only a matter of time before we'd see each other in town. You bought the Crawford mansion, after all."

Our brisk walk came to an abrupt halt. "H-how did you know that?" he asked.

I smirked. "Because Jake and Jen suck at keeping a secret like that. Neither of them told me outright, but I can read body language and those two are terrible at being discreet."

He laughed, which helped ease some of the remaining tension I'd been feeling. "But you still helped with the historical design. Jake showed me the 3D model you had made from the old photos. It's amazing, and pretty much exactly how I want the place to look when it's finished."

"I'm glad to have helped. It's been a treat watching the old place come back to life, and I should thank you for being the one to make it happen," I said, pausing to look down at our intertwined fingers. "You know, I don't hate you, Roth. I've never hated you. It's just complicated."

We walked toward the library, then sat on the little bench I'd had installed under a huge oak tree near the corner of the building.

"If you don't hate me, why would you never return my calls or texts?"

I took a deep breath. "Roth, we're not cut from the same cloth. You're a famous singer and I'm a small-town librarian. How could that work long-term with you being gone for weeks and months at a time? Looking at your face on magazine covers in the library doesn't count as me seeing you."

"This is an old argument. I thought we overcame this."

I shook my head. "No, you convinced me to ignore it. It was hard enough for me when you were just becoming more famous. But Roth, when all the commotion happened after Amsterdam and the media was having a field day at your expense, I realized I just can't be a part of your life, not as your partner. Cameras stuck in your face. People screaming your name. At first, I admit I thought you were guilty of cheating on me with those prostitutes, but after I calmed down and thought about it, it just didn't seem like you. I'm sorry I didn't believe you or give you a chance to explain, and that's on me. But I still felt hurt by the whole thing, and it didn't change the fact that you and I have incompatible lifestyles."

Roth sighed. "I figured that's what was going on. I just wish you felt like you could've talked to me instead of avoiding me. You shutting me out was the worst part of all of it."

I gave up trying to put on a brave face and let a teardrop I'd barely been holding back drip from my eye. Roth cupped the side of my face and brushed it away with his thumb. "Not a day has gone by that I haven't waged an internal war with myself about letting you go. I missed you so much at first, it felt like my heart might literally break in half. If I didn't break it off like I did, I knew I'd just be creating a revolving door of heartache for myself. Roth, honey, I can't live like that. It'd end up a mess the moment the press found out about you and me. The fulfilling little life I've built for myself here would come crashing down around me. Can't you see that?"

I could hear myself pleading. I needed him to understand and not push me. If he did, I was sure I'd give in and come to regret it.

Roth sat back with a sigh. "I understand, I really do. That's why I tried to shield you from it as best I could, but clearly it wasn't enough. I wish the circumstances could be different."

"Me too," I replied.

"I promised to perform at the carnival tonight. I hope you don't mind, but I went through Doc, and he scheduled me last-minute as the closing performer. We need to talk more, though, 'cause I'm going to be in town a lot now that my tour is over."

"It'll all be okay," I said, and stood as he did. "Welcome back to Crawford City, Roth."

We looked at each other for several long moments before we embraced. Roth pulled back, but kept his arms around me. I couldn't help it, I just needed one last kiss. One last time to feel his soft lips caressing mine.

Without thinking, I leaned into him, capturing his mouth. He let out a surprised gasp, then took charge.

The kiss was hot and intense as we unleashed months of pent-up passion and stifled feelings for each other.

I broke our kiss before it had a chance to break me. I rested my hand on Roth's chest and hiccupped the tears back as they began to flow uncontrollably.

"I'm going to head home," I said, taking a step back.

Roth nodded and sighed sadly before he turned and walked back toward the event.

I wiped my eyes and turned in the opposite direction toward home. Movement out of the corner of my eye caught my attention just then and I saw Lorna Bailey driving by in her car. She slowed and rolled the window down, flashing a creepy smile at me.

Somehow, I knew she'd caught sight of Roth and me kissing. "Damn," I whispered. I only hoped we'd been shaded enough under the old tree that she hadn't been able to make out who exactly I'd been kissing.

My heart was beating hard despite my hopes. I more or less sprinted to the cabin and rushed up to my bedroom. I kicked my shoes off and crawled into my bed fully clothed, safely back in my sanctuary. Fully expecting that I'd dream of the man who had just walked back into my life and turned it upside down, I cried myself to sleep.

THIRTY-TWO

ROTH

OF ALL THE SCENARIOS that went through my head of how seeing Chris again might go, ranging from him throwing library books at me to swooning in my arms like an actress in some old black-and-white movie, how it actually played out was probably as good as it could've gone realistically.

I understood. I didn't like it, but I did understand. Dealing with the press and the paps could still be a lot for me, and I'd gotten fairly used to it. And that was with a very intense manager in the form of my no-nonsense sister and bodyguards to keep me from having to deal with them much, at least not directly.

When I mentioned all that to Zania, Lettie, Jesse and Jen later that night, they offered their support, and then Jen reminded me that the paparazzi drove Princess Diana to her death. I mean, I was no Princess Di, but her point about the vultures with cameras was well taken, especially considering what happened in Amsterdam.

After I'd given the BBC interview about the incident, there'd been a huge break in the investigation. The private investigator we'd hired had helped authorities uncover an unregulated prostitution ring run out of the hotel. They had shady ties to the event company hired by the arena where I'd performed and some unscrupulous Dutch media outlets with closely associated sister companies in the US.

Apparently, the Dutch authorities had been investigating it all for some time and I hadn't been the first celebrity targeted in that way, but my case helped put all of the pieces together, partly because I'd been so vocal about it. Years of litigation awaited, both overseas and in the States since the feds had launched their own investigation into the sister US media companies, but I felt satisfied that at least what I went through wouldn't happen to any more unsuspecting famous guests at that hotel.

Jen sat next to me, put her arm around my shoulders, and side-hugged me. "Honey, you are moving here, give it time. Once the celebrity stuff wears off a bit, he'll probably come around."

"Provided you're still interested," Zania said, causing us all to look at her.

She shrugged. "What? It's not like he's John Boyega or anything."

"Oh my god, are you still going on about John Boyega?" Lettie said, causing me to laugh.

Zania had met the *Star Wars* actor while we were in the UK and had been obsessed with the poor man ever since.

As Lettie and Zania argued about her celebrity crush, I snuck into Jesse's kitchen and poured myself a glass of wine. I hadn't let myself drink anything other than bottled water that I could twist the sealed top off since the Amsterdam incident. Being drugged once was enough for a lifetime.

I also didn't like how alcohol slowed me down the next day, but now that I had a break, I figured I deserved to spoil myself a bit.

Jen came in behind me and held her glass out for me to fill.

"So, are you okay?" she asked.

I shook my head and willed myself not to become emotional in front of my brother's girlfriend.

"You know, they're never going to get it, not totally. Even Lettie and Zania, they don't know what it's like to have cameras pointed in their faces or have their every move watched. In our line of work, there's so many people expecting you to either give them your time and attention, or waiting for you to slip up just so they can delight in raking you over the coals. Either way, it takes a lot out of a person."

I took a seat on the stool across from her and we both just sat silently for a moment. "I get why Chris can't handle the spotlight, but famous people keep their spouses hidden from public view all the time," Jen said. "I mean, look at Amelia Denton. She's been a star for longer than any of us have been alive, and I still have no idea what her husband looks like. Come to think of it, I don't think I even know his name."

"You're an Amelia fan?" I asked, surprised. Jen, the few times we'd hung out, listened to loud European techno music. Not homespun country.

"Of course, I am. I did grow up here, you know. But more so as the years have gone on. She stands up for what's right. Not many people do that, especially if it could hurt their career. I respect that."

"Yeah, me too," I said. "Do you ever regret pursuing the spotlight?"

Jen looked at me, then down at her hands. "I mean, yeah, sometimes. I'm at the end of my career. Thirty-something is the downward slide for a model, and I've got no illusions about doing this forever. I think about all that I missed, but I got a lot out of it too. Not just my career, but also real friends I can contact at any time and who'd drop everything to support me if I needed it. I've met people I'd never have met otherwise, including famous people and even royalty. I mean, that's cool. Had I remained here in Crawford City or even moved to Nashville, I'd have missed all those opportunities."

"Is it worth losing the love of your life over?" I asked, unable to hold the tears back. My heart felt crushed as I felt the weight of everything Chris had said tonight.

"If he's not able to make a concession for your life, then he's probably not the man for you, honey," Jen said. "But I really think he will. He's just afraid. I've seen pictures of what went down in Amsterdam, and that had to have scared him. Just give him time. If you want a relationship with him, that's the best thing you can do."

Our talk gave me a little hope, even if it was just a small amount. I pondered what it'd be like to live here in Crawford City without fear of rabid fans mobbing me or paps popping out of bushes. Would I trade in all the fame and fortune for the easier life? A life with Chris?

Despite the stage fright, I'd dreamed of being a professional singer since I'd been a little boy. I'd had to overcome a lot just to go on stage, but as I'd proven to myself over the past year, even my crippling fears couldn't hold me back from achieving my dream.

Could I really give all of that up for the man I loved? Would I truly be satisfied, creatively or otherwise, only singing in the shower, at a few local festivals, and at karaoke night at the café once a week? Those were rhetorical questions, because I already knew the answer, a resounding no.

That being said, I still loved being here in Crawford City. Watching neighbor helping and snooping on neighbor in equal measure. Everyone being up in each other's business, but mostly with genuine concern and affection behind it. I loved the people in this small town and even without living here full-time, I felt like a full-fledged member of the community.

I didn't know if it was possible to have both, my dream and the man of my dreams, but damned if I wasn't going to try. Hopefully, I could convince Christopher Asbell to try with me.

Thirty-Three

Chris

Following the carnival, I saw Roth pretty-much daily, and emotions simmered a bit after that first encounter. I could see him without wanting to weep. I'd managed to convince myself that was progress.

It seemed like the whole town was playing matchmaker, though. They were also fiercely protective of Roth since he'd arrived. When anyone pulled a phone out in his vicinity, someone would step between Roth and the camera. At first, I thought it was coincidence, but it soon became obvious that protecting his privacy had become a community effort.

I noticed other things, too. When Roth was in the café, for example, he was almost always seated in the back near Mrs. Cole's emergency exit. If any out-of-towners were in the café and seemed to recognized Roth, a group of locals would surround him, blocking him from view and affording him the opportunity to slip out the back unnoticed.

The group effort had become so coordinated that if you weren't in the know, it just looked like that part of the restaurant was crowded. Such were the lengths the people in this town went to, in showing how much they valued and cared about one another.

Even though Roth and I weren't a couple, it made me proud of Crawford City that its citizens could and would protect one of their own.

Roth stayed away from the library and if he visited Doc and Amos, it was when I wasn't around. So, besides seeing each other from a distance, we were able to avoid direct interaction.

Was I happy about that? I'd be lying if I said I didn't hate it. I missed him terribly and dreamed about him all the time. Almost every morning I'd wake up with him on my mind. When I wasn't asleep, I was thinking about him. I'd be in the middle of working and suddenly wonder how he was doing, how he was feeling, what all he had going on that day. It was almost as if I was stuck on love and nothing I could do would switch my mind back to seeing him as a friend. Not that I'd only ever thought of him as a friend, if I were being totally honest.

Todd came into the library two weeks after Roth's return and asked if I could help consult on some of the historical finishes on the Crawford mansion.

"I don't know, Todd. I mean, I really don't want to get in the middle of Roth's business, ya know? The jig is up, we all know he's the new owner, and he's back in town so he can decide all that stuff."

Todd sighed. "You know, Chris, I avoided Ash for years and we lost a lot of good years because I was an idiot. I would hate if you were making the same mistake with Roth."

I smiled, but it was forced. Ash had said basically the same thing to me a couple of days before. They both had my best interests at heart, I knew that, but only I knew exactly how I felt about the situation. "I know what you're saying, Todd, but I'm a simple guy. I'm not made for globetrotting and fancy parties and dodging paparazzi while they're snapping my picture every time I walk down the street."

"Do you see them snapping his picture right now?" Todd asked.

"Not blatantly, but they are. Just the other day while watching TV, I saw photos of him going into the café. One of those stupid *celebrities are just like us* segments. So, the paps might not be in town, but someone's taking his picture and selling it to the media."

"You should talk to Lettie," Todd said quietly, looking around to make sure no one else was within earshot. "Roth's team is leaking pictures to the press in an agreement to keep everyone else at bay. It's some sort of agreement Lettie concocted to give Roth some peace. It goes to show there's always a workaround, even if it's not perfect."

I patted Todd on the shoulder and thanked him. It was sweet that he was concerned. Since I'd moved into the cabin with his dads, he and Ash had become a second family to me. Truth be told, Mom and Dad had all but adopted Amos and Doc as their family too.

It felt good to have a friendship with Todd and Ash that resembled what I guessed an older sibling relationship would feel like.

"Oh, Todd, why don't you have Lance come by to look through all the historical stuff with me. I can show him the reference section with all of my research notes on the property."

Todd nodded, but I could tell he was disappointed I didn't just agree to meet with the Crawford House Team, as they called themselves. Lance, Tom, Jake, when he was in town, Todd and his righthand man Linc, Amos, and even Doc met weekly to discuss the progress on the house and the property overall. Occasionally, Jesse would sit in for his brother, but now that Roth was back in town, he'd filled that seat himself. Even my dad had gotten involved, helping rehab the gardens as part of Amos's landscape crew. Shortly after Dad and Mom moved to town, Dad had gone to work for Amos full-time. So, it was a bit strange my father was doing the gardens of my... well, whatever Roth was to me.

I used to sit in on those team meetings, too, but now with Roth attending, I decided to keep my distance and only consult when someone needed me. I missed the camaraderie of it, though.

Todd said his goodbye and headed out the door. He was no-nonsense and did a much better job than Ash, and especially Jen, at taking my no for an answer.

Jen spent most of her time in Crawford City these days. She would occasionally fly off to some exotic part of the world for a photoshoot or fashion show, but for the most part, she stayed put. She and I had actually become pretty good friends. I mean, we didn't spend a lot of time together, mostly because I didn't have a lot of time, but that didn't stop her from dropping by the library every freaking day, as she'd done for months, to update me on how Roth was doing. His moving back here had done nothing to stop her.

Some days it took everything in me not to tell her to buzz off, but I could tell if I ever did, I would see the ugly side of my friend very quickly.

"Jen," I said when she walked in to give her daily update. "Looking out the window, I can literally see Roth standing across the street right now. You don't need to fill me in on his every movement today."

She squinted her assessing eyes at me, which I'd learned over the months to ignore, even though it still made me squirm uncomfortably inside. "If you can see him standing there, why haven't you gone over to talk to him?"

"Um, I'm working. Just because I don't have a line of patrons at the circulation desk doesn't mean I'm not busy."

"Bullshit," she said, with no concern or regard for anyone in the library. Of course, everyone in town adored her, so if anyone got shushed in this conversation, I had no doubt it would be me.

I sighed and went back to organizing books behind the counter. I could feel her staring at the back of my head, willing me to turn around, but I could match stubborn for stubborn.

"You really should give him a chance," she said after an awkward amount of time.

"I have and it didn't work out."

"So, give him another one."

I laughed. "Jen, just because you've got goo-goo eyes for his brother doesn't mean everyone is looking for or ready for love."

When I glanced at her, she stuck her tongue out at me, making me laugh again.

Finally, she sighed and leaned on the counter. "He's such a good guy, Chris, and he really cares about you. I know you care about him too. It's just a shame you two can't make it work."

"Love isn't for everyone, Jen. I never thought I'd settle down with someone, if I'm honest. I'm a loner, and I've always been that way. Roth is a great guy, I would never dispute that, but I don't see a reality where he and I can ever be, um... a thing."

She shook her head and straightened back up. "I think you're a blooming fool, Christopher Asbell. Throwing a man like Roth Gallo away is stupid and careless. I'm not talking about him being a famous or a talented musician. He is a quality person, one who I know could make you happy if you would just get out of your own way for both your sakes. But it is your life."

She turned then and headed out of the library. Even when she was upset, she was regal and beautiful. She was also forthright and tough as freaking nails, and I felt the sting of her words.

I closed up the library after she left, plopped down in my office chair, and thought about what she'd said. Was I a fool? Maybe, but I was not so much of a fool as to get involved with a man who was unavailable most of the time, and who, through no fault of his own, could cause me to lose everything I'd worked so hard for. But as I replayed the broken record of excuses of why I'd broken things off with Roth, the flimsier it all sounded even in my own head.

That night, I tossed and turned, unable to get Jen's words out of my head. The following day, I didn't have to be at work until the afternoon, so I got up early and ran down to the barber to get my hair cut. James Pipkin usually arrived early at his shop. He'd told me back when I was trying to run the library by myself, if I needed a haircut, he could squeeze me in even if the shop was closed. Just knock on the door until he came out.

After he cleaned me up and made me look presentable again, I rushed home and got ready. If I was going to do this, I was going to look my best.

Yes, I was going to do it. Sometime around dawn, I'd awoken and finally realized I was indeed a fool, just as Jen had accused me of being. I was head over heels in love with Roth, and if he could manage to live in a small town without people harassing him, surely they wouldn't give a damn about a nerdy librarian. A lightbulb of understanding had switched on for me in realizing I'd been trying to solve a problem that didn't even exist yet.

After getting cleaned up and sprucing my hair up, taking advantage of Mr. Pipkin's talent as a barber, I darted out of the house and up the street toward the café, where I fully intended to snag one of Mrs. Cole's huge cinnamon rolls to woo him with, I hoped it wasn't too late for us. I'd certainly understand if he'd moved on, since I'd all but kept him at arm's length since he'd arrived, but he'd forgive me.

When I neared the cafe, I saw a crowd gathered outside of the library. Shit, I hoped my assistant Caroline was okay. I quickly rushed over and was about to dart up the stairs to check on her when I heard someone shout, "Hey, there he is!"

I looked around to see who they were talking about, then turned back to see about fifteen cameras stuck in my face. Then the question onslaught began.

"Chris, how long have you and Roth Gallo been dating?" someone yelled out.

"Chris, will you be living together in his new mansion?" another asked.

"Chris, do you and Roth have a third lover?" someone else shouted.

The mob of bodies and cameras had me surrounded before I registered what was happening. The paparazzi had descended on my town, and they knew my name and where I worked. I began backing up but stumbled into more of them.

Then someone grabbed me, making me trip backward, and I ended up landing on my hand as I hit the sidewalk hard. Pain rushed up my arm as I cried out in agony. Cameras continued to snap my picture until I heard a familiar voice demanding the crowd disperse. I looked up to see Darren, Sheriff Cross's deputy, looking every bit the authority figure.

"Who injured this man?" he asked, and the cameras immediately stopped snapping. He kneeled down to me but didn't touch my arm.

"Sheriff Cross, I'm requesting backup," he said, speaking into a handheld radio. "I witnessed a group of people accost our librarian out in front of the library. He's injured and I need to get him over to the clinic to see Doc Ash. We've got at least twenty people here who need to be questioned."

I heard mumbling as the crowd began to try and disperse, and then the voice of Sheriff Cross, along with the other deputy, telling everyone to freeze.

My hand was screaming in pain, but Darren managed to help me get up. No one was snapping pictures now, as I heard the sheriff giving strict orders for everyone to remain in place while I was escorted away.

"Are you okay?" he asked me after we crossed the street.

"No, it feels like I did a number on my hand," I said, cradling it against my chest to keep it from moving.

By the time we reached the clinic, my head was spinning. "What happened back there?" I asked the deputy when he sat down next to me in the waiting room.

"No idea, but Sheriff Cross will get to the bottom of it. Did you see their faces when she told them to freeze?" He chuckled a bit.

"No, I was eating pavement at that point. I heard the woman who pulled me down loud and clear, though."

"Thank God we were just finishing breakfast at the café, or I'm not sure what those vultures might've done."

I shuddered at the thought. Of course, that just caused my hand to throb even more.

Within a few moments, Ash showed up and asked me to come on back to the exam room. I was poked, prodded, x-rayed, and determined to have a fracture. Ultimately, I was given a cast and drugged. Ash also informed me I wouldn't be going back to work anytime soon, at least not to sling books around like usual.

The sheriff herself escorted me home, and although the paparazzi were still milling around, no one dared snap a picture as I was driven back to the cabin. Sheriff Cross told me she'd given all of them a warning and threatened to arrest them for assault if they tried anything like that again.

She had confiscated their cameras and said, in glancing through the images, many of them showed me being pulled down and everyone continuing to photograph me instead of helping. "That's against the law," she said. "As far as I'm concerned, they are all guilty of assault and if they act like that again, we'll begin the process of arresting them. We did arrest the woman who actually put her hands on you and caused you to fall."

I sighed. "What's this mess about? Why are they all here?" I asked. I could feel the meds beginning to kick in and I didn't know how coherent I'd be for much longer, but I wanted to know.

"No one would say, but I'm guessing someone got wind of you and Roth," she said sadly.

"Then why aren't they snapping his pictures?" I asked, though I wouldn't have wished what I'd just experienced on him or anyone else.

She shrugged. "I'm sure they are, or would if he was out. We called his security detail as soon as all this went down, and his bodyguards are on full alert. I doubt anyone will be getting much access to him for now."

"Damn," I said, but that was about all I had in me. With Doc's help, I went up the stairs immediately after getting home and crawled into my bed. "I'll check on you later," he told me, then disappeared.

I didn't remember falling asleep or much of anything else, except waking up to Mom sitting next to my bed, rubbing my head. "Hi, honey," she said when I opened my eyes.

"Hi, Mom. Why are you here?" I asked.

"Well, Amos called and said you had an accident and broke your hand. So, naturally, we came to check on you. Your dad is downstairs."

Doc came in then and said I needed to take my next dose if I wanted to avoid another nasty rush of throbbing pain, so I sat up and swallowed the pill.

When I'd downed all the water, I handed the glass to Mom and lay back down.

"Mom, you don't need to be here. Ash says it's just a small fracture, it'll be fine."

"But it probably won't be fine for you, not here at least," I heard my dad say as he entered the room.

I propped myself back up. "What do you mean?"

"I guess someone took a picture of you and Roth kissing. It was broadcast on TV , and that's why those photographers showed up in town. Considering they just attacked you like a pack of wild dogs, it's a serious situation now," Mom said, concern etched on her face.

"So, what can I do? Hide here in my room until it all blows over? Ash says I need to take it easy for a while anyway."

"Sheriff Cross and Roth's security team have advised us to get you out of town for a while."

"But my job? I mean, I can't be shoving full book carts around, but I've still got a library to run. I can't just leave," I said, thinking maybe this was all being blown out of proportion.

"We've got that handled," Doc said. "I've already talked to Mrs. Elliot at the library and she's going to cover for you. Between her and your assistant, Caroline, they'll keep the place running smoothly."

"Where will I go?"

"Well, word has traveled fast about what happened. Jake called and offered up the condo he still owns in Nashville for as long as you need," Doc said. "The place has good security already, and no one would think to look for you there anyway."

I sighed, feeling frustrated and tired. "So, I guess I should pack?"

"No," Mom said. "I already did it. Sheriff Cross is downstairs waiting, and she and her deputy are going to tail us to the county line. If anyone follows, they can be pulled over for interfering with law enforcement escort."

"That's good, I guess."

I was still too high to fully comprehend what was happening or to complain too much. My parents helped me down the stairs and into their car. I fell asleep on the drive and only vaguely remember waking up outside what I assumed was Jake's condo, and being led to a bed.

It wasn't until the next day, when I woke up late in the afternoon, that the impact of all that had happened hit me, along with the throbbing pain in my hand.

I got up, came down the hall to the kitchen, and sat down on the stool across from where Mom was cooking. Apparently, my parents had plans to stay here with me, at least for a while, which was comforting.

"Morning, honey," she said, and came over to kiss my head.

"Morning. So, have you heard anything new about all this?" I asked.

She sighed. "Roth came by about an hour ago. He's worried about you."

I took a deep breath and let it out slowly. "Is he coming back?" I asked.

She shook her head. "No, I don't think so. He seemed pretty upset and just wanted us to tell you he was sorry he got you dragged into this. I'm not sure, but I think he might be staying at his parents' place across town. He didn't say and I didn't ask."

I put my good hand up to my forehead and rubbed. It was the move I tended to make when I was stressed and unsure what to do.

"Mom, I was headed to his place to talk with him and see if we could make up. On the way, I saw the crowd at the library, which obviously derailed my big plan."

She looked at me thoughtfully while she stirred what smelled like soup on the stove.

Finally, she said, "Honey, I think that's probably a good idea, considering you're in love with him."

"Mom, I never told you..."

She laughed. "You didn't need to tell me or anyone else for that matter. Anyone can see you've been moping about for a long time, and everyone who knows you both clearly understands Roth is the cause."

"You don't think we're too different? That our lifestyles won't mesh?"

She chuckled. "Well, you do have different lifestyles, but you have a lot more in common than not."

I looked at her funny. Maybe the drugs were affecting my head. "Mom, what do Roth and I have in common?"

She set the spoon down on the little saucer she kept near the stove, put the lid on the pot, and sat on the stool next to mine. "Baby, you love music and even sing karaoke nearly every week. He's a singer. He's a professional, but if you'd wanted that, you could've had that too."

I laughed. "I doubt that."

"I don't. I know I'm your mother, but trust me, if you couldn't carry a tune in a water bucket, I'd have told you. You've always had a crystal-clear voice, Chris. That's why you had a shelf full of singing competition trophies in your room growing up. You could've taken it further if you'd wanted, but books were always your real passion."

"So, okay, we can both sing and we both like to perform. That's not enough to build a life around."

"Perhaps not, but you also both love books. Look at how many hours he put in at the library, volunteering for you for months on end."

"Everyone should like books," I countered, although I knew I was starting to sound obstinate. I couldn't deny that my mom had raised some good points, and I'd met dozens of happy couples in Crawford City who seemed to have even less in common than Roth and me.

"You both enjoy local history," Mom continued. "Look at how he's saving that old mansion in town, all because you said preserving it was important. You both love working with the public, you both have sweet, caring personalities, you both are family-oriented and keep us all close to you, as much as you can, at least. I hate to tell you this, sweetheart, but you and Roth are really quite perfect for each other."

I stared at her through watery eyes, and didn't even try to stop the tears from rolling down my face. "I miss him so much, Mom."

"I know, sweetie," she said as she gently guided my head to rest on her shoulder. "I'm pretty sure he misses you as much."

"How do you know?" I asked.

Before Mom could answer, Dad came up behind me and slid one arm across Mom's shoulders and the other across mine. "Son, he's told us he misses you, desperately. Quite frankly, I think he's told anyone who'll listen."

That just caused me to cry even harder. "I should call him."

Mom and Dad held onto me a moment longer, then Mom said, "Why don't you take your painkiller, get some more rest, and let us invite him over for dinner. I'm making chicken noodle soup because that helps heal all that ails you."

For generations, my family had turned to homemade chicken noodle soup to deal with anything from the common cold to broken bones and sprains. I should've known she'd be making that for me today.

"Thanks, Mom. Thanks, Dad. I love you guys," I said, and leaned into their hugs once more.

I popped a pain pill and went back to bed to get a little more rest. I was so tired, not just from the injury, but from the emotional upheaval that'd been a part of my life since I'd met Roth, most of it my own doing. Sleep, and knowing my parents were just down the hall if I needed them, seemed to be what I needed most right now.

Thirty-Four

Roth

I FELT UTTERLY MISERABLE. The very thing Chris said he didn't want to happen did, right in the middle of little Crawford City, right in front of his library. Lettie, Jake, and my record label were all working overtime to determine what exactly had happened and why.

It didn't take long for them to unearth a picture of Chris and me kissing on the bench outside the library. The picture was already sweeping across social media, with more than a few nasty trolls calling me a fraud and a liar about being gay, and a few TV entertainment news shows had broadcast it as well.

Of course, if those trolls had cared to look a little closer rather than make assumptions, they'd have seen I'd never lied about being gay. In countless interviews, I'd deflected questions about my sexuality and specifically said it wasn't relevant to my career. More than once, I'd told reporters flat-out that it was no one's business but my own, and I still felt that way.

"You need to contact Chris and work out how you're going to deal with this," Jake told me, his usual playful personality now all business. "I'll try to talk to him to-morrow. I offered him my condo in Nashville, and he'll be staying there with his parents until this dies down a bit. Seriously, you both need to talk and soon. We need to get a jump on this before we can't contain it. Right now, it's just a news flash and everyone's enjoying the buzz, but if you aren't sitting in front of some interviewer in the next twenty-four hours, it's going to explode and not likely in a good way."

I nodded. Jake had already told me that when I came out of the closet publicly, I'd need to be prepared for the press to zero in on it, at least at first. Luckily, other country stars had been coming out lately, so it wasn't nearly as big of a deal as it would have been even a few years ago.

I felt prepared to face reporters. What I hadn't pre-pared for was how Chris would be sucked into the fray.

I'd shown up early the following morning at Jake's Nashville condo, and after Chris's parents invited me in for coffee, it became clear that Chris wouldn't be waking up anytime soon. After chatting with them for a bit, I drove to my parents' house to see if they could offer a bit of advice.

"You've got to be yourself, honey," Mom said after I explained the situation.

"I'm not sure Chris is very interested in me being myself," I said miserably. "I feel fortunate he's even talking to me at this point. Well, he was, sort of, before he got injured. Now, who knows?"

"That's not the kind of man your sister and brother have described," my father weighed in. "From what they've told us about Chris, he's smart, kind and understanding. If that's the case, he'll work with you to sort through this."

"You missed the part where he dreaded being caught up in any paparazzi madness. And that was only regarding having his picture taken, not being thrown to the ground and breaking bones."

Dad looked concerned. "Have they ever done that to you?" he asked.

I shook my head. "No, nothing like that. The paps have gotten too close for comfort a few times, but that's why I have bodyguards. The sheriff thinks the person who grabbed Chris hasn't been in the business long enough to know you photograph but don't touch. She's already been charged and will have to appear in court, provided Chris wants to press charges."

"I'm glad you have security," Dad said. "But you probably need to provide some security for Chris now, too, at least until this blows over."

I nodded. "Lettie is already on it. As soon as Chris okays it, we'll have a detail staying with him around the clock."

"Good boy," Mom said, and patted my leg.

I was just about to get up and head back to my old bedroom when my phone rang. Chris's dad was calling. He and I had exchanged numbers before I left the condo this morning. He had promised to send me updates on Chris's health, if nothing else, after seeing how concerned I'd been.

"Hello," I said, feeling my heart begin to race.

"Hi, Roth, It's Brandon, Chris's dad."

"Hi, Mr. Asbell. Is Chris okay?"

"Yeah, he's fine. We would like to invite you over for dinner tonight. Joanne's made chicken noodle soup, and we'll probably have grilled cheese sandwiches too. Nothing fancy, but Chris would like to see you."

"Yeah, I'd like to come," I answered quickly. "What time?"

I could hear the amusement in Mr. Asbell's voice, when he replied, "How about five. Chris is sleeping now, which is good for healing, but I'm guessing he'll be up by then."

"Thank you, sir." Then, before I forgot my manners, I asked, "Should I bring something?"

"No, son," he said, his deep chuckle resonating over the phone. "Just bring yourself."

I spent the rest of the day freaked out and excited at the same time. I was convinced this was it. Chris was going to yell at me about messing up his life and getting him injured. Then he'd likely tell me to get lost and never come within fifty feet of him again. And yet, I clung to a tiny shred of hope that maybe the opposite would happen.

Despite my overall dread, I couldn't help but feel excited about seeing him. Even if it proved to be one of the worst nights of my life, at least it included spending time with him again. I felt that desperate to try to smooth this awful situation over as best I could, even if it was the final nail in the coffin regarding our relationship.

Seeing him in Crawford City for the past couple of weeks and not being able to touch him, feeling like I couldn't even talk to him, had been excruciating. I knew sharing a town with him, but having to keep my distance would be difficult, I just hadn't been ready for the pain to be so visceral. Despite the mansion project nearing completion, I began questioning if I'd be able to remain in Crawford City long-term if we couldn't even count each other as friends.

If things didn't improve between us, I had all but decided I'd try to sell Crawford House once we finished its restoration. Even if I lost money, I'd have at least saved a historically significant home, one that mattered to Chris and the community.

I pulled up to the condo around four thirty. I knew I was early, but I just couldn't help myself. I wanted to be in the same room with Chris again, even if it was awkward or tense as hell. Before I could knock, his father opened the door.

"Hey there, Roth," he said, and pulled me into a hug. I'd long ago realized that Tennessee folks fell into two categories: huggers and the *don't you dare touch me* people. I learned early on that Chris's mom and dad fit into the hugger category. My family fit into that as well, but I'd never gotten used to all the affection.

I smiled, though, and if Chris's dad was hugging me, that had to be a good sign.

As soon as we walked into the living room, Chris's mom, Joanne, came over smiling from ear to ear. "Oh, it's so good to see you, Roth," she said, giving me a hug as well. "Now, I put the sandwiches in the oven and put out saltines on the counter. You'll find the bowls and silverware easily enough. You just make yourself at home." She then grabbed her purse and the two of them walked toward the front door.

"You're leaving?" I asked, dumbfounded.

"Oh, you and Chris need some privacy. There's karaoke tonight over at Lula's Duck Club, that's where we'll be. We'll be home around nine, so y'all have the place to yourself till then. If you need us, you have Brandon's number."

Mr. Asbell pulled his wife out the door, and I wondered what she'd meant by all this. Not wanting to get my hopes up, I headed toward the kitchen, hoping to find Chris.

Instead, no one was there. I smiled when I saw the notes on the oven door about the grilled cheese sandwiches. There was also a note on the refrigerator in the same handwriting explaining to Chris that they'd left for karaoke, as well as a list of directions for heating up the soup and sandwiches.

I chuckled at the very motherly act of leaving those notes. My mom would've done the same.

I heard movement and turned around to see a very sleep-mussed Chris standing behind me.

"Hi," I said self-consciously. "Your mom and dad just left for karaoke."

"Really? Why didn't they wake me up?" he asked, and I shrugged.

"I'm guessing they were making way for us to talk."

"That sounds like them. I should've guessed they'd pull a stunt like this."

"Your mom made us dinner She left directions on how to heat up the soup and the sandwiches."

Chris looked over my shoulder and chuckled. "I've been out on my own off and on for over six years, but she still writes out cooking directions like I'm fourteen."

I laughed. "Once a mom of a teenager, always a mom of a teenager. Just ask mine."

"So, um, I need to get a shower. Can you entertain yourself for a minute while I clean up?" Chris asked.

"Yeah, sure," I said. As he turned to leave, I added, "Chris? I'm really sorry about what happened."

He turned back around and walked up to me, then pulled me into a hug. He felt so good in my arms. "It wasn't your fault, Roth. I should've anticipated it, now that I think about it. Maybe not a broken hand, but I should've been more on guard."

"Really? Why's that?"

He stepped back, breaking my hold. "Do you remember Lorna Bailey?"

"The woman who threw the bottle at us?" I asked.

He nodded. "Yep, that's her. On the Fourth of July, when we kissed under the oak tree, she drove past me smiling from ear to ear afterward. It creeped me out. I figured she'd probably seen us, but hoped she hadn't gotten a good look at you since the tree had shaded us. Anyway, thinking back now about her reaction, I can only assume she's the one who snapped a picture of us."

"I saw the picture. Apparently, she's got a good night-vision camera 'cause that image is about as clear as day."

Chris cringed. "I'm sorry, Roth. We should've been more careful. Is this going to cause you a lot of trouble with your career?"

"I mean, the picture was pretty hot," I said, and succeeded in getting a smile out of him. "Seriously though, no, I think my career will be fine. Jake thinks if we get ahead of it, it'll actually help."

Chris smiled, clearly relieved. "That's something goodish to come out of this mess."

Things got awkward then and Chris turned like he was about to leave, so I burst out, "I miss you so bad. I know you probably hate me, and I don't blame you if you do, but I've been in agony these last couple of weeks. Seeing you in town, but you ignoring me... it hurts."

Tears sprang from my eyes, and I should've been embarrassed to be making such a spectacle of myself, but I couldn't not tell him or show him how I felt any longer.

In two quick strides, Chris was in front of me, pulling me back into an embrace. "I could never hate you. I've missed you just as bad. I'm stupid and an idiot for not holding onto you with all my strength, because I love you that much, Roth. I know haven't shown you that enough, and pretended like I didn't care, but I've never stopped loving you. I should've grabbed ahold of you the night of the carnival and never let go."

"I love you too, baby," I whispered into his ear as I squeezed him tighter.

We stood like that for several moments, clinging to each other and letting our bodies speak for us, before Chris finally pulled away. "I know I stink. I really should go get a shower."

I laughed, then gave him a quick peck on the lips. "I've missed you, but I think I can give you enough time to shower. Meanwhile, I'm going to follow these very detailed directions your mom left and heat up the soup and sandwiches, which, just so you know, smell amazing!"

"Make sure she hears you say that," Chris said, laughing. "She's a terrific cook. I was a sickly kid, so she's mastered the whole chicken noodle soup thing too."

Chris kissed me again before disappearing down the hallway. The thought that he wasn't going to kick me out and was willing to have a conversation with me was exhilarating. That he'd admitted to still loving me and missing me just as much as I had him left me feeling like doing a victory dance. The evening had gone better than I'd dared hope, and all because I cut the bullshit and spoke from my heart. I'd do well to remember that.

For the moment, though, I had soup and sandwiches to reheat without burning the place down, so I focused on the directions.

Thirty-Five

Chris

W E'D MADE OUT FOR over an hour after talking through dinner, and now, mostly because we were anticipating my parents returning at any moment, we sat cuddled up on the oversized couch in the living room.

"You sure you're okay with coming on TV with me? I mean, they'll probably ask you all sorts of personal questions. It doesn't mean you have to answer anything you don't want to, though," Roth told me. "I can't promise anything, but once you've done a big interview and it has cycled through, the press and the paps will probably leave you alone. There's always someone more interesting, more famous, or more controversial to chase down."

"Yeah, being gay is so last year," I said, causing Roth to laugh out loud. "But, yes, I'm okay with joining you for the interview. As you said, I'll answer what I feel comfortable answering, and leave the rest."

"Jake and his assistant Charlie will run us through like a million roleplays so by the time it happens, you'll feel prepared. But when we're in the interview, if you ever feel uncomfortable, you can just lean on me, and I'll do most of the talking."

"Hey, I've been famous for what, a few days, and you're already trying to steal my limelight?" I said jokingly.

"Oh, no, you can have it all. This is the stuff I hate. In fact, why don't you do all my interviews from now on? I'll just go sing and make music. You know, do my actual job."

"Speaking of making music," I said shyly. "I love the song you wrote. The one you first recorded on your phone."

Roth grinned at me and kissed my temple. "You know it's your song, right?"

"I thought it might be. I'm sorry I couldn't get over my hang-up about the whole fame thing sooner," I said, not remembering my broken hand until I gestured with it, causing a jolt of pain to shoot through my arm.

Roth gently took my hand in his own and kissed it, then draped my arm back across my tummy.

"You were swarmed by a group of paps. I can't blame you for trying to run the other way."

I sighed and positioned myself so I could look him in the face. "I'm not going to run away ever again, Roth. I mean, I know we have a lot of work to do on us. We've been on and off again for so long, I want to take some time just getting to know each other again, as friends and boyfriends. So, I'm not expecting a marriage proposal, but I'm in this now. I'm committed to you and to us. In fact, when the mob descended on me, I was on my way to Mrs. Cole's. I'd planned to bribe you back into my life with one of her delicious cinnamon rolls."

"Really?" Roth asked, surprised. "I thought you were done with me for good."

"Honestly, I did, too, until your soon-to-be sister-in-law came over and knocked some sense into my head."

"Soon to be sister-in-law? Do you know something about Jen and Jesse that I don't?"

I laughed. "You have to know those two are about as close to being engaged as you can get without wearing a ring."

Roth chuckled. "I'm not sure Jesse knows that yet. Maybe I should talk to him. He's incredibly smart, but can also be surprisingly dense sometimes... like all of us, I guess."

"Well, Jen knows. Hell, she's looking at wedding magazines every damned time she comes in to harass me about you. Then I get the pleasure of reshelving them all after she leaves."

"Oh god, I can't wait to tell Lettie," Roth said, sounding practically giddy. "We're going to have so much fun with this."

"Siblings," I said, rolling my eyes as he chuckled. "I do owe Jen, though. She helped me see how stupid I was being. She really laid it on me, then paps accosted me the next day. It all made me realize that although what happened was scary, it's not anywhere near as scary as losing you."

Roth's smile contrasted with the tears in his eyes. "You never have to worry about that. I'm yours, Chris, for as long as you'll have me."

"Then we'll have each other for a long time 'cause I'm done with letting you go."

THIRTY-SIX

EPILOGUE—ROTH

ONE YEAR LATER

"**L**ADIES AND GENTLEMEN, I'D like to introduce you to my boyfriend, Christopher Asbell, who has graciously agreed to sing a duet with me tonight."

The crowd screamed as Chris shyly walked onstage to join me. There'd been a lot of hoopla around my sexy librarian ever since we publicly came out as boyfriends. That TV interview, which, in keeping my word, we'd done as an exclusive with the BBC interviewer Julia, had gone viral. The vast majority of my fans had embraced Chris while remaining respectful of our privacy, and my boyfriend slowly got comfortable having a tiny bit of limelight shined his way.

Jen had even talked him into doing a photoshoot with renowned British photographer Elenore Langdone. The photos were amazing, of course, because he was such a handsome man, but also because she captured him working in his element.

I used the stunning black-and-white photograph of him working in his library while sunbeams shone in on him for the cover of my latest album, titled *Love's Net*.

I'd written the first single, "Broken Yearning," shortly after Chris broke his hand in the paparazzi melee. I'd designed it as a duet with our voices in mind. The fact that he agreed to sing it publicly with me went to show how much progress we'd made in our relationship over the past year.

I think the fact that he was so handsome and could also sing so well shocked the nation, my record label included, and he kept being asked when he'd release his first album. He'd always just laugh and reply, "I'm a librarian, not a singer."

Unfortunately, his working the circulation desk at the Crawford City Library was still not a safe option for him, so he'd taken over running the newly added second-floor reference section that had recently opened thanks to a large donation from an anonymous donor.

Of course, Chris knew that donor was me, but he didn't complain. He loved expanding the regional history section in particular, including adding as much information about our new home as he could. There was more than enough money in the donation to ensure his position was safe while also funding a full-time librarian to work under him, ensuring the library would be open and functioning at full capacity for years to come.

The band began playing and my focus returned to the song I was about to perform for the first time in public with the love of my life.

"You are not an object to be tossed out or thrown away."

"You are not my imagination or a person just for play."

As we took turns with the verses, the crowd seemed to be holding their breath. I silently tooted my own horn that the song was good. Great, really. It perfectly encapsulated the love I had for this man, and singing it with him made me emotional every time.

Of course, tonight was not only special because of us singing it together, but also because of what I had planned afterward.

As the strong harmony ended, the two of us confessed our love once and for all. As the band quietly played the last part of the song again, I fell to one knee. A hush fell over the entire stadium.

"My sweet Chris, I have a very important question for you," I said and lifted the ring box out of my pocket with shaky hands. "In front of my band, my fans, our families backstage, and the rest of the world, please do me the honor of becoming my forever duet partner. Will you marry me?"

Chris looked down at me in shock, wiped at a tear, then winked at me before looking out at the audience and asking, "Should I say yes?"

The crowd's response was deafening as they all screamed "Yes!" in unison.

When the noise died down, Chris, who had begun laughing and crying at the same time, said, "The fans have voted, and I concur. Yes, my love, I will marry you!"

The stadium erupted in cheers as I slid the ring on his finger and we kissed, then rushed off the stage to take a quick break before I had to finish the final set of my show.

"Was that too much, baby?" I asked.

"Of course, but I would've expected nothing less," Chris said, and kissed me again. "Now, go finish wooing your fans while I go show off this ring to our families."

Chris had never looked so happy, and it felt as if I floated back onto the stage to the cheers that hadn't stopped since we'd walked off. The crescendo of noise indicated my fans had noticed my return, and grinning from ear to ear as I strode across the stage, while my band started playing the song I'd written for Chris following the Amsterdam incident. Chris, my love, my fiancé, my future husband.

I smiled as I caught sight of him walking toward our families, who were sitting in a cordoned-off section of the arena near the stage, with security placed around them. They all looked like they'd been crying happy tears, especially Lettie, which almost had me getting choked up mid-song. My sister and I had been through so much together since I'd begun my professional career in music, and I couldn't imagine having succeeded like this without her.

In fact, I wouldn't have been up onstage at all, singing about my love and feeling the happiest I'd ever been, were it not for that small group of the most important people in my life, plus a handful of dear friends back in Crawford City. At different points in my life and in their own ways, my family, my fiancé and his parents, and my friends had all taken me into their hearts, embraced me as theirs, and made me feel like I truly belonged. *They were my home.*

The Coming Home Series will continue with
Returning Home

To be notified of this release and others, sign up for
Blake's newsletter at

https://blakeallwood.com/signup

Join Blake's email list to get advance notice of new books and receive his occasional newsletter:

www.blakeallwood.com

MM Romance
By Blake Allwood

Transitions Series
Aiden Inspired
Suzie Empowered (MF Romance)
Bobby Transformed

Chance Series
Love By Chance
Another Chance With Love
Taking A Chance For Love

Romantic Series
Romantic Renovations (1)
Romantic Rescue (2)
Romantic Recon (3)

Melody Series
Melody of the Heart
Melody of the Snow

Road to Rocktoberfest Anthology
Changing His Tune - 2022

Coming Home Series (2023)
A Long Way Home
Family Home
Discovering Home
Finding Home
Bound For Home
…and many more

Novellas
Tenacious
Moon's Place

Romantic Fantasy
By Adam J. Ridley

Big Bend Series
Love's Legacy (1)
Love's Heirloom (2)
Love's Bequest (3)

The Witch Brothers Series
Emerald Earth (1)
Diamond Air (2)
Ruby Fire (3)
Sapphire Water (4)

Science Fiction
By Adam J. Ridley

Superhero Series
Emergence

Blake Allwood was born in west Tennessee, then moved to Kansas City MO after earning a degree in Early Childhood Education from Graceland College in Lamoni, Iowa. He met his husband Shaun in 1995 and they officially married in 2015, once gay marriage was legalized; although they still consider Valentines Day 1995 as their true "anniversary date". Twenty-two years later (2017), after fostering 12 children together, he and his husband sold their home, purchased an RV and began traveling the country with their two dogs.

Typically, Blake can be found relaxing in the RV or by the fire with his laptop and their Jack Russell Terrier, Buddy, curled up between his legs demanding attention. Denver, their Siberian Husky mix is often asleep at his feet or playing tug of war with Blake's husband.

Most of Blake's stories are inspired by the places they have visited in their ongoing travels. His first book, **_Aiden Inspired_**, was released in 2019 and he has now written over 20 books. In 2023 he is releasing the **_Coming Home_** series which is comprised of ten-plus sweet contemporary romance novels that are based on a fictional town in his home state of Tennessee.

Blake also writes under the pen name of Adam J. Ridley for his urban fantasy fans looking for stories revolving around gay characters. His first series is The Witch Brothers Saga, starting with ***Emerald Earth***.